A MYTHN

C000072150

ECHOES

OF

DRAGONS

AWAKENINGS
BOOK ONE

C. BORDEN

The characters, places, and events portrayed in this book are fictitious. Any similarity to real persons, living or dead, is coincidental and not intended by the author.

Copyright © 2022 C.B. Writing Solutions

All Rights Reserved

No part of this book may be reproduced, or stored in a retrieval system, or transmitted in any form or by any means, electronic, mechanical, photocopying, recording, or otherwise, without express written permission of the publisher.

First paperback edition: March 2022

ISBN: 9798405734484

Cover Design and Formatting: C.B. Writing Solutions
Editor: Lisa Binion
Printed by Amazon KDP
Printed in the United States of America

To those precious souls who kept pushing me,
who kept encouraging me,
who kept believing in me even when
I stopped believing in myself...

This one is for you.

TABLE OF CONTENTS

PROLOGUE

On the southern continent of Mygras, the place where all fears and rumors come from, a dark ceremony began in a temple in Croglinke. The temple's ceiling, which sloped to the north, was dismantled so that the unusual crossing of the suns could be clearly observed while the ceremony took place. A black obsidian altar was covered with a red sheet, a white cloth draped on one end and a golden tray on the other. Behind the altar were two large thrones identical to the ones in the Elven temple far to the north in Elmnas, but while those thrones bore artistic depictions of Elven gods, these thrones were empty. Instead, looking down on them with horrible gaping jaws and glaring red ruby eyes was a huge dragon carved out of the same stone as the thrones.

There were only the priest and one of his pages, both dressed in pure white gowns with silver sashes. Both wore sacrificial knives at their sides. They looked warily around as they waited for their master. As the suns drew near their zenith, the aging priest busied himself smoothing the red fabric on the altar. Without warning, the doors to the temple flew open with a bang. The young page at once flung himself to his knees, visibly trembling while bowing to the large figure towering in the doorway. The priest paused in his preparations to turn to his master and offered a deep bow before turning back to the altar.

The White Lord was fearsome to look at. Rumors and myths said that he was a direct descendent of the gods. To look at him, it did not seem a far stretch. Standing well above most human men, he had the well-defined and powerfully built body of a human warrior. There his similarities to the human race ended. His neck and face were reptilian with a rough pebbled texture. He had slits for nostrils and yellow reptilian eyes. No lips covered his sharp teeth, and a pair of thin fangs showed dominantly as they overlapped his lower jaw. Every inch of visible skin was albino white, so white that he seemed to glow as random rays of light from the suns above washed over him as he walked. Strangest of all though were his ears, which were shapely and pointed, showing his Elven heritage.

Terrifying even in his calm stature, he strode to the front of the temple. His traditional white robes were held closed with a platinum girdle where his sword hung. His large white hands bore a black stone ring, and his fingernails were polished and sharpened to give the appearance of claws. While his reptilian face gave away none of his emotions, his upright stature and the hold of his head showed his complete confidence and fearlessness. He found it enjoyable to disconcert his subjects, so he decided to come to the ceremony in his bare feet. Normally sheathed up to the knee, his feet, also a pale white, were large and misshapen. Both feet sported six toes rather than five, and the toenails were sharpened similarly to his fingernails.

He was known as the White Lord to the world, but his real name was ancient and long forgotten to all but himself and his god. No one seemed to know exactly where he had come from, so no one knew his exact age. In addition to rumors that he was a son of the gods, there was plenty of speculation through the years as to where he really came from and why he was the only known surviving Heridon.

The Heridon, a strange race of beings that were one-quarter human, one-quarter elf, and half Drake—a strangely humanoid race of dragons— were rumored to have been wiped out during the Cataclysm that resulted from an advanced mix of magic and technology gone wrong. The Heridon, historically of the same stature as most humans, were rumored to have been as intelligent and graceful as the elves. However, they had been a greedy people and were accumulators of all kinds of wealth. During the time of the Great Cataclysm, the rocky island home of the Heridon had been destroyed under an onslaught of explosions, which were blamed by the surviving races on the Heridon's own powerful technology. In the destruction of the island, most of the culture, heritage, and art of the Heridon and their supposed dragon mounts were a huge loss felt throughout the world.

Like the elves, the Heridon had been one of the oldest and most advanced races. They had long lives like the elves, living an average life of eight to nine hundred years, though their ancients were rumored to have been easily over one thousand years old. It was thought that the White Lord may have actually been around during the Cataclysm, which would have made him at least 750 years old. Not that his age mattered among the tenants of the rest of the world. What mattered was that whenever and wherever he made his presence known outside his own realm, which spanned the entirety of Mygras, he brought nothing but fear, mayhem, slavery, and death.

He was a powerful sorcerer and drew great power from the misery and death of any who opposed him. Over the centuries, tale after tale had been told of his attempts to spread his rule beyond Mygras. However, for every tale fraught with fear and dread, there was also a tale of bravery and sacrifice as heroes from the other races rose up against him and held him at bay. With the strange event of the suns and the unusual currents flowing through the entire world, the White Lord was sure his time had come.

The White Lord made his way to the front of the temple. His eyes flickered to the altar and then to the open roof above where the suns were just beginning to touch at their edges.

"Tell me, High Priest, what have the stars told you of my future?" He came to a halt in front of the altar, standing alert and tense with his hands clenched as though expecting at any moment to be attacked from behind.

The high priest turned and raised his head to look at the White Lord. Nodding his head in submission, yet standing fearless and tall in front of him, it was clear that while the White Lord was his ruler, this man was a powerful creature in his own right. After all, the White Lord would not have known of the coming of this spectacular event without the visions of the high priest.

"My Lord, we have not the time right now to talk of the future. We have but a few moments to ready ourselves for the ritual. The timing is crucial." Glancing at the page to his side, the high priest nodded his head. He then stepped toward the White Lord.

"If you please, my Lord, I need to gather some of your blood for the ritual."

Waiting for the White Lord to give his approval, the high priest reached out with one hand and displayed a small dagger in his other.

Not afraid that the high priest would attempt to harm him, the White Lord extended his hand, never letting his eyes drop from the priest's face, searching the man's eyes, reading his posture, smelling for the odor that would give away if the man was nervous or fearful.

Knowing that while they shared a truce of sorts but also knowing the White Lord would tolerate no accidents and no excuses, the high priest took the White Lord's hand in his own. He flipped it over to reveal the soft side of the Heridon's hand that was not covered in the rough pebbly skin covering the rest of his body and sliced deeply through the palm of his hand. Taking a small bowl presented by the returned page, he allowed the White Lord's wound to bleed thick violet blood into the bowl. Unsure of how much blood he would need to complete the ritual, he let the wound bleed freely into the bowl until the White Lord's innate healing abilities caused the wound to seal itself and heal.

The high priest glanced into the face of his Lord and nodded a silent thanks. Letting the Heridon stand where he was and offering no more explanation, the high priest turned back to the altar. Glancing up at the suns and seeing that they were nearly completely eclipsed, he began the powerful chanting of the spell for this ritual. As he chanted, he put the bowl of blood on the altar. He looked to his page for the last essential item.

The page labored under the load of the sack he carried and heaved it onto the altar, untying the strings at the top. Letting the sack fall away from the object, the page gasped, his eyes wide in awe at the beautiful oval gem revealed. The high priest gently touched the gigantic gem as though he would the small face of a babe. His chanting still uninterrupted, he removed the sack and handed it to the page, signifying the page's completion of his part in the ritual.

The page glanced again at the gem in wonder, then at the high priest with his bowl of blood, and then at the imposing figure of the White Lord as he waited. Deciding to clear out before anything else was needed, namely his own blood, the page cowered and made a hasty retreat.

The White Lord's attention was drawn away from the altar and the high priest. The gem was fascinating, but he was not impressed by its deep red color or its size. He knew it wasn't an actual gem but a dragon egg. He had willingly sacrificed many resources and the lives of many of his men to come by it, yet the egg and what it contained was merely a means to an end.

What drew his attention now were the suns overhead as they reached their full eclipse. While his own memory from before the Cataclysm was sketchy at best, he was very intelligent. The suns on their normal paths, moving opposite of each other in the Mythnium sky, was unnatural. He knew it but could not explain it. He imagined that no one on the planet could explain it either.

The one sun rose in the northwest and moved in a straight path across the sky before it settled in the northeast, a brilliant blue light in the heavens. During its short time alone in the sky every morning, Mythnium appeared to be a planet of ice and cold. However, that frigid cast only lasted for an hour before the bright red sun rose in the east to make its way diagonally from the southeast to the northwest. It's red hue when combined with the hues of the first cast Mythnium in all its shades of lavender and purple, causing the world to have an almost ethereal appearance. That the suns were moving in such a way as to make an eclipse further confounded the White Lord, who scowled in frustration that he could not make sense of it, and he felt he should.

Frustrated but also awestruck by its undeniable beauty, he watched as the brilliant light, auras, and colors mixed and flowed; almost a visible and iridescent heat could be seen shooting away from the suns as they stood one in front of the other. Never in his life had the White Lord seen such an incredible phenomenon, and he knew he most likely never would again.

Deep down, he knew that the seemingly uncaring gods actually did care, and that this phenomenon was sent by them to give hope to the world. He suppressed a deep desire to chuckle. He had no allegiance to any of the gods of the races of Mythnium except one. In general, he knew that the other gods cared not for him or for his aspirations. More often than not, they worked in unison to unsettle his plans by sending his opponents special gifts or talents or by setting in motion a series of events that even his best counselors and psychics could not see or prevent. No, he cared not for most of the lofty gods. Whether this event was caused by them or not, he intended to use it expressly for his own purposes. Someday he knew he would accomplish his goals, and nothing could stop him, not even the gods. He smiled grimly because he knew he was touched by his god, and his god supported his goals even if he did not outright help him see that those goals were met.

While the White Lord was lost in thought watching the eclipse, the high priest poured the blood from the bowl into a shallow tray. He then picked up the heavy egg and set it in the blood. Using his hands to rub the viscous blood all over the egg, the high priest continued his chant, allowing it to rise in volume and cadence. He was not beseeching the White Lord's god for this ritual, not for any ritual performed in this temple. He was beseeching a mystical and dark force that he believed moved within the currents of magic. He dealt entirely with the dark currents of magic. Nothing else could bring the dragons back besides the gods, but over the centuries, it was apparent that the gods' playtime with dragons had long ended. Chanting faster and faster, rubbing in the blood, spreading it all over the egg until the egg no longer showed its deep ruby coloring, the high priest took the same knife he used to wound the Lord and poised it above the egg. Pausing for a split second and ending his chant with a powerful word of magic, the high priest slammed his blade into the top of the egg.

Drawn back to the ritual being performed at the altar, the White Lord checked himself as he expected to see the blade shatter against the egg's crystallized shell or slide off the top, yet it passed through the layer of blood and through the shell as though it were soft and yielding flesh. At that instant, there was a high keening wail, something so loud and terrible the high priest had to stop himself from pressing his hands to his ears. The priest kept his hand on the hilt of the blade and twisted it, making a circular hole in the shell of the egg. Removing the blade then using his fingers, he scraped out the last of the blood and guided it into the hole in the egg. Once done, he replaced the bowl and began chanting anew.

He wiped his hands clean and stepped back from the altar, walking backward until he was next to the White Lord at the base of the altar. Never stopping his chanting, he lowered himself to his knees, beckoning for the White Lord to remain standing where he was. For many minutes of chanting, the high wailing continued. Then as suddenly as it had started, it stopped. The high priest's voice echoed hauntingly off the stone walls of the temple. The suns up above were already past the perfect eclipse, touching at the edges on their opposite sides.

The high priest, not revealing his concerns over this made-up ritual, droned on with his chanting, his voice rising and falling in a strange cadence. When the White Lord had asked him how to hatch the dragon egg several days before, the priest was honest but was certain he could find a way in some ancient texts. When nothing had revealed itself after he had spent sleepless nights scouring his books and scrolls, the high priest used an old ritual that had been used to bring forth the dead. It was one he was familiar with and hoped beyond hope that the necromancy spell would work. While he chanted and prayed his use of magic had done its work, the White Lord stood ready and waiting.

Time passed. The White Lord was aware of time passing and was beginning to grow impatient. He again glanced up to see that the suns were not touching at all, then a little later were quite a bit farther from each other. He glanced at the high priest, who was still chanting his annoyingly repetitive chant. He looked to the altar. There was nothing coming from the egg: no sound, no

17

movement, nothing to give him and his heightened senses any notion that this ritual had worked. Having no problem at all standing in wait for an opponent or for his prey when it obviously afforded him the thrill of the win or the hunt, this was beginning to seem foolish. He, while being quite a lot of things, was no fool. The White Lord glanced again at the high priest and was about to verbalize his disappointment when a cracking sound caught his attention. Looking back to the egg with a slow smile spreading across his pebbly face, he found that there was now a crack in the shell.

He watched in growing fascination as the crack widened tiny bit by tiny bit. A sucking sound emanated from the crack, and he was able to see the layer of blood disappearing from all over the egg as it was being absorbed or sucked from within. The crack gradually grew in length, stretching from the top of the egg where it had been punctured to the bottom. It was not very wide at first but soon grew wider and wider in areas. Not paying much attention to the high priest kneeling at his side, he was momentarily distracted as the priest changed his chanting and prostrated himself on the ground in relief.

He doesn't kneel that way for me, the White Lord thought grudgingly.

He refocused his attention on the egg. New cracks formed all around the shell. He held his breath. How he had longed for the day when he would bring the dragons back. He would be undefeatable with dragons at his command. He imagined the conquered cities, countries, peoples, and kings, and his eyes blazed with an unnatural combination of rage and desire. Deep down though, the thought of conquering the world paled in comparison to the promise of complete revenge he hoped to exact on those who had destroyed his people, who had left him so utterly alone and incomplete. He tensed up, his hands clutching his belt eagerly as he leaned forward, willing the dragon to burst forth so he could begin working towards his ultimate goal.

All of a sudden, the little dragon poked its head out. Bright and brilliant red, it had eyes almost identical to those of the statue behind it. As it pushed its head farther out of the shell, its eyes glowed ruby red, a fire burning within the slitted reptilian pupils. Next, its front claws reached through the cracked shell, and it braced and pulled itself forward onto the altar. It was shiny and wet, small patches of the White Lord's violet blood appearing on its glistening red scales. The dragon paid no attention to the shell or other items on the altar.

It ignored the priest bowed in front of it on the ground. Instead, the dragon looked right at the White Lord, its eyes seeking, finding, and boring into his eyes. For a split second, the White Lord felt a horrible unfamiliar feeling of fear flash through him. Reigning it in, he forced his own gaze back at the dragon.

The dragon, still looking at the White Lord, raised itself up on its rear legs. Standing, the baby dragon was only waist-high to the priest with its nearly body-length tail trailing behind. It stood for a moment, testing its strength and then unfurling its leathery wings. The wings were already thick and full, capable of offering flight if the dragon chose to do so. They were a shade of deeper red than the rest of the dragon, and on the left one, a strange mark was etched in white.

Breaking his gaze from the dragon's eyes, the White Lord looked closer at the white mark. Shock caused him to inhale quickly. There on the wing of the dragon was the White Lord's own mark, a white dragon curled around a skull. It was small and imperfect, but it was obviously his mark. The White Lord looked back at the dragon's face and found himself looking into its strangely familiar eyes.

"High Priest, stop your groveling. The dragon is born. Get up! Get up!"

The high priest stopped his chanting and raised his head to look at the dragon sitting on the altar. The dragon didn't pay any attention to him, and the priest had no idea how to further proceed. He rose to his feet, thankful for the first time in his life at the presence of his Lord.

"My Lord. The dragon was born in your blood. According to lore, you have but to speak to it, and it will do your bidding.'

"Really." The White Lord paused in thought, his eyes never leaving the creature in front of him, "Tell me, Priest, what do young dragons eat."

"Oh, well… Let's see. According to my research, the dragons had specific diets. The dragons that were used for war were kept on a blood diet during their youth and then raw, preferably living, meat as they progressed to and reached adulthood. However, those dragons used for menial tasks that had to work alongside any of the Heridon, were fed vegan diets, never eating anything of meat or flesh."

"So, with our little pet here, what do you think would best suit my purpose?"

The high priest responded at once, "Fresh blood to be sure, my Lord."

"Hmmm… Very well. Call in your new page."

Disgruntled at knowing he was about to lose yet another page to the White Lord's whims, the high priest muttered, "Yes, my Lord."

He called out to his page at once, loud and clear, which caused the young dragon to drop to all fours while pressing its wings tightly to its sides. It lowered its head, now looking at the high priest. It backed up and wrapped itself around the base of its shell, crouched and waiting.

The young page ran into the sanctuary from the side door he had left through and came to an abrupt halt in front of the priest. Because all temple pages had their tongues cut out, he could merely stand mutely to wait for his priest's bidding. When the high priest merely looked at him saying nothing, the page grew confused and looked fearfully up at the White Lord. The White Lord didn't glance at him or address him. Instead, he called out to his new pet. "Please, help yourself to your first meal."

With lightning speed, the White Lord whipped out his sword and sliced through the unsuspecting page's neck, sending sprays of blood over the altar and the young dragon. Straightaway, the dragon responded to its master's command, and to the undeniable urge to eat. Moving quickly and smoothly, the young beast landed on the ground where the page's body lay with blood pooling around his head. The dragon moved to the pool and started lapping it up. When the pool was dry, it moved to the jugular of the body and sucked out all the rest, leaving a withered husk in its place. Licking its jaws and teeth, the dragon emitted a catlike purring sound as it moved away from the now empty shell and cautiously approached the White Lord. It moved to his feet and curled around one of them as if to rest its head on the White Lord's foot.

"Thank you, High Priest, for your assistance. I trust you will do more research about our dragon friend here. One dragon is incredible indeed, but I will need more if my goals are to be achieved. By the way, how fast will my little pet here grow to maturity?"

The high priest moved away from the White Lord, making plans to clean the mess as quickly as he could. Blood sacrifices were commonplace in this temple, but he abhorred the stains left and was eager to have them cleaned before too much longer.

"Your dragon will mature fairly quickly. Depending on its sex, it will reach its adulthood in six or seven years, but you can already start training it for battle. However, my Lord, like I told you before, dragons supposedly are as smart as any of the races, and once you are able to communicate with it, I would advise listening to its own ideas and opinions on matters. It could have very definite ideas about things dependent on how you raise it."

He started to move back to the altar but thought of something and turned back to the White Lord. "Sir?"

"What is it?"

"What will you call it?"

The White Lord looked down at the dragon at his feet and thought for a few minutes, images of all that lay before him flashing through his mind's eye.

"Ah, but is it a female or a male?"

At his question, the dragon picked up its head. Inspired, the White Lord asked it directly, "Well, my pet? Are you a lady?"

The dragon looked into the White Lord's eyes, and he stiffened as he felt the mental intrusion. He had been given a firm impression even though it was not in the form of words that the dragon was a female. With eyes wide in wonder at this forgotten skill of the dragons, the White Lord let a smile cross his face while he took care to hide the entire truth of his intentions.

"I see." With that he looked over at the priest who was watching in obvious confusion at the one-sided exchange.

"It appears that our little friend here has some abilities that I had long forgotten. She is in fact a female and has the ability to share thoughts. A most valuable asset. Don't you agree, Priest?"

Stammering at the news and struggling to protect his own self-incriminating thoughts, the priest nodded his head. "Most impressive, my Lord. Will you name her right away or shall we make a ceremony of it?"

The White Lord paused for a moment. "No. No ceremony will be necessary. I will name her now. A name of power. A name that will inspire fear and respect. Let me see… A name that promises death. Libitina. Yes, the Old Elvish word meaning death. I think such a name of power will be more than adequate for our little fiery friend. Do you not agree, Priest?"

At the decree of her name, the Red Dragon picked her head up from the White Lord's foot. She moved away to stand on her hind legs, stretching to her full height and demanding the White Lord's attention.

Looking down at his new and powerful ally, the White Lord mentally thrust a question to her.

Libitina. What do you think of your new name? Do you understand what it means? Does it suit you?

23

A subtle tugging at the corner of his mind grew louder. It wasn't quite a voice but with a strong sense of communication that he could clearly understand, the dragon responded, *Yes. Death will suit me as a name. I will be your ally. I will not be your slave. Red Dragons are never slaves to anyone. I sense you are a powerful being with a strong link to the magical currents.*

The White Lord struggled to keep from reeling at the mental intrusion. He realized that this alliance was going to be much more complicated than he had intended or expected. For such a young dragon to so eloquently state so much knowledge of his own plans while simultaneously crumbling his plans for keeping the dragon as a war animal, he found himself reinforcing his mental walls.

Of course. I understand. Dragons have been gone for hundreds of years, so much of the dragon's partnership with the Heridon has been lost. I will treat you with as much respect as you show me, and I hope that you will refrain from assaulting my thoughts without some sort of forewarning.

Looking all around in obvious concern and dropping to all fours, Libitina crouched to the floor in a protective stance.

What do you mean dragons have been gone? Where did they go? When did they go? Have the Heridon gone to find them?

Now speaking aloud so he could better organize his thoughts, the White Lord responded, "Come, my dear. Let us leave the priest to his tasks, and I will tell you what I know of the dragons' disappearance."

He turned and started walking out of the temple. Libitina scurried alongside the White Lord as he left the temple and started the long walk to his fortress.

Along the way, he told the shiny Red Dragon all that he knew of the dragons' demise during the Great Cataclysm.

The White Lord walked beside the young dragon as they left the temple, which sat on the edge of a cliff outside the city of Croglinke. As they walked side by side over rocky terrain toward the fortress city, he pointed out the thick walls of the fortress and explained the basic layout of the city that was now the dragon's home. Just outside the fortress walls were the hovels and rugged rock dwellings of thieves, robbers, murderers, and criminals that were not worth their salt. In other words, they got caught for not doing their crimes well enough.

Along the interior of the fortress walls, the White Lord housed most of his military. His military forces were comprised of people of all races who were prone to the things that were thought to be bad or evil. Among them, the White Lord encouraged and valued anger, violence, hatred, and all the chaos those traits inspired. His only rule among his forces was to not get caught. He knew his troops had set up hierarchies and rulers among themselves. He knew it kept them from completely falling into anarchy and total chaos, but he never once imposed those rules on them himself. His only expectation was their obedience when he called on them. He did not even care for their loyalty.

Farther still inside the walls lived those who were more successful at being unscrupulous. Their dwellings were more lavish. More opulent. More audacious. They all attested to the airs and egos that so many of the best con artists, murderers, and thieves held. It was all a grand delusion. They all knew that at a whim, the White Lord could choose to evict any or all of them just for breathing the same air as him. But he found a sick delight in keeping the arrogant in suspense, sometimes showing them extreme favor and indulging their often strange whims. Other times, he would execute the most faithful of them for no reason at all except his own amusement.

Centered in Croglinke but extending back to meet the base of a tall mountain, the White Lord's intimidating fortress of white stone rose against the contrasting natural black stone of Mygras's northern cliffs. It towered over the rest of Croglinke and was rumored to extend well below the fortress city all the way to the cliffs. He proudly expressed to the dragon that from the tallest spires, he could see out over the ocean in one direction and also out over the vast mountain range that he had chosen as his home.

Realizing he promised to tell her of the dragons, he changed the topic and shifted gears.

As far as he knew, he told her, the Heridon had created an incredible technology that was thought to be combined with the magical currents of Mythnium. In working with the device, boosting it with magic, and testing its capabilities, something went wrong. There had been no warning, but the destruction of the device had been so powerful that it had affected the entire world of Mythnium.

In the wake of the explosion, the Heridon and the dragons had been destroyed. The continent where they resided, mostly removed from the other races except for trade and travel, had disappeared into the vast ocean taking the technology, the culture, and the wealth along with it. In addition to the incredible loss of the two races, the magical currents had been upset. Before the Cataclysm, magic was inherent to Mythnium but largely unused by most of the races. After the Cataclysm, with the sudden loss of useful technology and the increase in magical currents, more and more races began to use and rely on the currents to some extent.

Only one known survivor remained from the Cataclysm. Despite his amnesia and led by his god who consumed his mind in the time directly after the traumatic event, he had taken great care to find what he could of his heritage before he fled the burning island. As he devised a plan for his own future, parties from the other races sped to any locations they could recall that had once belonged to the Heridon or to the dragons. In a large cavern, a hoard had been found. Sitting in the treasure was a grossly large elliptical-shaped ruby gemstone. The humans gathered as much of the treasure as they could, including the ruby stone, and returned to their own ravaged lands to begin rebuilding.

During that time, the White Lord revealed to Libitina, he came to power little by little. He could not recall exactly how he had survived or where he was exactly at the time of the Cataclysm, but in the conquests and battles that he waged throughout the years at the urging and direction of his god, Naga, he learned of the story of the ruby stone. He knew from his shattered memories that it was not a gemstone but possibly the last dragon of the world. From that point on, he battled with one goal in mind: to retrieve the egg, discover how to birth the dragon inside, and continue on.

The White Lord finished his tale and found himself at the bridge to his fortress.

Libitina had been silent during his discourse but was still at his side.

I'm not the last dragon. I am the only birthed one. There are echoes of dragons calling to me from every direction. I can hear the souls of others that are yet unhatched. They are far away. I can sense that they long to be free. What a shame we have been gone so long. I think though that we can find them. But I will have to mature a lot more before I can focus my mind enough to locate them.

"Ah. You are indeed a very valuable ally, Libitina. I have no doubt that we will make a very powerful and successful alliance. I suspected there might be more eggs hidden around Mythnium! When you know more, I hope you will share what you learn so that we may find more of your kin."

Libitina scurried across the gleaming white bridge and into the fortress with the White Lord and followed him as he made his way through several rooms, which were sparsely yet opulently furnished. Finally, they stopped in a large throne room where a huge onyx throne sat facing the door.

The White Lord moved to the throne and sat. He reached down and allowed Libitina to scamper up his arm to the left side of the throne. Once settled there, she looked at the White Lord.

You do know that not all dragons will align with your cause? As I said before, we are not slaves. Some will gladly join us. Others will not. Some may even oppose us.

"Hmmm. Can you tell from the minds that you touch now which will help us and which will hinder us?"

No. I will not see their minds that clearly until after they are hatched. Even then, many of them will have gleaned enough of their heritage to know how to shield their thoughts. It will be instinctual for the most part. We will have to birth each one and then wait and see.

"We won't just be able to destroy the eggs of the ones that would hinder us outright. Of course. It would never be so easy. Ah, but then it never is," he said out loud and paused to think before continuing. "Well, I have waited this long, and my waiting has won me your alliance. I think I can wait some more. In the meantime, let us look for the other eggs and see what we can do about raising up the dragons again! Ah-hah, and we'll see about the conquest I have been longing for!"

PRAYER OF MYTHNIUM

Progress through unity,
World, nature, people;
We progress with deeds
Not words.
Faith carries us;
Justice preserves us;
Integrity guides us.
We serve and protect
With hearts as one.
~With hearts as one.

"In the days when the dragons resided beside us, we overcame fear one step at a time. The fear never left, but we were always one step closer to overcoming it."
~Of Faith and Fear,
from the archives at Farcaste Reach

1

A ldrina sat alone at the edge of the nomadic camp and stared through the mountain pass that spread out below her. She swatted away flying bugs as she mused over the new life she had found among the Willow Elves, which was a far cry from the life she had grown up in. It had only been ten years but already seemed so long ago. She remembered the day she left Jackob's inn, which sat on the edge of a small village not far inland from the western coast of Mythos. He had claimed to be her uncle, but if that had been true, he had proven to be a most heartless and immoral man.

Her life at the inn had been hard for as long as she could remember. Her earliest memory was of the night her uncle, Rackas, had taken her to the inn. She had both loved and hated Rackas for many years after that. He had visited his brother from time to time during her youth and would always ask about her, but she only ever saw him from a distance because Jackob and his wife were careful to keep her away from him during his visits. While Rackas emanated warmth and concern for her, Jackob was hard and cold. The only thing Jackob and his wife cared about was how she, even as a young child, could benefit them.

They had started her off as their helper and housemaid. She had been expected to help clean, prepare foods, lead guests to rooms, and run errands, but otherwise, she was to be completely invisible to the inn's patrons. They had initially had her sleeping in a corner of the attic that was not much larger than the cook's pantry in the kitchen. But it had been warm and the only place she could disappear to where they largely left her alone.

However, as she grew older and turned into a young and fairly attractive woman, Jackob began to demand other things from her. He started working her as a bar wench, outfitting her with low-cut dresses, gaudy make-up, and itchy wigs. Immediately popular with many of the seedier patrons, she got more than a few carefully placed beatings for avoiding the men's groping hands and slobbery kisses. Over time, Jackob insisted she do more than merely pour ale or wine, and he moved her into a lavishly decorated room where she was expected to entertain the more private, primal desires of Jackob's wealthier patrons.

By that time, Rackas was no longer visiting the inn. Rumor had it that the older man had fled to some of the islands off the western coast of the continent due to his smuggling. It didn't matter much to her though because she knew that Rackas had washed his hands of her when he had taken her to his brother. She could not imagine that he would've approved of his brother forcing her into a life of abuse and prostitution, but she also doubted that Rackas would have done anything to stop it if he had known.

The day she decided she had had enough, she had just overheard the other girls wondering over the strange phenomena of the suns. She had run outside to see the event for herself and was awestruck as the suns moved closer and closer as though they were going to collide. She remembered the strange colors of the sky and the stranger still tingle in the air as though lightning were about to strike from the very air around her.

Jackob had called her inside to prepare for her night, but she had stood rooted in place until the suns moved together in the most beautiful joining she ever could have imagined. Warmth and hope flickered deep in her heart, a feeling foreign to her but one that could not be ignored. Inspiration compelled her to leave. Not waiting to see the end of the eclipse, she ran into the inn and stuffed her meager belongings into an old pillowcase. She stuffed the little bit of coin she had been squirreling away under the bed into a pouch sewn into her skirt, and she simply walked out of the inn.

She still wondered that no one had seen her walk brazenly out the front door and that Jackob had not sent anyone after her. But she had left the inn and the small town of Weston without incident. It had not been till that evening as the suns had moved along their paths and were low over their horizons that she realized she had no plan and no direction on where to go. She had not passed any travelers because she had unknowingly chosen the road that led east into the Alisyan Mountains instead of the road that led south to Farcaste Reach, the largest known settlement on that side of the Walker Mountains. That time of year, few people traveled into the harsh terrain of the mountain chain that stretched to the east along the southern edge of Mythos.

She had no idea how to make a fire, so that first night she spent alone and cold in the dark at the base of the mountains. Afraid, she began seriously questioning her resolve and her decision to just leave. She ended up falling into a fitful sleep only to be awakened just before first sunrise by a strange-looking elf who was staring down at her in obvious concern. That elf, who had introduced herself as a Willow Elf, invited Aldrina to a simple meal of gathered berries and dried meat and then invited her to join their tribe for a while.

That wispy Willow Elf was known as Olphara. She was the eldest of their nomadic tribe, just over a century old, and the most skilled with the healing magic that the Willow Elves were most known for. She was just short of Aldrina's height though much skinnier. Her rather ruddy complexion was from her time spent on the slopes of the Alisyan Mountains, but she had a kind face that matched her kind heart. She had become Aldrina's dearest friend as well as a mentor and was nearly like a mother to the young woman. Over their ten years together, Aldrina often forgot she was not one of the Willows, as people referred to them, and they were not the sort to remind her.

She had spent her time among them and was at once taken in by their simple nomadic way of life. Most of the tribes moved throughout Mythos, offering their healing skills wherever needed among the rich and poor of the scattered peoples of all races. As a rule, the Willows never turned an injured or sick creature away even if the creature was a member of one of the more brutal warmongering races. This charity usually allowed them safe passage, especially among the most dangerous regions on the continent largely inhabited by brutal, less-civilized races.

The almost holy nature of the Willows was a comforting balm to Aldrina's soul after so much of her life had been cruel, hard, and both physically and mentally abusive. She found herself admiring their work. Then during one of their journeys to a small village of goblins, a race notorious for its brutal nature, she discovered she had a talent and a desire for healing as well.

The goblin village had been attacked by another goblin tribe. This was common for them, especially as tribes often held deep blood rivalries. The attack on the village had left many of the younger members mortally injured. The timing of the Willow's arrival made all the difference to the small village. Aldrina's assistance and her almost intuitive ability to sense the severity of some of the injuries had made a great impact. From that point on, she was no longer a guest of Olphara's tribe. Instead, she was treated as one of them and taught their ways, their beliefs, and their skills.

She was also accepted more fully by Olphara herself. As the matriarch of the tribe, Olphara was unmated and bore no children. Like the matriarchs before her, she had been chosen during a ceremonious coming of age celebration to begin training under the previous matriarch, sacrificing love and family for the good of the tribe. Once the other matriarch had passed on, Olphara took over the care of the tribe and had spent her life improving their skills to the point they were often sought out over many of the other Willow tribes. She had often taken in strays like Aldrina, lost souls who had no other place to go. Olphara had taken a special interest in Aldrina though. While she encouraged other people she had taken in to get back on their feet and finally go on about their own path in life, she allowed Aldrina to remain, forming a close bond and treating her as the daughter she would never be able to have.

During her time among Olphara's tribe, Aldrina learned a great deal about herself. Not only did she learn her own strengths and talents, but she learned a great deal about her own heritage as the Willows could sense the Elven blood in Aldrina's veins. Olphara had been curious about Aldrina's heritage. Half-elves were not uncommon. Aldrina's outward appearance did not give away her race, but her aura belied a lineage that was deliberately and carefully mixed. Olphara learned of Aldrina's bloodline because of her sensitivity to auras. Her bright and lasting aura hinted not just of her Elven heritage but of a heritage linked to royal bloodlines. Olphara's skill in reading auras allowed her to recognize the link in Aldrina to that of the royal line in Elmnas to King Mronas. She wanted to be certain, so she had sent out inquiries. In her research to verify her readings, she discovered the king had a niece living in exile. Though it was a secret even among the elves, she was certain efforts were in place to protect the girl from the people who had removed her parents from the Ebony Isles. Once Olphara was certain Aldrina was who she suspected, she informed and encouraged the young woman to go to King Mronas because he was her true uncle and could help her return to her rightful place – a queen of the Ebony Isles.

Expectedly so, Aldrina could not fathom that she was the daughter of an Elven princess and a human prince who had been in line to be the next king of the Ebony Isles. She could not imagine herself to now be the rightful heir, but the entire royal family other than herself was dead. Memories of her escape from the islands were long forgotten, not even foggy remnants remained. Her knowledge of the world had not expanded beyond Jackob's inn and the things she was learning with Olphara. As Olphara pushed Aldrina to make the journey to Elmnas, Aldrina grew more and more determined to remain among the Willow Elves and become a healer like they were. She thought of what her life might be like as a princess or a queen for that matter. It took Aldrina months to accept what Olphara said as truth. Since accepting it as truth, she found the idea of being a ruler ridiculous. She had no idea what it would be like, and since she had no desire for the implied creature comforts prestigious families and royalty likely enjoyed, she continually denied Olphara's push. Nothing could dissuade Aldrina, and after a time, Olphara ceased in her nagging.

Aldrina continued to stare down the mountain pass and let the memories and revelations of the last ten years wash over her. She had grown attuned to life among the haggard mountains and the hills and valleys that stretched out below them back toward the small town of Weston where Jackob's inn was. She still wondered whatever became of him and of Rackas, but Olphara had helped her rid herself of any bitterness she held toward both men. Now she was a woman at peace with her choices.

As she considered the rewarding life she had built among Olphara's people, movement along the pass caught her eye. She rose to her feet and watched with interest as two heavy-laden wagons bumped slowly up the pass toward the camp. Turning her head, Aldrina whistled over her shoulder to get one of the guard's attention. He ran over and lifted his eyeglass to view the caravan better.

"Very interesting," the guard muttered under his breath.

"Who is it?" Aldrina asked.

"It appears to be a small caravan of Silver Dwarves. Most unusual."

"Why unusual?"

The guard handed his glass to Aldrina so she could see the approaching caravan more clearly.

"Unusual because their home is the Silver Isles, and they very rarely venture to Mythos. That they are so far south and west is, as I said, most unusual. They must have had business with Farcaste Reach."

Aldrina stared through the glass at the approaching dwarves. They certainly looked unusual to what she was used to. Willows were sought out by everyone for their healing magic, so even dwarves would visit the camp from time to time. But these Silver Dwarves mostly had black or dark red hair and beards, and their faces were red skinned. They were very unlike the Deep Dwarves that came south out of the Walker Mountains to trade with their pale, almost albino, skin, light-colored hair, and pale eyes.

Aldrina put the glass down and moved to join the small group of Willows that had gathered to meet the caravan. The lead dwarves hollered a boisterous greeting and moved the first wagon into the center of the camp while the elves directed the second wagon to one side. Aldrina watched the first wagon in particular for it was being driven by a female dwarf. Curious, she moved closer and watched the stocky woman tie up the reins and hop to the ground. The woman had thick black curly hair bound tightly in several braids that hung down her back, but even with the braids, several strands had broken free and frizzed about her head like a fuzzy crown. Her face was sunburnt and her lips chapped, obvious signs she was not used to the suns or the winds of the surface. Still, her eyes twinkled, and there was a tilt to her mouth that gave away her friendly, even jovial, demeanor.

The dwarf dusted herself off and squinted curiously and boldly at the elves that stood around her.

"Well. Old Pruzin told us right! We found the Willows." She stopped abruptly as she took in Aldrina, who was noticeably taller than the dwarves and most of the gathered elves. "But you're not a Willow."

Aldrina could not help but laugh as she met the woman's stare. "No."

The dwarf shrugged her shoulders in a carefree manner, and she extended her hand to Aldrina with a warm twinkle in her eyes.

"I am Estryl. With hearts as one."

Aldrina shook the dwarf's hand and knew instantly that she liked this exuberant dwarf as she echoed the common greeting, "With hearts as one."

*"Yesterday will forever be beyond our reach, but
tomorrow will always be there for us to catch and
grasp firmly and deliberately with both hands."*
~ Master Mage Fralizan, 425 AC

2

*T*he suns beat down on the camp causing most of the dwarves to linger in the shadows of their carts or the tents offered by the Willows for the duration of their stay. Aldrina walked between the tents on her way to the main cart that Estryl shared with her brother, Stranick, and one of the elders of their Dwarven council, Elder Martan.

Aldrina had learned from Estryl that she had been blessed with a unique ability that helped her shape metal and imbue it with magical properties. The very reason that the Silver Dwarves had left the vast tunnels and caves of their home on the Silver Isles was because her magic had not been seen among their people since the time of her great-grandmother. They hoped that in addition to the Dwarven histories and the research they conducted at Farcaste Reach that the Elven histories kept by the Willows might offer further enlightenment for Estryl.

They knew the Willow Elves had caches they guarded that were full of historical texts that would have been lost following the Cataclysm had it not been for their quick movements from tribe to tribe to collect, preserve, and protect whatever texts they came across. Aldrina had heard Olphara mention the many caches that were hidden across Mythos, but she had no concept of their importance or the vastness of the collection compared to well-known localized libraries at Elmnas, Wargate, or Farcaste Reach. The fact that Elder Martan had insisted Estryl's party visit Olphara before continuing on to any of the other more well-known libraries impressed Aldrina.

As she neared Estryl's wagon, she could hear Elder Martan groaning in frustration while Estryl and Stranick appeared to be laughing heartily over something. Looking to see what they were laughing at, she smirked to see that Olphara was performing her relaxation techniques on the grizzled old dwarf though her efforts appeared to have exactly the opposite effect on him.

"You must relax, Martan."

Martan grimaced and squirmed on the table where he lay on his stomach while Olphara walked nimbly up and down his back digging her toes into various pressure points and other tense spots in an effort to release the tension.

"If you do not stop digging your toes into my back like I'm a stuck pig, I will show you just how tense I really am!" growled Martan in irritation.

Olphara frowned and effortlessly jumped to the ground. Meanwhile, Stranick and Estryl regained their composure and helped Martan stand up.

"I think I will start you off with some of our herbal teas before trying to massage your back again."

Martan grumped, "Just get me a good ale. That is all the help I need."

Olphara rolled her eyes, and as she walked past Aldrina on her way back to her tent, she muttered, "Stubborn old mule."

Elder Martan got to his feet and dusted himself off. He called after Olphara, "Don't bring me any of that mess you gave me when we were at Wargate either!" He grimaced in memory.

Aldrina couldn't help the smile that touched her lips. "You knew each other before?"

The old dwarf harumphed in response. "A lifetime ago, but yes. She thought I'd appreciate an ale she had found that had been some foul concoction those weird rana make. It was worse than drinking mud!" He spat on the ground in distaste.

Aldrina laughed. "I think I know what you are talking about, but I believe she has some honeyed ale she kept from a Deep Dwarf who stopped through a couple years ago. She never drinks it."

"Oh, yes. That would be the good stuff."

Aldrina nodded and moved past him. She waved at Estryl. "May I join you?"

Estryl sat on a rough-cut bench and waved Aldrina over. "Of course! I have so much to ask you! Is it okay if we play that question game again? I feel like I'm learning so much more than I ever could from some musty old books."

Martan hmphed at her but walked away, while Stranick sat nearby and began sharpening some tools and blades for the Willow Elves in return for their hospitality.

Aldrina sat down near Estryl. "Has Olphara agreed to take you to the closest cache?"

Estryl nodded enthusiastically while she blinked rapidly in the bright light of the suns.

Aldrina nodded to the wagon. "It's so bright out here for you. Would you rather sit in the wagon or in the shade of one of the tents?"

Stranick overheard and laughed. "Oh, no. Not her. She enjoys being blinded by the suns."

Estryl threw a small pebble at her brother. "You too, you big dolt, or you would be doing that in the shade of the wagon, not out in the open as you are."

Stranick shrugged dismissively, "If my baby sister can handle the suns' rays, then so can I."

Estryl rolled her eyes and looked at Aldrina. "I'm quite excited. Olphara is going to take me and Elder Martan in the morning and has granted us a week to visit it and glean what we can. We just had to promise to handle everything with great care. I guess some things we might not be able to handle at all but will have to rely on the elves to open and turn pages and such because they are so old. The care these elves take with these written things. It's very interesting to me."

Aldrina nodded in agreement. She had learned to read during her time with Olphara's group, and while she enjoyed the poetry and songs, she did not care as much for the books, scrolls, and tomes that dealt with what Olphara called educational topics. "Do you make only weapons and shields?" Aldrina asked.

Estryl shook her head. "Oh, no. That would be so boring. I have made pots and serving trays, horseshoes and metal tools. I've even made a mirror for one of the elders as a gift for his wife. I had a lot of fun creating that mirror. Why do you ask?"

Aldrina reached into her tunic and pulled out a rough gemstone approximately the size of her thumbnail. It was nothing much to look at, but if it had been cut and polished, it might have made someone a nice ring. She looked at it a moment and then held it out to Estryl.

Estryl took it and looked at the stone for a few minutes before looking back at Aldrina. "What is it for?"

Aldrina shrugged, "It's just something from my past life that I'd like to put to use if I can. Olphara saw it among my belongings and asked if I knew

45

what it was. Of course, at the time, I had no idea. Some stranger had given it to me as payment instead of gold…" Aldrina's face clouded over for a few seconds as memories of life at the inn flooded her mind, but she recovered and continued. "Anyway, Olphara told me that it is a rather common gemstone. One of the visiting healers from someplace called Watercastle said I might be able to use it to help me focus my healing magic, which would actually help me a great deal. I learned a lot about healing from the Willows, but I struggle with focusing my abilities. If that healer was right… Do you think you could create an amulet with it that I can wear around my neck?"

Estryl looked closer at the unremarkable gem. It was milky white in color, not clear and pretty like stones she had inset in many of the weapons and shields she had done over the years for the dwarves back home. As she flipped it around in her hand, she noted the cuts and gashes on the stone and the way that the sun caught them and refracted the light. She had a sudden inspiration and felt a unique song building within her. Meeting Aldrina's gaze, she nodded.

"I can make you something that will hold this just right so that in certain lights it will catch rays of light and refract them beautifully. I don't know how that will affect your healing magic, but I know just the metal to use and how to set the stone within it. I will set the Ab-nar sigils on the casing and the chain. Though again, I don't know how it will help you focus your healing abilities."

Aldrina smiled widely. "I will have to learn, I'm sure, but the way you describe it, it sounds beautiful already, and that would be wonderful in itself!"

Estryl was thoughtful as she continued to stare at the stone, "I better get started before the song disappears. If you will excuse me, I think I can have it completed by tomorrow evening."

Aldrina objected, "But you have your trip to the cache…"

Estryl smiled as she got to her feet, "This won't take long. If I can't complete it before we leave, then I can when I return in the evening."

Aldrina grinned in excitement. "What do I owe you for your work?"

Estryl thought a moment, "Let me think on it. I am sure we can think of something."

Their game of questions forgotten, Aldrina nodded and rose to her feet while Estryl hurried to the portable kiln-type forge they had brought with them and began rummaging through the metal ingots to begin on the amulet and chain.

"Knowledge, to learn, to grow, to become a better citizen of Mythnium is so often limited by how far we allow our imagination to stretch; for it is only the imagination enhanced by knowledge that shows true intelligence."
~Elder Martan, *The Pursuit of the Lost Magics* – Dwarven History

3

Stranick and Estryl picked up book after book. After carefully examining the titles, they set some back in the rock cubbies in which they were stored. Others they stacked on a cart to push to a stone table in the center of the hollowed-out cave.

At the table, Elder Martan sat with several candles burning to give him clear light as he searched books and scrolls for the knowledge he sought. He worked methodically. On one side of the table were the books, scrolls, and tablets Estryl and Stranick found that they hoped might have pertinent information. On the other side of the table was the stack he had already worked through. They were ready to be recataloged and replaced in their cubbies. In front of him, he had several pieces of parchment on which he had jotted down snippets of references or notes that further referenced other books and scrolls. He frowned at the notes in front of him. So far, he had found nothing that was directly helpful to Estryl. All his notes were merely vague recollections of rumors and legends regarding types of Dwarven magic, but none of it gave any insight into how she could hone her abilities. Nothing compared to the scrolls that had been in her house the entire time, but even those were obviously missing huge gaps in knowledge and training, speaking more of warnings and hazards than of the practical use of her magic.

The elder rubbed at his eyes, and Estryl appeared at his side, shooing away some tiny lizards that had gathered to find warmth by the candles. "Why not take a break for a minute? Rest your eyes."

Elder Martan looked at the young dwarf. For being such a hardy, tough, and skilled blacksmith, she was also especially feminine, gentle, and thoughtful. He nodded at her and rose to his feet.

Stranick emptied the cart at the table and then rolled it to the other side and piled the read books onto the cart. Rather than replacing them where he knew they belonged, he took them to Olphara.

Olphara then took each book and carefully reviewed it, taking note of its condition. Then after writing her own notes in a massive ledger, she put it away herself.

Elder Martan grabbed a flask of ale and sat on a bench that had been carved along one short wall of the cave. He leaned into the rock wall and motioned for Estryl to sit beside him, watching Stranick and Olphara as they continued to work.

"Have you found anything useful?" Estryl asked while Martan took a long swig of the ale.

He wiped his mouth and shook his head. "Lots of reference to it but nothing specific about it."

Estryl didn't seem too worried even though their ten years of research while at Farcaste Reach had proven to be just as unfruitful.

Elder Martan sighed.

"Are you worried?" Estryl asked.

"Aye. You know that I am. The scrolls that were handed down to you are just tiny fragments, and I worry that taking them as they are, out of context, will force the council's hand regarding your use of this magic."

"You don't think it is something we should be afraid of?"

Martan looked at Estryl, his gaze boring into her. "No. Treat it with caution. Learn its limitations. Use it with respect and keep in mind of the magic inherent all around us. All of that. Yes. But be afraid of it? No. That is not how we should look at this talent. Fear holds us back. We never reach all that we are capable of doing or being when we allow fear to dictate our actions. If you let fear into even a single part of your life, it is all too easy to let it seep into every other aspect. It can affect not just you but everyone around you and can become contagious. Fear is far more dangerous than misused magic for it can quickly permeate the minds of entire communities, turning from just internal fear to outward suspicion then to distrust and onward to hate, anger, and even violence. When fear takes hold, so much more goes wrong."

Estryl remained silent, taking in what the elder said. She did not worry about the magic. She had been using it for so long, it was part of her. It was only at a contest among the blacksmiths with her people that she had been made aware that other blacksmiths did not use magic the way she did if they used it at all. Since learning of her family's historical use of magic and the revelation that it had revealed itself in her after two long generations, the other blacksmiths and the council were divided on how they felt about her use of it. Elder Martan was her biggest supporter—after her brother—and when she decided instantly that she wanted to journey to the surface in an effort to learn more about this magic, it had been Elder Martan who insisted they leave as quickly as possible before fear caused the council to stop her.

She found it hard to believe that she had been on the surface for nearly ten years. It had taken time to find transportation from the Silver Isles across the sea to Watercastle. Once they reached Watercastle, they had to decide if they wanted to go straight to Farcaste Reach, a city that was known for its schools and centers that focused on magic, its rules and uses as well as much of the lore and history surrounding it, or go to Elmnas, the city of the Forest Elves, which was rumored to have the oldest texts and histories on Mythnium.

They had decided to go to Farcaste Reach first, and their journey there had been long and arduous as Elder Martan insisted that they travel with no guides. His own suspicions of the other races motivated his desire to travel with as little interaction with the surface races as possible. They traveled southeast with only maps and verbal directions from people they passed along the way. If he had been embarrassed at all by the number of roundabout ways they took, wrong turns that sent them several days and a couple of times weeks out of the way, and other misdirected routes, he gave no indication. While the travel fascinated Estryl so that she was not put off by the long journey, Stranick had been flustered and irritated so much along the way that he nearly decked Elder Martan on more than one occasion. Only his deep respect and realization that Elder Martan was helping his sister kept him from lashing out at the old dwarf in frustration.

Once they had finally reached Farcaste Reach after nearly a year of travel, they learned a lot about the magical currents moving about Mythnium so similar to weather patterns. Some people at the Reach were specifically studying how to track those currents. Estryl's mind felt as though it would explode from all that she learned about the currents of magic, how they ebbed and flowed across the surface of Mythnium, and how they were absorbed by certain things or repelled by others. She had learned how to recognize the magic moving within her and about her, and that helped her already with how she used it. She thought she was beginning to understand the reason for the song and the image that often intertwined within her when she looked at a new project to be made, but there were definite areas where she felt she was working more from instinct rather than using the magic as a tool. That did concern her a little.

They had been at Farcaste Reach for nine years before Elder Martan finally decided he had exhausted their libraries and schools, concluding they had found everything that dealt specifically with Estryl's inherited abilities, which was not much at all. Those few references he found referred to her gift as song magic. It was exceedingly rare and was exceedingly valuable but just as equally dangerous to both the gift bearer and those around them. Beyond that basic information, every reference recommended further research with the Willow Elves or the Forest Elves.

Now it seemed every reference kept among the caches of the Willows echoed the same limited knowledge of Farcaste Reach and merely pointed them to Elmnas. Estryl was excited by the prospect of visiting the Forest Elves for they were by far the most noble and honored of the surface races, but she sensed a reluctance in Elder Martan that she did not understand. As she sat next to him in silence, she tried to let the matter drop, but she could not help but worry about the older dwarf. If he was reluctant to go to Elmnas, it had to be for a good reason.

She considered confronting him at a later time, but as they sat in silence, the question nagged at her. Finally, she blurted it out. "Why don't you want to go to Elmnas?"

"What?" started Martan as he sat upright at the unexpected question.

"I sense you're reluctant to go there. Why?"

Elder Martan stared at Estryl for a moment. The woman was uncanny in her observations of the people around her sometimes and that unsettled him.

He turned his gaze downward. "Might we save that for another time? My reluctance is my own concern…"

"But it's not. It's not your own concern, I mean. Not if we have to go there next. I think we should all know why."

Elder Martan remained quiet for a few moments before he shrugged his shoulders and sighed inwardly. "I am reluctant over something that happened when I was a much younger dwarf. I caused offense, and I do not know if the elves have forgotten… or forgiven."

Estryl's mouth dropped open. "You? What could you have done...?"

"I really do not wish to recall such embarrassing events. Suffice it to say I was a brash young dwarf."

53

"But is it something that will make us unwelcome?"

"It's something that might make me unwelcome, aye. I doubt the elves will hold my past actions against you or your brother."

Estryl frowned. "I don't understand."

Elder Martan leaned back against the wall. "I know. You don't need to understand, my dear. You need to focus on you and your gift, and let me worry about the things that are ahead of us. Even if I am unwelcome, I am the official emissary from our people on your behalf, and that will weigh heavily with the elves. They may decide one thing for me but will most certainly decide to honor our people by allowing you to research and maybe train with them."

Estryl was not satisfied. "I don't want to be among them if they will not also welcome you."

The old dwarf leaned toward Estryl and spoke sternly as a father might to his child. "This is not about what you want, Estryl. This skill, this magic, is your responsibility. It matters not how the elves respond to me. What matters is that you get all the knowledge and skill you can in order to master your magic even if it means I cannot be beside you. Do you understand me?"

Estryl shrank inwardly at the hard edge to the elder's voice, but she nodded silently. She still didn't like not knowing why the dwarf was reluctant, but she knew he was right. No matter how they were received by the Forest Elves, her mission to learn all she could was of the utmost importance.

"How little she could have known the destiny before her in that first step she took away from her past, one full of pain and sorrow toward one of hope and redemption, not just for her but for thousands of her people."
~ Master Pruzin, Historian of Farcaste Reach

4

Several days later as the Dwarven group sat eating their evening meal among the Willows, Estryl handed Aldrina the amulet she had been working on. Aldrina held it in her hand and gasped in delight. Estryl had wrapped the gemstone seamlessly in an intricately woven cage with the nature rune, Ab-nar, depicted plainly over the smoothest part of the milky stone. The rune was tiny and simple yet elegant: a basic carving of a leaf with its stem curving out to the side with a circle at the end. Even the chain appeared to be woven rather than linked so that it moved smoothly and silently like a metallic rope.

"How did you...?" Aldrina asked breathlessly as she handled the delicate necklace.

Estryl smiled at Aldrina, delighted to see her genuine happiness with the finished piece. "Metal sings to me. This is the first time a gemstone has spoken to me, but when I chose the metal and set the two together, I saw a very distinct image. I started working. Then the song that I told you was building when I was holding the stone came out, and the magic really did the rest. I feel as though I am more of a vessel or a channel to it than I am a user of it."

"You have knowledge of runes?"

Estryl shook her head. "Only a rudimentary understanding from our time at Farcaste Reach. Of course, we dwarves use them, but rarely, and I was not aware of how to use them in my metalwork, even with this one. I have never added runes to my work before, but I was inspired to add it while the song was building within me. I can't tell you if it will make the amulet more powerful, but maybe someone more versed in use of the magical currents can help with that."

Aldrina paused, appraising the dwarf woman before her. This was an incredible artist that the gods had clearly blessed with a unique magical talent. She looked back at the amulet in her hands and had no words to express how incredible the workmanship was or how thankful she was to have it. As she stared at it, she thought of the few visiting healers who had relied on amulets to help them with their healing magic. There were none among the Willows, so she'd have to wait until another spent some time with them before she could learn to use the amulet. Still, now that she had it, she felt an increasing sense of excitement and eagerness to return to the healing tents to help the Willows at their work. She took the chain and carefully clasped it around her neck, noting that the amulet hung perfectly just below her collarbone. She tucked it securely out of sight into her tunic as she stood up.

Estryl noticed immediately and started to ask, but Aldrina responded first. "My Elven heritage helps me with magic so I can direct it better than most humans, but even with that natural intuition, I struggle to focus the healing magic. With this amulet, and I think with the added rune, I can hold magic in reserve and learn to better focus it so that my attempts to heal someone are more successful. I have a lot to learn though."

Estryl nodded in understanding. "The Willows do not use such talismans?"

Aldrina shook her head. "No." She lowered her voice and leaned in toward Estryl. "In fact, if Olphara knew I had it…"

"Oh!" gasped Estryl in dismay, her hand to her mouth.

"What is it?" questioned Aldrina in confusion.

Estryl turned deep red in embarrassment and sudden concern. "Oh, I wish I had known, Aldrina."

Aldrina felt a sudden dread in the pit of her stomach. "Why?"

"Oh. Maybe it will be okay. I just… Well… While we were on the trail to the cache today, Olphara asked me if I was currently working on anything special. She was so interested in how I use song magic in my blacksmithing, and… I was… I was just so eager to share with her since she has been so forthcoming with any information we might find in the cache that I… Well, I told her exactly what I was making and that I was making it for you!"

Aldrina sat back down abruptly. "Oh," she whispered.

"Will you be in trouble?"

Aldrina met Estryl's gaze. "Oh, not in trouble exactly, but sort of, I guess… Yes. I will likely be asked to leave."

Estryl moved closer to her new friend and stared into the campfire between them and the wagon.

"Oh dear," she said in a low voice "That bad? I am very sorry."

Aldrina shook her head. "Please. Don't be. Olphara knew I was struggling to direct the healing

57

magic.   Besides, I knew what the consequences would be for having one made.   Honestly, I was planning on moving on anyway.   I know using talismans in the healing process is unacceptable among the Willows.   Plenty of visiting healers have them and use them though not among the Willows out of respect.   I would never disrespect Olphara or her people by trying to use it under their noses after all they have done for me during my time here. But I figured I could have it and keep it safe, maybe learn a few things about how to use it from visitors, and then someday when I move on…"

Estryl was quiet.   She felt bad as though she had brought doom upon her friend.   Before she could think of something comforting to say, there was a rustle behind them.   She and Aldrina turned to see Olphara standing quietly behind them, a withdrawn look in her eyes.

"Aldrina. May I speak with you?" Olphara asked formally and stiffly.

Aldrina sensed the hurt of what Olphara considered a betrayal, and she felt ashamed for having the talisman created.

Rising to her feet, she smiled thinly at Estryl and responded to Olphara, "Of course."

The following morning, Aldrina fought to control her crying as she packed her belongings.   She had more now than she had had when Olphara found her, but it still all fit into a pack that she could easily sling over her shoulder.   Her conversation with Olphara the night before had been uncomfortable and painful for both women, but there was no way around the fact that Aldrina had gone against the traditions and expectations of the Willow Elves. Olphara could not allow or excuse a healer to remain among them using tools to aid their healing magic. To the Willows, it was unnatural and opened the door to accidents that could affect not just the healer and the person who needed healing but could also affect others in the immediate area in adverse ways. Olphara didn't need to ask Aldrina to leave, but a part of Aldrina had hoped that her friend and mentor would find a way to make even a slight concession. When none was made, the two parted ways most awkwardly.

"Aldrina? Are you in there?" a low voice asked from outside her tent.

"Yes. Come in, Estryl."

Estryl drew the tent flap aside and stepped into the dim interior to see Aldrina already dressed for travel. From the dark puffy circles under her eyes and the wet streaks down her cheeks, Estryl knew that she had been crying. She was dressed in an earth-colored garb, different from the whites and creams that the Willow Elves wore as a sign of their profession. Her blonde hair, which she kept long but bound to keep it out of the way of her work, was tightly braided and coiled on top of her head. Her lips were set in a grimace that gave away just how hard it was for her to leave.

"You don't have to go," Estryl blurted out triumphantly in hopes of bringing a smile to the other woman's face.

Aldrina raised her eyebrows in doubt.

Estryl continued, "What I mean is that you don't have to go right away. That is, I have a proposition

59

for you. Well, we have a proposition for you. I mean, it was Elder Martan's idea. He does come up with the very best solutions, you know. I mean, he is an elder for a reason, right?"

"Estryl… What are you talking about?"

"Oh. Right. Sorry. So I told Elder Martan what had happened, and he had an idea. We discussed it at great length, and we are all agreed. After we agreed, we went right away and talked to Olphara about it. She told us you planned to leave this morning, and you said last night that you had intended to leave in the future anyway… but I know you don't feel like you are ready to leave just yet… so if you like our idea, then you can stay a bit longer."

"What? How?" Aldrina asked, confusion on her face as she tried to process everything Estryl just spewed out. She had been speaking so fast and so excitedly that it was like only one word had been spoken.

"What if you came along with us? Joined our caravan? I mean to go to Elmnas, which is where we are going from here. We could use a healer among our group, and you could use time to practice your skills with the amulet, and…" Estryl paused when she saw Aldrina cover her mouth with her hand.

"Well… Okay, maybe it's not a great idea…"

Aldrina dropped her hand and grabbed Estryl in a spontaneous hug. She let her go almost immediately, but her face was radiant even as new tears streamed down her face. "I'd love to join you! What a generous offer!"

Estryl shrugged. "Isn't that what friends do for one another?"

Aldrina sat on her bed in relief and nodded.

Estryl, overcome with emotion and shy about it, turned to leave. "Well, that settles it then. When we leave in a couple days, you leave with us. Okay?" she said without looking at Aldrina, unwilling to show the emotions she knew were exposed on her face.

Aldrina stared at Estryl's back, replying, "Okay."

As Estryl stepped out of the tent, she commented over her shoulder, "Only one condition: Olphara said the amulet must be kept packed away while you are here. You can still help the healers but not with the amulet." Without another word, she stepped out of the tent, leaving her friend filled with excitement at her newfound prospects.

Aldrina sat on her bed and grinned. But then her smile slowly faded. Elmnas? They were going to Elmnas? Aldrina looked upward and sighed inwardly.

"Okay," she thought outwardly to Siki and Cria, gods she wasn't sure she believed in, "is this your doing?"

She sighed again and shook off her reservations. She had to move on; there was no other choice. She smiled to herself again as she realized she was looking forward to this adventure with Estryl and the other dwarves.

"He wages war on the whole world as though he wishes the planet itself to implode. Does he not realize all he seeks to destroy includes the fabric of his own existence?"
~ *Investigations of War by the Drow Council, 380 AC*

5

*H*orns blared around the battlement walls as fire lit the night sky. Chaos and terror overtook the suddenly roused citizens of Farcaste Reach. Fireballs and bolts of lightning arced from the tall walls across a wide ravine to a sea of orcs, goblins, and mercenaries, who in turn sent volley after volley of arrows, stones, and even the bodies of their own dead over the Reach walls.

Various wizards and sorcerers stood at key points along the walls in magically shielded towers as they prepared powerful fighting spells and directed their students on which areas to focus their attacks. Farcaste Reach had never been breached. The localized magical power within its walls made it the most fantastically protected settlement on Mythos, and the citizens safely inside her walls typically drew comfort from that fact. Still, arrows, rocks, and bodies cleared the walls, killing many defenders and causing havoc among the ranks.

While its residents were knowledgeable and skilled in magic, Farcaste Reach was not a militant society. They had no army. They did not focus training on battle and warfare, and they were used to a life of little disruption and very little violence. As a result, while they were making great strides in repelling the surge of attackers all about them, they were not prepared for an attack such as this.

The White Lord stood on a jagged rise on the other side of the ravine that served as a natural moat around the Reach. He surveyed the towers and the shielded magic users within. As wave after wave of his army fell before the magical defenses, he merely watched and took note. He was in no hurry for the battle to be over, and he was confident he had the resources and the bodies to keep pushing to the Reach as long as he desired.

He had no intention of destroying the ancient school of wizardry. He sought information. He sought to learn where more dragon eggs might be found, and he was certain the Reach would have that information. He knew the capital of the Forest Elves would as well, but he was not prepared to traverse the great span of Mythos to attempt to capture that city. Not yet.

Conjuring a portal large enough to bring his armies and Libitina through was taxing enough. Conjuring portals was never easy. One had to have been to the place they were trying to create a portal to. They had to picture it and where they intended to come out with nearly exact clarity, and they needed to understand the magical currents and have an idea of how the currents were acting at both ends of the desired portal. While he had the skill and knowledge and the ability to get to Farcaste Reach, the distance across the Donovan Sea from Mygras to Mythos meant he had to draw on his own strength as much as the magical currents themselves. Once he had the portal open, he was easily able to tap into the currents on both ends to help widen the portal and extend its limits to give his armies enough time to pass through. However, after they were all through and he was able to let it shut, he knew it would be at least a full day before he was able to open it for the return trip to Croglinke. Considering a portal to Elmnas, a place he had never been to himself, was out of the question, even for him.

An arc of white lightning pounded the ground below the point he stood on, shaking the rocks under his feet. Eyes narrowing, he held his hands together before him and whispered a few words of magic. He felt the magic in the air around him move to him, into him, and through him. As he felt the magic move, he sensed the point of release and spread his hands wide, looking toward the minor tower on the center of the wall he was facing where the lightning bolt had originated.

With a single word, he released his spell and directed a powerful shockwave, invisible to the eye, across the ravine and into the small tower. Smiling in satisfaction, he stood taller as the tower he targeted simply exploded in every direction, sending stone, wood, and people flying. He knew the shockwave was instant death to anyone who stood in its path, so he didn't bother looking to see if there were any survivors in the ravine that he could later interrogate.

He stared beyond where the tower stood and looked into the city beyond the wall, marveling at the grand scale of Farcaste Reach. He knew it was actually a city from before the Cataclysm, the only one that had remained standing mostly intact. It was also one of the first places that the races had run to for shelter and a new start as Mythnium shook for decades in the aftermath of the Cataclysm. He marveled how the elves, humans, dwarves, and other races had joined together to turn Farcaste Reach into the only place on Mythnium to hold each race as equal with equal opportunity to learn anything in general or magic. By all accounts, Farcaste Reach was nearly idyllic in its politics, social justice, and overall quest for knowledge in order to bring lasting peace to Mythos as a whole.

He laughed into the night, the sound of his mirth sending chills down the backs of those closest to him though not making it to those who stood on the walls of the Reach. The noises of battle overcame what had been the stillness of the night.

He turned his attention to a massive orc standing just behind him. "Take the amaroks and go into that breach."

The orc nodded its understanding and ran down the steep bank to a group of his kind where they waited with their giant wolflike mounts. Jumping onto the back of one, the orc let loose a war cry that spurred the others into action. Leading the way down into the ravine and across it to the other side, he and his amarok easily scaled its steep walls and what was left of the wall under the obliterated tower.

Watching with mounting excitement, the White Lord heard the wails of terror as the orcs and amaroks decimated the defenders that had raced to protect the breach. While they made short work of the defenders, the White Lord turned his attention to the sky.

"Now, my friend, reveal yourself."

Finally! came the response filled with impatience and fury.

From somewhere behind him, he could sense Libitina approach. At ten years, she was fully grown in size though not necessarily mature. He could feel her excitement and bloodlust that matched his own. He looked up to watch her as she soared over him and the Reach. He knew the people on the walls would see her, but they had no weapons that could harm her. He doubted any of their wizards would be of sound mind to cast any decent spells that would hinder her once she was spotted. Sure enough, he could make out people along the walls pointing in her direction. Some foolishly sent arrows her way. Some cast swift spells of lightning and fire toward her. Nothing had any effect on her as most missed her completely.

He watched her dip over to the left as she lined herself up with the wall. Clenching his fists in grotesque delight, he watched as she spewed flame onto the wall and at the towers that rose up ahead of her. Then she veered off into the main part of the city itself. Staring into the smoke, he lost sight of her for several long moments.

"I lost sight…"

She rose up over the smoke billowing up from the Reach. Her wings flapped lazily as she floated on the updraft of the intense heat.

Shall I continue?

The White Lord nearly let her. His sensitive nose could smell charred flesh even across the chasm. His sensitive tongue could taste the copper of blood on the air. Closing his eyes, he savored the taste and smell of war. His blood quickening in his veins almost caused him to lose control. He shook his head before taking a long deep breath and surveyed the damage done before him.

"No. We came here for a reason. I need survivors."

He could sense her intense frustration and her need to feed. "On second thought, I am sure you would enjoy a snack. Go where you will, but leave me the tall tower there in the center. And do try not to eat everything in sight. We still need recruits for our growing army."

The dragon perked up and flew to the northern side of the Reach. Snapping his fingers, a nearby human heard and raced to his side.

"My Lord?"

"Assemble my guard. I am ready to visit the tower."

The man nodded. "At once." He dashed off, sounding a horn.

In moments, a large contingent of orc and human mercenaries filed in line behind the White Lord as he led the way around to the main gate of Farcaste Reach. He met no resistance; his original forces had dispatched everything outside the Reach with ease. Once he reached the gates, he found that Libitina had burned the massive wooden doors right off the hinges with heat so intense the metal dripped down the stone walls. Inside the Reach, few challenged his advance, and those few who did, he easily cut down. Only once did he meet a human warrior mage whose fighting skill caused him to put forth effort. In the end, he knocked the mage unconscious and nodded for him to be bound and gagged to make the return trek to Mygras.

As they moved toward the tower, he instructed his guards to fan out on side streets and alleys, either killing the young, old, weak, and infirm, or capturing those who could be good fighters in his army. Screams and wails, pleas for both death and mercy echoed through the Reach from every corner. He smiled widely in their echoes.

Finally, they reached the door to the tower. Knowing it would be magically warded, he called for Libitina to join him and blast the heavy iron-studded doors down. He could have used his own spells, but this was the first time he had allowed the young dragon to venture beyond Croglinke and across the Donovan Sea to Mythos. Utilizing her brute strength and her ability to burn and blast through things was a unique opportunity he wanted to witness to judge her powers and limitations.

The Red Dragon landed on the pebbled street in front of the doors. She stood taller than the huge doors, and her massive body forced the White Lord and his contingent backward the way they had come. He watched the dragon measure the strength of the doors and expected her to pull back her head, drawing in air to help fuel her inner fire. But he was surprised when instead of trying to burn or blast them, she merely placed her two front feet on the doors then pushed against them.

Groans of wood splintering, metal rubbing against stone, and shouts from behind the doors warned the White Lord of what was about to happen next. His lips set in a thin line of satisfaction. Leaning against the doors as she was, her body weight alone was putting immense pressure on the doors. She set her hind legs firmly beneath her, and with a great flap of her wings pushed against them. A resounding crash and cries of terror from inside the ground floor of the tower flowed out onto the street toward the White Lord. Once the dust settled, he observed Libitina standing to the side staring at him, amusement and pride flashing in her eyes.

Next time, give me a challenge, she said to him. Then she launched herself into the air on a mission of destruction.

Watching her fly off to another corner of the Reach, the White Lord snapped his fingers and his guard rushed ahead of him to rid the tower of any people. He watched as some tried to escape. Others rushed toward him, imploring him for mercy. Those he dispatched himself with calm disconnect. After a while, his guard marched out of the tower with a dozen men of various races, all dressed in the garb of the esteemed historians of Farcaste Reach. His guard lined men up in front of the White Lord, and he moved along the line assessing each of the men. He singled out two of them, and ordered that the rest be executed.

Turning his back on the executions of the unarmed men, he followed the guards who retained his new prisoners away from the tower and out of the Reach. Once he had reached his camp, he ordered the two men to be brought to his tent for questioning.

The first man, a middle-aged human, was forced to his knees before him. The man was shaking from head to toe and smelled of urine and vomit, both staining his breeches and tunic.

"What is your name?" the White Lord demanded with no pretext.

The man trembled and muttered something.

"Louder so I can hear you, or you will be killed on the spot."

The man shook uncontrollably and tears ran down his face. He gulped several times and lifted his head though he avoided eye contact with the ancient Heridon standing before him. "My… I am… unnamed."

69

The White Lord growled in anger. "You aren't a historian?"

The man shook his head emphatically.

"How long have you been among the historians?"

"Only ten years… since… since the eclipse."

The White Lord paced in front of the man thinking.

"The other man brought with you, the Willow Elf, he is a historian?"

The man trembled even more, but didn't answer. His head bowed downward.

The White Lord moved to stand in front of the man. "Get up," he commanded.

Slowly, the man rose to his feet, still avoiding looking at the White Lord.

"Now. Look at me."

The man shook his head and kept his eyes cast downward.

In a lightning-fast move, the White Lord grabbed the man's chin and forced his head upward, lifting the man off the ground as he did so.

The man instinctively grabbed the White Lord's wrist only to impale his hands on the deadly spiked gauntlets he wore. Screaming in pain yet unable to remove his hands without ripping them to shreds, he still managed to keep his eyes lowered.

The White Lord squeezed the man's lower jaw and smiled grimly as he heard and felt the jaw shatter in his hand. "I imagine it will hurt you to talk now, so you will have to nod your head to answer me. Now. I will not say it again. Look at me."

Nearly unconscious from the pain in his jaw and hands, the man met the White Lord's reptilian eyes.

"There. That wasn't so bad, now, was it?"

The man simply stared.

The White Lord resisted shaking the man, knowing he was on the verge of passing out.

"A nod 'yes' or 'no,' please."

The man shook his head no, blood flowing out of his broken mouth.

"Very good. Now answer my question. That Willow Elf, he is a historian?"

Tears flowed from the man's eyes, but he nodded in the affirmative and then tried to say something. But the pain was too much, and he passed out.

The White Lord tore the man's hands off his wrist with his other hand and tossed the unconscious man to his guards.

"Get him out of here. Give him to the dragon. I'm sure she will enjoy a new treat. And bring me the Willow Elf."

The guards nodded and left, dragging the man between them.

"The ambitions that drove him were not understood for too long. The desires that motivated his bloodthirsty ravages across our lands made us cower in fear, not because he seemed to be gaining power, but because we could not find an answer to the never-ending question: why?"
~ King Mronas, *Interviews of Elven Kings, Vol 3*

6

*T*he White Lord stood at the entrance of his tent watching as his forces began to leave Farcaste Reach. Soon he'd have to reopen the portal to take them back to Croglinke. He desperately wanted to raze the Reach, but his communion with his lord recommended otherwise. There was some implication that events could spiral before they were ready to take action. He frowned, feeling he and Libitina were ready to take on all of Mythnium, but he trusted his god and sought to obey him because he was the only god who gave a damn about him. Still, while it was not completely destroyed, he and Libitina had left a definite mark on the Reach. Most of the city burned. Wailing and crying rose up above the city walls even as hundreds of men and women of all the races were led in chains up the ridge to wait for him to open the portal. He looked up and saw Libitina flying toward him, coming to land just before his tent, a sense of sated rage within her.

Hearing a dry cough behind him, he turned back into the recesses of his tent and moved to stand in front of his prisoner. Excitement flowed through him as he observed the Willow Elf that stood trembling before him. Discomfort and fear emanated off the old historian in almost tangible waves. He stepped toward the Willow who he had stripped down to a loin cloth that was now soiled and bloody after hours of brutal interrogation. Clicking his clawed hands together, he noted with pleasure the way the elf cringed inwardly as though he could somehow hide within himself. The White Lord stopped in front of the elf and whispered promises of pain and terror. He stepped backward as the scent of urine mixed with blood and feces filled the air, and he licked his pebbly lips in sudden hunger.

Turning on his heel, he moved away from the old elf, knowing he had not yet gleaned anything of true import. He leaned against a heavy table that stood at the back of his tent.

"You will tell me more. You hold on to some secrets still. I want those secrets. I want to know all that you know. Particularly whatever you know about dragons."

The historian trembled and nearly fell over, but two guards quickly moved to support him, forcing him to remain standing.

The White Lord watched as the old elf struggled to remain conscious, his eyes constantly rolling around as he fought the pain. He watched the old man lick his lips over and over, wincing even as he did so for his lips were broken, dried, and chapped.

Finally, the man rasped out, "I know nothing of dragons."

He gasped for air, making great effort to fill his lungs even though several of his ribs were broken, his chest blue and purple from the severe beatings.

His head sagged, but he continued, "All we have is old lore from just after the Cataclysm. All I have read question where the great beasts went. There is speculation and a sense of loss, but nothing at all that tells for sure that the dragons were anything more than ancient beasts. They were exceedingly rare. Some thought they were sentient though most scoffed at the suggestion, but everything says they were completely eradicated in the Cataclysm."

After the last word, Pruzin took in a ragged breath and started to say more but was interrupted.

"No!" The old elf and even the guards holding him trembled at the vehemence in the White Lord's impatient scream. He narrowed his eyes, taking a deep breath to calm himself. He longed to rip the elf from limb to limb himself.

"They still exist, Pruzin," he whispered with forced calm. "You have seen the proof of them this very day. You would still deny me the secrets you know? You would still dare to defy me?"

Pruzin lifted his head and peered through swollen eyes. He opened his mouth then snapped it shut again as pain overwhelmed him. He stared at the White Lord, willing his terror to stop betraying him. He gulped out, "I swear to you, I know nothing more of the dragons. To see…" He glanced over his shoulder to where the large Red Dragon stood peering through the tent flap with what appeared to be satisfaction equal to the White Lord's. He forced his gaze back to the White Lord even as his own blood ran like ice. "To see a dragon alive and… and… terrible. I never imagined the tales were ever anything more than exaggerated legends. More mythical than factual."

The White Lord sneered, "How wrong you were, old one."

Pruzin sagged and nodded in dismal agreement.

74

"There is no sense in trying to help everyone, but in the act of helping just one person, a glimmer of light shines in the darkness. A decision is made that changes the course of history."
~ Mythnium Proverb

7

*H*e stood in the door that led out onto the small balcony and felt the ocean breeze wash over him as he stared east across the Cresia Ocean toward Mythos. He longed to be home again and to have a peaceful night's sleep without worrying he had been found out. Time was running out, but the last message he had from Elmnas asked him to remain a while longer. Rubbing his face and combing out his graying beard with his fingers, he sighed. His mind wandered. He wondered what Aldrina was like now as a woman. He had not seen her in nearly twenty years, the last time he had visited his younger brother's inn. He had very nearly killed his brother over the way Jackob and his horrible wife treated Aldrina, but he had no choice but to leave her there. He knew that no matter how bad things might have gotten for her under his brother's care, at least she would be alive. Unknown and alive.

He sighed again.

Over the years, he often wondered if he had done the right thing by the girl. He often imagined other ways he might have been able to keep her safe. They could have left his little home and settled farther west on Mythos, beyond even King Mronas's reach. He imagined raising the girl as his own. The attachment he felt for her in just the short time they were together baffled him, but then he had no children of his own anymore. Her trust in him after she was found on the beach had touched his heart so deeply; it was as if the gods had given him a second chance.

It was no wonder that when King Mronas's emissaries had found him and asked for his help to undermine the tyrannical rule over the Ebony Isles, he jumped at the opportunity to try to help Aldrina return to her rightful home. Since then, he had left everything behind on Mythos toward that end, only writing his brother once because King Mronas planned on sending his guards to fetch Aldrina to be cared for among his own people. When he learned she had run off and was later found among the Willow Elves, his contact divulged that the king thought it best she remain there for a time. He had no idea how she was faring in the Alisyan Mountains among the nomadic healers. The concern and worry he had over her was strong with him even now, knowing she was a grown woman and likely well cared for.

He leaned on the balcony railing and breathed in the ocean air that wafted over the island he now called home. A door clicked open behind him, and feet shuffled onto the balcony.

He glanced at the person joining him, a woman nearly his age with graying hair, bright eyes, and a bright smile in a tanned face. "Rackas, you old goat, I have been looking for you everywhere."

Rackas smiled at the woman and turned to give her a quick hug and a peck on her cheek. "Ryma, my dear. Am I neglecting something?"

Ryma pinched him under his ribs gently. "Yes. Your shipment for General Duwo arrived. Jasper just

76

brought word. He wants to know if you want to deliver it yourself or should he take it?"

Rackas shrugged out of his wife's embrace and glanced at the suns as they retreated to their setting points. "No. It is too late today. Tell Jasper to go home. I will send a messenger to the general. He'll want to receive it at the docks, I'm sure, so he'll likely want to meet me there at first sunrise."

Ryma raised an eyebrow at Rackas, noting the gauntness to his cheeks and the dark circles under his eyes. "I'll tell Jasper, but you come in and eat something. You look like you haven't slept in weeks." She stepped toe to toe with him. "You know if something is bothering you, my love, you can tell me. Maybe I can help."

Rackas smiled and kissed Ryma then spun her around with a slap to her bottom. "I know," he replied as he pushed her toward the door leading inside. "I'll be in shortly. I enjoy the fresh air, you know."

Ryma winked over her shoulder as she hurried off to find Jasper.

Rackas's smile faded after she left. He knew she was a spy for the general, who in turn had long suspected Rackas of being a spy though he had not indicated who he thought Rackas was a spy for. It had taken him years to build his reputation and fortune among the people of the Ebony Isles. All during that time, he planted himself in the general's path in as many ways as he could.

Being a shrewd businessman, Rackas had no trouble transitioning his smuggling enterprises from western Mythos to Niphas, the main island of the eight that made up the Ebony Isles. He had worked his way up the ranks of the smugglers and the black market. He was forced to shed a lot of his ideologies in order to gain respect and favors from other smugglers, who were a deadlier lot on the Isles than they were on Mythos. Once he had earned a reputation among the other smugglers, he began working on building relationships with the merchants of the Isles. While he worked his way into different circles, he also worked to gain a reputation among the constantly scheming wealthy families who held ties either to the general himself or to the royal family who had been deposed.

He had found and wooed Ryma, a spinster from among the general's own extended family. Her own family was one of the wealthier families though they lived on another island surrounded by a large estate that grew and sold exotic fruit. He had chosen Ryma to be the target of his affection at first just to gain closer access to the general. But as he got to know the woman better, he did feel genuine affection for her. Once they were married, he finally found himself established among the people of the Isles with a sizeable estate that kept him near the general. This allowed him to gain the man's interest and business though not his trust.

Rackas didn't care to gain the man's trust. He also didn't care that his own wife, who he genuinely loved now, was a spy against him. He cared only about his purpose to gain information that Mronas could use to put the Ebony Isles back in the control of the Rina family, to put Aldrina in her rightful place on the throne.

With a final longing look to the east, Rackas turned and went inside in search of strong wine and his wife's spicy foods.

"Pursuit of power, the downfall of our world, the catalyst of the Cataclysm. That pursuit corrupted the best of us, and the results created the worst of us. What then will the continued pursuit of power cost the White Lord?"
~ *An Early History of the Great Cataclysm,* 150 AC

8

*H*e watched the old historian squirm on the rack. Licking his lips at the sight of the blood oozing from the various wounds inflicted on the old elf, The White Lord looked down at the short blade he had been using to cut at his prisoner. "Now, about this Silver Dwarf. What does she call herself?"

Pruzin muttered something, blood and spittle dripping from his split lips.

The White Lord stepped closer and leaned down to hear the elf better. "What was that, old one?"

He stared into the bright eyes of the historian and found himself caught off guard at the vibrant defiance he saw in the pale blue orbs that bravely met his own. "What do you want with her?"

The White Lord stood tall and tapped the blade against the historian's shoulder, watching the elf flinch under the feel of the cold steel sticky with his own blood. He considered peeling off another inch of the elf's skin, but the defiance he saw in his eyes made him reconsider. Since returning to Croglinke, he had spent several days having his men interrogate the elf before he stepped in and took over himself. It was only in the last day that he got the old elf to reveal anything at all, and it was all about this Silver

Dwarf that could use the currents of magic to shape metal using song. The White Lord was curious about the skill itself, but he was more eager to get to the wielder, to have that skill at his command to use as he saw fit. He was determined to find that Silver Dwarf. Seeing the defiance in the elf's eyes, he knew he'd have to use different tactics to get the information he wanted.

He leaned back against a rock table where he kept various weapons and tools used for interrogation or just to torture when the mood struck him. He lifted the blade that had rested on the elf's shoulder to his nostrils and breathed in deeply, his eyes never leaving the face of his prisoner. He savored every twitch and grimace that betrayed the old elf. To make him even less comfortable, he ran the blade over his tongue, making a slow show of how he savored the taste of the elf's blood. Seeing the disgust and fear mingle together to replace a bit of the defiance in the elf's eyes, the White Lord nodded, satisfied for the moment.

"Let the elf loose," he instructed his guards, who waited at the door behind him.

As they moved to undo the chains and bindings that held the elf to the rack, he watched him try to summon the strength to remain upright. The groans and unsolicited cries of pain as the elf fell to the floor in a heap made the White Lord's blood run hot. Still, he simply stood watching. The guards on either side of the elf stood, waiting for their Lord's next command. Finally, he motioned for them to leave the room.

"Get our prisoner some bread and water," he called over his shoulder as they left, then he crouched before the elf.

"Farcaste Reach is gone, old one," he lied. "No one will be coming for you. For a while, no one will even know to miss you. This, of course, means I have all the time I want to play with you until I get everything I want from that brain of yours or until I grow bored. Then I will go find another historian and do the same to them."

At his promise to find someone else to torture, Pruzin looked up sharply, horror in his eyes. The White Lord chuckled and thought to himself, *so that is how to play this one. Play on his desire to protect others. Very well.*

He stood up. "Now that I think about it, I think that is what I should do. You clearly have nothing else to offer me. I hope you enjoy your last meal, old one. Once you are done, I will feed you to that brilliant red beast you saw at the Reach. And then I will capture someone else more willing to share their knowledge with me."

Without another word, he turned on his heel and moved to the door. Stepping through it, he stopped when he heard the faint cry behind him, "Wait…"

He pored over maps of the Alisyan Mountains that stretched east to west across the southern edge of Mythos. He pondered the various trails that led away from Farcaste Reach on the southwestern side of the continent and eastward toward mountains known to be home to the Willow Elves, the healers. Pruzin had given him much information, enough to plan on capturing an addition to his own forces.

Heavy steps shook the room, and he smiled, "Welcome, Libitina. I am planning another excursion to Mythos."

I am to come along? the dragon asked as she lowered her head to gaze at the maps that were spread across the vast table.

The White Lord considered her question. *No, my dear. Not this time. This time, I will go alone. Though I will take that old elf with me. He may prove useful. I underestimated the strength of the will central to the Willow Elves.*

What do you mean? The dragon inquired.

Willow Elves are healers by nature. Their touch on the magical currents allows them to heal just about anyone of any ailment, including even the most severe wounds. They are quite skilled though they are also incredibly wary. They separate themselves from the other races in order not to be drawn into politics, disputes, and wars. They have an insatiable desire to help, but that desire is in stark contrast to their equal desire to have no part of anything that could bring harm to others. So they are a scattered people.

He paused for a moment, but then continued.

Anyway, I digress. That central desire to help also makes them eager to prevent pain and illness in others if they can. With Pruzin, I was finally able to get him to reveal more of what he knows by using that desire against him.

The dragon, still peering over the maps, moved her head eye-level with the White Lord.

And..?

The White Lord looked her in the eye, With proud and serious determination in his voice, he responded,

"And he directed me to the leader of the Willow clans. He directed me to Olphara herself."

What does she matter?

The White Lord looked back at the maps and traced a claw down a particular mountain road.

She matters because Pruzin directed the Silver Dwarf to seek her out by name. This is important, my dear, for two reasons.

Pausing for effect, soaking in the full attention he was getting from the massive beast before him, and thinking at the back of his mind how proud his god would be to learn of this new development, he stretched his arms wide and lifted one finger.

"First," he said out loud, in order to keep his thoughts in order, "finding Olphara means we find that dwarf. Second, finding Olphara means we find the one person on all of Mythnium who can give us access to scores of historical data we have not had access to. Imagine it! Among the caches the Willows protect, we could find more about your kind. Maybe where more eggs were kept hidden. Maybe more of what really happened prior to the Cataclysm!"

Libitina moved away from the maps and made to leave the room.

But you won't need me this time?

The White Lord frowned. "Do you not understand how important this is?"

The Red Dragon looked over her shoulder at him and mentally shrugged.

I understand the dwarf could be useful. I understand more dragons like me could be useful. I don't understand how knowing the cause of the Cataclysm could benefit us. I sense that is important to you, but I don't know why, and you shut off that part of your mind to me.

The White Lord's gaze narrowed as he watched the dragon amble through the massive door and out into the light of the suns overhead. She knew he was blocking things from her? He mentally rebuked himself. Of course she knew. She was a very smart creature after all. Clenching his fist on the table, he slammed it down in frustration. Was he underestimating her mental abilities? Immediately, he shook off the question. No, he thought. She was just a dragon. Fierce. Powerful. Able to communicate. But just a dragon. Nothing more.

Settling his sudden trepidations, he looked back at the maps and continued to plan his next visit to Mythos, to the Willow Elves, and to Olphara.

"Trust not those who speak eloquently and at length without first revealing their honest intentions through actions."
~ Igma, Goddess of Wisdom

9

*H*is eyes glittered with pride as he watched her gorge on her meal. He clenched the arms of his throne and leaned forward to watch with amusement and excitement near to longing to get into the mix with her as she tore her victim apart. Blood sprayed across the vast throne room, droplets of it splattering across his face. He raised a hand and wiped his face, seeing the blood staining his hand. He held the hand to his face and took in its coppery scent. He noted that it was still warm. He flicked his tongue out and reveled in the taste of the fresh kill. His heart raced wildly in his chest, and the urge to join her nearly overwhelmed him.

In his mind, her thoughts touched his.

Why fight it? Come. Join me.

He saw her roll a blood-red eye in his direction. Its iris, a mere slit in a large red orb, narrowed on him, a sign of the frenzy that had overtaken her.

He spoke out loud. "No, my dear. Your excitement is enough for me."

Mmm... Your thoughts betray you. Come. Eat with me.

The White Lord smiled indulgently at Libitina. He rose, careful not to slip on the blood that had sprayed onto the steps to his throne, and approached the beautiful dragon. Her eyes rolled back in her head as she tore another chunk of meat from one of the merchants that had been presented to her.

What did these do to displease you? she asked between large gulps.

He stepped closer to her, his feet saturated in the thick blood of her victims. He laid a clawed hand on her flank and felt the heat radiating from beneath her scales. He looked down at the flayed bodies of the three merchants. He kicked at the one she was currently gnawing on.

"This one promised to bring me word of any import regarding the north. In the ten years since the crossing of the suns, I imagined the peoples to the north would be clamoring about prophecies and omens and reawakened skills or gifts like with the Silver Dwarf. He brought me nothing that I didn't already know about creatures from the past, increased goblin activity, all cyclical occurrences." He paused and then admitted, "Although as you know, we have been stirring the pot a bit. Still, I expected to hear of reaction to our attack on Farcaste Reach. Yet… he had no news at all."

Libitina sucked the brain matter from the back of the merchant's head.

You know how shortsighted the other races are. How easily they forget the cycles of this world. Besides that, no word about our attack may be word in itself. If I am the first dragon they've ever seen and if we are the first to ever penetrate the tower, the people of Mythos may not actually believe it happened at all. Was that truly why you were displeased?

The White Lord patted the dragon and then reached down to gather a gold chain from the dead man. He let the chain catch the light from the torches on the walls, getting lost in the glimmer and sparkle of it before he replied to the keen animal and let the chain fall to the ground.

"You are perceptive." He paused. He was making more of an effort to keep certain thoughts blocked from the intrusive dragon. She had not yet learned an honest appreciation for her role in the White Lord's plan. Like any juvenile, she was wise in some ways but thoughtless in others.

"Maybe I will fill you in another time, my dear."

Libitina raised her head and turned to level her eyes with the White Lord's. There was no defiance in her eyes, but she clearly did not think of him as her master despite her deference to him. She stared into his eyes, and he stared back with no fear. She knew that while she had sharp teeth and claws, she could never use them against him as he had great influence over the magical currents that would protect him. Still, she stared into his eyes and tried to decipher what he might be hiding. She could not break through his mental block. She shook her head at him and without another word, she returned to her meal.

The White Lord took in a deep breath, catching the thick smell of the blood both through his nostrils and along his tongue. Hunger nearly overcame him, but he never ate with an audience.

For him, his meal times were a sacred rite. He chose to worship during his meals in order to spend them alone with his god. He envisioned his own meal just hours before. He had been presented a young woman directly from the temple. She had been an acolyte, chosen for her purity but was past the age the priests preferred for their rituals, so the priest led her up to the fortress for the White Lord, another willing sacrifice fulfilling her last duty. The woman had been prepared with great care. Her hair had been shaved off. Her entire body had been shaved, washed, and rubbed with a thick oil that enhanced her particular aroma. She had been led willingly as most of his meals were so mentally manipulated that they never thought to question. To dine with the White Lord and then to be sacrificed to his god was a great honor for any acolyte, so there was never a need for chains or ropes that would mar the skin; she had been wrapped in gauzy robes so she would not sweat in the heat of the desert.

He had welcomed her to his table as though she were an honored guest and enjoyed watching her eat her last meal. She had enjoyed the fruits and vegetables that had been laid out before her and had drunk deeply from the goblet of wine. That was one of his favorite parts. The wine was laced with an herb that would render his dinner guests paralyzed and yet leave them completely aware and with all feeling.

As the young woman lost the ability to control her limbs, he saw fear and panic grow in her eyes, but her body betrayed her. At that point, the White Lord moved to her side and whispered exactly what he intended to do to her as he fed on her. He relished the terror that flashed in her eyes as realization dawned on her what was about to happen to her. This manner of sacrifice was not anything the priests had shared with her nor any acolyte. He savored the salty tang of her tears and the bitterness in her flesh from the adrenaline that fear caused to burst through her helpless body.

By the time he had finished consuming the young woman, the only thing left of her was her carefully removed skin. As he stood naked in her still wet blood, his alabaster body glistened. He raised his eyes to the heavens, which he could see through an open panel in the ceiling and offered his thanks silently to Naga, the god of the Heridon. Naga had revealed himself to the White Lord in the aftermath of the Cataclysm, imparting bits of information and knowledge that helped the White Lord learn more of his forgotten history.

It was when he was in communion with Naga that he laid out plans for the future. Those plans had helped him develop patience as he considered the short-term goals that would help him achieve his ultimate goal. He had spent hours communing with Naga before he allowed his servants to remove the skin to be preserved and added to his collection. They never cleaned the blood from the room. He insisted it remain. The stench of the drying blood soothed him. The room was his personal shrine to the perfectly malevolent god he devoted himself to.

Libitina stirred and gulped out a belch, drawing the White Lord from his thoughts.

Thank you. Maybe one day you will allow me to commune with your god as you do.

The White Lord smiled at her indulgently, his toothy grin nearly matching her own. His god was selfish and did not want to share communion with anyone but him. When his god had imparted that to him, the White Lord had promised that he would never allow the communion they shared to be opened up to anyone else.

"My god prefers the sanctity of our private communion. Perhaps, someday, as he observes you and all that you are becoming, he will take you into his fold. But for now, you need not worry about it.

Come, dear Libitina. Let us go for a walk and let the servants clean up in our absence."

The dragon, who had been lying on the floor to eat, lifted herself up. She walked beside the White Lord, and together, they left the throne room, ending up at the top of a short but wide series of steps that led to a vast courtyard. She moved her head from side to side taking in the numerous guards. Some stood on the walls of the fortress and others were scattered throughout the courtyard.

More guards these days, she commented, not considering the White Lord's refusal to include her as a slight.

The White Lord nodded. "It's time to begin preparations beyond capturing Olphara. After our successful attack on Farcaste Reach and with my plan to gain the knowledge of the Willow Elves, we should expect the people of Mythos to start looking our way. The time is coming for me to stretch out to the north once again."

To what end? mused the dragon, her eyes glinting in the light of the two suns.

The White Lord cocked his head to look her in the eye. He reached up to her face and wiped some residual blood from the scales on her lower jaw. He moved his hand to her nostrils and saw her eye dilate as the scent aroused her insatiable hunger.

"Blood, my dear. I do it all for blood."

Libitina bared her teeth in an effort to mimic the White Lord's grim smile, and the pair stood overlooking the courtyard for several minutes before they continued down the steps and out of the fortress.

"If you see yourself in the actions of a stranger, if you hear your voice in the words they speak to you, if you find that the stranger in front of you is like a reflection of yourself in a smooth pool of water, be prepared for the reaction you will inevitably have within yourself. For if you love that stranger, you must love yourself, but if you desire to kill that stranger, you must come to terms with killing that within you that needs killing."
~ *Reflections of the Water Woman*, a Mythnium Fable

10

"C aptain! Look out!" someone shouted from behind, and she ducked to the left just as a goblin's spear whizzed by her ear so closely that she instinctively checked to see if she was bleeding. She turned to face the goblins that stood behind her. A quick thanks was nodded to one of the young men who was part of her unit while she swung her short blade across in front of her and nearly sliced a goblin's head off. As the goblin fell to the ground, she nimbly leapt over it to the spindly goblin that threw the spear. Its eyes widened in fear as it scrambled backward, looking for something to fend off the tiny elf warrior who was no bigger than it was. She didn't give it time to find a weapon, throwing herself forward at a sprint. Before the ugly goblin could complete its turn to run away, she had slashed its belly open and then stabbed it cleanly through the throat. She stopped to get her bearings, catching her breath, and taking note of the nicks and cuts all over her arms and legs before she turned to face the main fight where her unit of three humans, two Forest Elves, two more White Elves, and a dwarf were fighting against several dozen goblins. Though they were outnumbered—her unit was comprised entirely of Wargate graduates—she knew that with their extensive training in combat, they would make quick work of the disorganized goblin band.

Then a deep rumbling that shook the ground under her feet and caused birds to take flight from the trees at the edge of the forest caught her attention. She gasped as a group of trolls moved to join the fight. She watched sudden concern touch the faces of several of her party, and she knew they were overmatched. She watched in slow motion as one of the larger trolls waded through the sea of goblins, knocking them aside with ease, and simply plucked one of the human fighters from the ground. Her blood ran cold as the troll ripped the soldier apart as though he were a parchment doll. Meanwhile, another troll had clipped one of the elves in the head with its studded club so hard that the elf simply crumbled to the ground, dead from the impact.

Seeing their new allies abruptly change the tide of the battle, the goblins rallied and began rushing forward in renewed determination with shouts and tribal calls and whistles.

Seeing red and her breath coming in short gasps, she tightened her grip on her blade and found herself struggling to keep her rage in check. While she had learned how to control her rage and impulsiveness for the most part, it was still a struggle. When the safety of her unit was compromised, it was nearly impossible to control. She forced her rage down and took a deep breath.

As she was about to whistle for her unit to retreat to the relative safety of the rise to the south of them, a bright flash of light flew out of the forest behind her and into the clump of trolls. Less than a second later, each troll was outlined in fire as though they had been trapped in glass and the fire burned them within it. She watched in awe and disgust as the trolls burned away. The goblins instantly took that as their cue to run and hide.

She and her remaining unit stood in silent wonder, staring at the smoldering remains of the trolls. A light crunch on the ground behind her startled her out of her observations. Spinning on her heel, her sword ready to dismember whoever stood behind her, she froze as she was hit with a paralyzing blast of magic.

"You're welcome," greeted a human dressed from head to toe in animal skins. His head was half-shaven with elaborate tattoos showing on his shaved scalp. The elaborately carved staff in his hands identified him as a mage. "I'd like to let you go, but do you intend to stab me with that little sword?"

He didn't wait for an answer but flicked his wrist, and she could move again. Eyeing the man suspiciously, she frowned as she wiped her blade on her tunic. She stared up at the mage for a few minutes. Something about him told her he was no threat to her or her unit, so she tucked her blade in its sheath.

"Thank you for helping with the trolls," she commented.

The man shrugged. "I think it's my fault they joined the fight."

She raised her eyebrows in question, noting that her unit had silently gathered around her in protective stances.

The man continued, "Well, I was tracking them. They had something I was interested in having, so I've been following them for a few days. I never intended to chase them to you, but…. Well, it's a concluded matter now, isn't it?"

"Who are you?" the White Elf demanded.

"Oh! Yes. Introductions are considered polite. I'm sorry. I hadn't intended on being around anyone quite yet. I still have so much to do. Yes, I have so much to do. I still have to find…"

"Hey!" she yelled up at him impatiently. The mage blinked in surprise.

"Oh fine… I'll start. I am Captain Tristal White Stone. This is my unit from Wargate." She nodded at the remaining members of her unit, and they each nodded their heads in greeting but did not offer their own names.

The mage looked at each member of the party closely as though measuring them up. Then he focused his gaze on Tristal. "I know who you are."

He stepped past Tristal, and she sputtered in bewilderment as she stared up at the tall man.

"Excuse me?" she demanded. "How exactly do you know me? I know we have never met. I would've remembered."

The man walked over to the dead trolls and began digging around in the ashes of their bodies in search of something. "Well, that is because we never met, you see."

Tristal glanced around her unit and realized they were as dumbfounded as she was. Finally, she could take it no more. "Who in the bloody blazes of hellfire are you?"

The man plucked something from the ashes, wiped it off, and tucked it into a pouch hanging from his belt. "We are back to that. Yes. Sorry. I really am out of touch." He sighed. "I was not ready, but maybe the gods have intervened for me to rejoin the living."

Tristal nearly burst in frustration at the man's cryptic way of talking, but before she could respond, the man stepped up in front of her. Meeting her eyes, he bowed to her and said, "Hello, Tristal. I am Orinus."

Tristal sat apart from the rest of the group and observed the human mage as she bit her lip in frustration. He appeared to be middle-aged, but for mages it was hard to know for sure. She sensed deep sadness in the man, but she also sensed a burning anger bordering on rage that matched her own. She wondered what his story was. What lit that burning anger within him, or had he always been that way? Of course, she knew him by reputation, which did not help with her natural trust issues at all. He had been expected at Wargate but had never shown up. Tristal had only been there a short while, but the speculation regarding his disappearance was all anyone could talk about for a while. Supposedly, he was one of the most powerful mages alive, which meant there were many at Wargate who were eager to train under him, to learn from him and see for themselves the scope of his magical abilities.

She frowned as she tried to think back over the years. There had been rumors that he had been in Watercastle at one point and had brutally murdered another mage and some of the locals, but no one had sought him out to question him. Even if they wanted to, no one knew where to find him. Yet there he was reclining against a dead tree with his feet stretched out toward the fire, his head leaning back, and his eyes closed as though he hadn't a care in the world.

Fine, she thought. He's a powerful mage. Great. How the heck does he know who I am?

She watched him for a few more minutes, completely ignoring her unit as they spoke lowly back and forth over their meal, still shaken over the deaths of two of their own. She moved to her feet and crossed the clearing to where Orinus sat, and she kicked his feet causing him to open his eyes.

"How do you know me?" she asked, her impatience obvious.

"What?"

She kicked at his feet again, and he pulled himself into a better sitting position, moving his feet out of striking distance. "You said earlier that you know me. How? We have never met."

Orinus glanced at her unit, who were silently watching as they kept eating. He motioned for her to take a seat with him.

Plopping herself to the ground, she crossed her legs and leaned forward, her elbows resting on her knees, her eyes searching his.

Orinus met her gaze boldly but with no hostility. Just as she sensed his power and his struggle with anger, he also sensed her anger and her ever increasing impatience. Both made her a dangerous fighter, not only to her opponents, but also to herself and to the people around her. Surely, her instruction at Wargate would have taught her how to diffuse this.

He caught himself as her eyes bored into his demanding answers.

"I expect you know of me to some extent?" he asked.

Tristal shrugged dismissively. "You are supposed to be some super powerful mage."

Orinus waited for Tristal to expand on that, but when she said nothing more, he nodded, "Yes, I am a mage. Whether I am super or powerful, I cannot tell you. I guess it would depend on who you asked. That doesn't matter in the grand scheme of things. But you want to know how I know you. One of the things I am skilled at is seeing people or events that will cross my own life. I cannot tell when exactly or even why, but I can see faces, feel emotions, determine places."

"You saw me? You have precognition?" Tristal asked incredulously.

Orinus nodded. "To some extent. I had not expected to cross paths with you so soon. I don't feel I am ready for whatever comes next, but apparently, there is an element to my path that even my foresight cannot discern."

Tristal glared at Orinus in exasperation. "You talk in riddles. What are you talking about? This doesn't answer how you know me. You said it like we have interacted with each other before. And what are you talking about whatever comes next? What does come next? Next to what? After this skirmish with these ugly trolls and goblins? After meeting you here?"

Orinus could feel Tristal's impatience feeding her anger and could feel the currents moving around her, and he had a sudden realization. "You know how to use magic?"

Caught off guard by the question, Tristal sat back and stared at him. "What?"

Orinus pressed, "I bet you know incantations and things that help you fight. But are you able to draw magic in and use it, direct it, control it?"

Tristal flashed him a withering look. "Of course not. White Elves aren't mages. Only clan leaders use magic beyond simple incantations."

Orinus leaned forward and said in a low voice, "But you have used magic beyond incantations. I can feel it on you and how you affect the currents around you. You didn't even realize you were doing it."

Tristal huffed in frustration. "You don't know what you are talking about."

Orinus shrugged indifferently. It was something he could explore more later. He leaned back against the tree and changed the subject again back to the original topic, catching Tristal off guard again. "I know you through my visions. I knew your face. I have seen flashes of conversations you were having. I have felt your anger build as you fight. Because of these visions, for me, it is as though we have known each other for many years. I know that puts you at an uncomfortable disadvantage, but that is the reality of that aspect of my precognitive skills."

Tristal felt her frustration diffuse ever so slightly as she pondered Orinus's response. She rose to her feet. She did not like that he had somehow been spying on her, but she sensed there was some reason he was here. What did concern her was his statement about her ability to use magic. That did bother her a great deal for she feared and distrusted the touching of the magical currents, but she tucked his comment away to address later if ever. Then another thought occurred to her. "What was that thing you picked up from the dead troll?"

"What?"

"What was it...?"

Orinus waved away the repeated question, realizing what she asked. He reached into his pouch and pulled out an ordinary looking pebble. He held it out to her.

Taking it, she gave him a look of confusion. "It's just a pebble."

Orinus nodded. "It certainly looks like one, doesn't it? Yet I've been finding these strange little pebbles on the bodies of the leaders of these little bands of roving mongrels and monsters."

Tristal held the pebble closer to her face and saw light purple streaks running through the tiny rock. "What's the purple stuff?"

Orinus held out his hand, and Tristal handed it back to him. "I have a suspicion but am not certain. Whatever it is, it is most definitely shaped by magic or imbued with magic, but it's purpose is still a mystery to me."

Tristal pondered a moment about why trolls or any of the lesser races and creatures, especially the malevolent kind, would have need of magic pebbles. "How many of those things have you found?"

Orinus emptied the pouch into his hand revealing more than a dozen.

Tristal's eyebrows shot up. "All from trolls?"

"No," he shook his head. "A combination of trolls, goblins, muligs, pixies, and a couple Wood Wraiths."

"Wood Wraiths," echoed Tristal. "But those haven't been seen this side of the Walker Mountains in centuries."

Orinus shrugged.

As she stood staring down at him, she asked, "I take it this means we will have you join our party then?"

Orinus narrowed his eyes and pressed a hand to his temple. "It appears that way. By the way, where are we going?"

Tristal glanced at her unit who had all gone back to talking over what was left of their meal. "We were requested to help a settlement called Middleton on the shores of Syan Lake. Their mage sent word that monsters were massing and attacking farms and homesteads in the area. The mage feared the settlement could not withstand an attack. We expect to be there in a couple days."

Orinus nodded. "I see. What sort of monsters?"

Tristal shrugged, "The mage didn't elaborate, so I guess we'll find out when we get there."

"Fair enough," Orinus replied, and then he leaned his head back, pulled his cloak down over his eyes, and crossed his arms. Obviously dismissed, Tristal glared at the mage before returning to her side of the camp and starting her own meal while she mourned the fact that she had lost two valuable warriors she could trust for a strange mage she did not.

*"It is through failure, it is through misadventure,
it is through hardship that one discovers their
courage, motivation, and value."*
~ Cria, Mother Creator

11

*T*wo days later, Tristal's unit reached the low hills approaching the shores of Syan Lake. They had already fought their way through several small groups of goblins as well as a swarm of pixies, plus a disorganized group of the strange frog-like race called muligs that looked like they'd been conjured up out of mud, their warty skin falling in flabby flaps down their bodies. Tristal had never seen one, so when the first one had stepped through the fog in front of her, she had taken pause not knowing if it was friend or foe. Thankfully, one of the older members of her unit had dealt with muligs before and shot an arrow through one of its eyes before it could spit its venomous bile into her face.

As they took stock on the low hills looking over the narrow beaches of the lake, cleaning wounds, filling water skins, and cleaning blades, Tristal breathed a sigh of relief even though she remained worried about the task at hand. They were supposed to assess Middleton's situation and help if they could, but if the last two days' battles were any indication, they were likely heading into a situation that was too much for them. Tristal had heard that all the monsters on Mythnium were suddenly growing bold. It was no longer a sighting here and there of a random goblin, troll, or griffin. It was happening all over Mythos as well as the Silver Isles, and rumor had it, even on the Ebony Isles, which were considered mainly removed from any threat of monsters because they were so far removed from the main continents.

The past two days concerned Tristal because it wasn't just that monsters were becoming bolder. While they were not fighting together, they were attacking only the higher races and were not falling into squabbles amongst themselves or against other monsters. That fact gave Tristal chills.

"Is something the matter?"

Tristal jumped at the intrusion, and she turned to face Orinus with a scowl. "Everything, I think."

As if reading her mind, Orinus nodded and said, "They are not infighting. They aren't attacking each other."

Tristal cocked her head to the side wondering how far his precognitive skills went. Could he read minds? "In your travels, how much of this have you witnessed?"

Orinus gazed out over the distant water of the lake, fog hanging suspended just above the water, allowing him to see to the opposite shore that rested at the base of part of the Alisyan Mountains. He clucked his tongue as he thought. "I didn't come across any groups like these while I was much farther north. However, as I have come south, I have witnessed more and more of the lower races and monsters moving about each other, grouping up even. Monsters like trolls and Wood Wraiths that are typically solitary are joining each other. Your group is the first I have seen attacked, but in listening to the talk of your unit, it appears that settlements all along the south have been attacked?"

Tristal sighed. "Yes. I fear what we will find at this settlement."

Orinus, still looking out over the lake, turned his steely gaze to meet the tiny warrior's. "Considering I collected two more of these curious pebbles in these fights, we should be quick on our way, shouldn't we?"

Tristal held Orinus's gaze, sudden respect reflected in her own.

Nodding at him in response, she called out to her unit to head out in five.

"Looks as though the settlement is completely surrounded, Captain."

Tristal agreed and turned to the elf scout. "Get to that hilltop and see if you can get a better vantage point." The scout saluted and ran off.

Orinus crouched on the other side of Tristal. "What's the plan?"

"Honestly? Not sure yet. We certainly can't just walk through that sea of cretins. We are a great fighting unit, but that is too much for us."

Orinus observed the open field that spread out between them and the settlement. Here, they had all been shocked to see the various monsters were actually attacking as one along with a large contingent of muligs. Orinus sensed there had to be magic at work, but if there was, he couldn't sense it or make out the source. Whatever it was, it had to be something more primal, more chaotic, dark. He suspected that it was the magic that was keeping the monsters from turning on each other, but he really couldn't be certain. Still…. He absently rolled the pebbles that he had collected in his pouch.

He turned his attention to the more pressing dilemma, which was how to get Tristal's unit safely to Middleton. After thinking about it, weighing the pros and cons of using different kinds of magic to assist, he settled on one that would be most effective even though it would tax his reserves and his energy the most. "I can help get us to the gate."

Tristal glanced at Orinus. "Out of the question. Didn't you hear what I just said?"

Orinus turned to Tristal a bit and pointed to the gate in the wall of the settlement. "I can help get us to that gate. And this unholy gathering won't even be aware of us passing through."

Tristal raised an eyebrow at the mage. "Is that so? Magic?"

"Of course. I can cloak us in the magic from the soil, the plants, the wind. Weave it together so that we will appear as the soil, move like the plants, and sound like the wind."

Tristal stared at the mage, trying to decide if he was being truthful or not.

"Oh, fine. I'll prove it."

Without another word, he rose to his feet, muttered an incantation, and waved a hand from his head to his feet and disappeared from sight.

Tristal gasped. "Orinus?" she whispered and stretched her hand out. Her hand touched his cloak that hung to his ankles and then the soft hide of his knee-high boots.

"See?" his voice mocked from above her.

Then with a snap of his fingers, he was visible and crouched back beside her.

Tristal considered his offer for a bit as she continued to scan the scene before her. There was no cover. There was no route that did not go right through the gathered horde. With great reluctance, she realized his offer was their only option other than leaving Middleton to its own devices, which would be catastrophic for its people.

"Okay. We will trust your magic. But once we get to the gate, then what? Someone has to open the gate for us, which means we have to be seen by the guards so they know to let us in."

Orinus smirked. "I do magic, not strategy. I can get us there; the rest is up to you."

Tristal rolled her eyes but turned to the hilltop where her scout was getting a better look. "We'll wait until he gets back with his report. Then we will go."

"Very well," replied Orinus, who then lay down on the ground, promptly closed his eyes, and fell asleep.

"You can't be serious," muttered Tristal.

When the scout returned, it was with solemn news. For as far as he could see, all the settlements along Syan Lake were being attacked by groups of monsters of varying sizes, this settlement having the largest congregation of trolls, goblins, and muligs. Taking that into account, Tristal was eager to get inside Middleton's walls before it was too late to help the people there.

Orinus stood before each member of the unit chanting his spell and waving his hand from head to toe on each one. When he got to Tristal, he looked her in the eyes. "Ready?"

"Yes," she replied shortly. "Get on with it."

"Okay. Remember, when you get to the gate, simply put some pebbles in an 'x' pattern, so I know you are there. When I see all the members accounted for, I will withdraw the spell, and then it will be up to you. I can support a little, but camouflaging all of us for the span of the field will tax my energy a great deal."

"Understood," Tristal replied.

Orinus cast the spell over Tristal, but he added a touch of something more so he could monitor her progress. He planned on following her step for step in case something unexpected occurred. Once she was hidden, except for a miniscule aura that only he could make out, he cast the spell on himself and followed her down the hill and out into the field.

Tristal moved with confidence and speed. Whether or not she trusted Orinus's magic, she trusted her ability to defend herself. She was not ready to just sacrifice her life, but if the monsters raised a weapon to her, she would die fighting her fiercest. As she approached the back lines of the mob of monsters, she took a deep breath. Coming up from behind, she was not surprised they didn't notice her, but as she stepped past one then around another and another, and then another and another, she could not believe that they could not see her, hear her, or even smell her.

She mused on the efficacy of the spell, but then a goblin not much shorter than herself walked right into her and fell back on its butt in shock. The surrounding monsters pointed and laughed, but the goblin reacted much faster than Tristal would have expected. It leapt to its feet and jumped in her direction. Tristal sidestepped, but the goblin, its hand outstretched, grabbed a part of her cloak.

Tugging at the cloak, not knowing what it held, the goblin began shrieking, "I caught it. I caught it. It's a ghost! I caught it."

An uproar rose up around the monsters that were watching for it appeared that the goblin was simply dancing a silly dance. Tristal pulled her short sword ready to kill the miserable creature but felt a hand on her arm and a voice whispered in her ear. "No. Killing the beast will only alert them all to our presence. Just yank the cloak back from it, and let's keep moving."

Tristal grimaced. How could Orinus see her? Inwardly, she knew he was right, but she so wanted to kill the ugly goblin. Instead, she just yanked the cloak out of the goblin's hand. While it sputtered nonsense about the ghost getting away, she quickly wove her way farther into the field and closer to Middleton.

When she arrived in front of the gate, she noted seven x's laid out on the ground. She bent down and made one for herself and noted another forming next to hers. She had barely stood upright when she heard Orinus say in a low voice heavy with exhaustion. "Be ready."

She turned to face the gate while she trusted her unit to turn to face the mass of monsters. She knew as soon as the spell was released, they would be vulnerable.

Instantly in her peripheral vision, she saw the seven members of her unit standing around her, their weapons drawn and ready. Orinus also faced the monsters, his hands held before him, his lips moving, but she could not hear what he was saying. She saw in just that quick instance though that the mage looked incredibly drained as he leaned forward on his staff working to cast more spells.

Feeling an increased sense of urgency, she looked up at the guards on the gate who were in the process of shooting more arrows into the horde of monsters. One of them caught sight of her party and let out a yell just as the monsters behind her saw them and rushed forward to crush them.

A guard leaned over the gate and yelled down to her. "Who are you?"

Tristal shouted up as she showed off a paper. "I've been sent from Wargate! Let us in!"

The guard disappeared without a response, and Tristal huffed as she tucked the paper back into her tunic.

She turned to face the rushing monsters and joined the ranks of her unit as they parried and slashed at their opponents. Orinus let loose the spell he had been casting and fell to his knees as the first row of monsters that stood before them instantly caught fire the same way the trolls had at the camp the day before. Those that stood nearest their burning comrades pushed backward against the frenzied mob at their back, but they too were pushed into the burning monsters, starting a short chain reaction along the lines closest to the gate.

Tristal and her unit stepped back toward the gate, helping Orinus to his feet as they went, and Tristal let out a sigh of relief as she heard the mechanisms of the gate being released. It opened just wide enough to let them in, and she motioned for her unit to go. She nodded at Orinus to go, and once he was through, she also stepped backward into the relative safety of the settlement walls and watched the gates close, blocking the monsters as they burned.

"Wow," exclaimed one of her unit, and she turned to face them. She looked each of them over, taking in that none of them had suffered any additional wounds. She turned to Orinus, who leaned heavily on his staff looking as though he was about to pass out.

"Thank you. My unit would not have made it through that mass without your help."

Orinus shrugged dismissively and then turned his attention to a man approaching them. The man wore heavy fur robes and a circlet on his head, identifying him as the magistrate.

Tristal stepped up to the man and handed him the letter from Wargate stating her unit's business there. "With hearts as one," she greeted formally. "I am Captain Tristal White Stone sent from Wargate at the request of your mage."

She glanced around at the men and women of the settlement who were all obviously scared, tired, and battle weary. "Where is your mage?"

The magistrate took the letter from Tristal, and without reading it, responded with the customary greeting. "Middleton doesn't need you. We… That is, I never requested your help. That young upstart had no right to write to Wargate. We have things well under control." He looked at Tristal and her unit, laughing as he noted their number. "There is nothing you can do for us. We are preparing to surrender and pray that those ungodly creatures will have mercy on us."

Tristal raised her eyebrows in surprise. "You plan to surrender? To that mob? Have you completely lost your mind?"

The magistrate stepped back, not expecting to be questioned and certainly not by a creature half his size. He bowed up, ready to backhand her, but Orinus stepped forward. He forced himself to stand his full height, which made him the same height as the magistrate. "You have not introduced yourself, kind sir. Please allow me to go first. I am Orinus. Have you heard of me?"

The magistrate blanched, visibly shrinking into himself. He stepped back again, glancing now at Tristal's unit as they all also stepped forward with intense gazes.

The magistrate stammered, "No one has heard from you in ages. It was rumored that you…"

"That I was dead, no doubt." Orinus finished. "Well, as you can see, I am most certainly not dead. Now you are?"

The magistrate clamped his mouth shut. He pulled his robes tightly around him and took a breath. "I am Magistrate Geraldt. I apologize for my abruptness. But as you can see, you have come too late, when there is no hope. Your unit cannot hope to help. We are so grossly outnumbered."

Orinus waved the man's statement aside. "I believe the captain inquired after your mage. Where might we find him?"

"Her," the magistrate corrected. "She is up on the wall to the south. I believe she was trying to keep

110

the muligs from burrowing under that side of the settlement where the mud from the lake meets that wall."

Orinus turned to Tristal and looked down at her. She could see the weariness in his eyes and how hard he was fighting the fatigue, likely to keep the magistrate from seeing him worn down.

"I will see if I have enough energy to assist the mage," he murmured to her. Without waiting for a reply, he strode off slowly through the people of the settlement.

Tristal watched him go, concern for the mage clouding her thoughts for a moment. Shaking herself, she refocused her attention on the magistrate. "I believe we have some things to discuss."

She turned to her unit and indicated for them to move to areas of the wall to help the local people protect their homes, and then she turned back to the magistrate who stared down at her as though she were a child he didn't know what to do with.

"Let's find a place to talk."

Without a word, the color drained from his face. He led Tristal to a building in the center of the settlement where they could talk without interruption.

"Come, you seekers,
seek what is hidden behind this door.
Come, you seekers,
seek for yourself the truth and the lies.
Can you determine which is what, or what is
which? Come, you seekers, for you seek to know,
but do you know to seek?"
~ Fairy Proverb

12

Geraldt sat heavily in a large chair. Even sitting, he was still taller than Tristal as she stood before him, but she was not intimidated in the least. The man was cagey and unsettled by her, and she wanted to know why. Why had he seemed upset by their presence, put off by their declaration to help fight the horde outside their walls?

She stood at ease before him, her hands resting easily on the hilt of her blade, ready to use it but not actually holding it.

Geraldt noted her stance and knew he had given too much away in their first encounter. Hoping he could undo the damage for he had too much to lose, he motioned for Tristal to take a seat in a chair opposite him. Leaning toward her, he offered her a drink.

Tristal looked at the clay mug he offered her and waved her hand at it, dismissing it. "This is not a social call. Your mage's message caught the attention of Wargate, which is why I am here. I am not just here to help if we can but also to assess this attack. Are you aware that Middleton is not the only Syan Lake settlement being harangued?"

Geraldt leaned back in his chair, a look Tristal could not decipher passing across his face. He stared at her for a moment before he took a long drink from his own mug. He wiped his face with the back of his hand and set the mug to the side on a small table. "I was aware, but we have not been able to maintain communication with any of them. That Meri's message to Wargate got through is incredible to me. All our birds have been methodically shot down."

He stared down at the ground and then looked back at Tristal. "Now that you are here and see what we are up against, what exactly do you hope to do? Surely you see that Middleton is lost?"

Tristal had already been considering what might be done. It did appear as though Middleton was either going to have to continue to fight a fight that did not look as though it could be won, or they would have to find a way to evacuate the remaining people. She started to say as much, but something in the way Geraldt stared her down made her cautious. She returned his stare, deciding not to answer him. After several breaths, he could not meet her stare any longer. He picked up his mug for another long drink.

Tristal watched him. The man was nervous. There was definitely something amiss. Until she could find out what it was, she decided not to trust the man. "I need to assess the town."

Geraldt laughed. "What is to assess? You came through the monsters. You hear the fighting. You saw our dead. Our injured. The few who remain who are able to continue to fight."

Seeing that she was not to be dissuaded, he turned angry. "Go then. Assess." He slammed his mug onto the table so hard the remains of his drink splashed out onto his hand. He took a rag out of a pocket and began drying his hand while Tristal simply stood observing him.

He bellowed at her. "Get out! Go! Now!"

Tristal bristled under his tirade, but she turned on her heel, leaving the man sputtering and cursing behind her.

Orinus stood, leaning heavily on his staff, beside the woman. She was a great deal younger than he was and had not been to Farcaste Reach. Her own powers were not nearly as great as his own, but she had natural talent with casting. He did not interrupt her as she continued her short chants that cast hardening spells into the mud at the base of the walls. Her hopes were that the hardened mud would hinder the muligs, allowing the archers to more easily pick them off one by one.

Orinus looked down and watched the monsters below him. While the woman dealt with the muligs, he decided to help by casting small spells that would help the archers along the walls. He wandered slowly along the walls, chanting as he went, waving his hands casually over quivers and arrows. Once he completed his circle around the settlement and stopped beside the other mage, he noted with satisfaction that more monsters were falling under more precise hits from the archers. The archers' quivers never emptied so they had arrow after arrow, taking out more and more monsters all around the settlement. He felt drained, but he could sense that Middleton was on a precipice. If the tide did not turn and soon, the settlement would be lost. So he pushed through his fatigue, drawing energy from stones he kept tucked away to help him keep casting.

The female mage leaned forward on the wall gasping for breath, her head hanging forward. Orinus laid a hand on her shoulder and asked in concern. "Getting a little drained?"

The woman looked up at Orinus. She had deep green eyes that complemented her wild red hair. Exhaustion etched dark circles under her eyes, but she smiled at Orinus and nodded.

"I am fine. Just tired. I have been casting and recasting that same spell since first sunrise. It doesn't last very long, and they seem to know that, so they keep moving from one spot to another."

Orinus understood all too well the draining effects of using magic. "Would you mind if I took over for a bit?"

The woman nodded and straightened up. "I think I am going to find something to eat. Can I bring you something when I come back?"

Orinus nodded his thanks.

The woman started to walk away but then turned back for just a minute. "By the way, my name is Meri."

Orinus bowed his head to her. "And I am Orinus."

Meri's eyes opened wide, but she said nothing. Instead, she spun on her heel and continued down the steps in search of food.

Meanwhile, Orinus turned his attention to the mud flats that stretched from the base of the wall to the edge of Syan Lake. Meri had been effective at hindering the muligs, but he could see why she was exhausted after having to cast and recast the same spell over and over. He watched the muligs finally begin to make a tiny bit of progress in Meri's short absence. Deciding on a different approach, Orinus thought of another way to keep the muligs at bay.

He reached into another small pouch on his belt and pulled out a blue gemstone with the water sigil, Bah-nar, etched into its face. Holding it out over the side of the wall, he started the first of two chants. The first caused the men and women on his side of the wall to pause in wonder as water started to seep upward out of the mud. It was just enough to catch the light of the suns, but then it appeared to be a finger's depth, then two fingers', and then up to the knees of many of the muligs. The muligs sneered, thinking the mage had erred. Surely he knew that water made the mud easier to work with for them.

Orinus stopped chanting the first spell and began chanting the next. The blue stone in his hand began to glow and a wide ethereal ray spread from it and onto the water that the muligs now found themselves standing in. Panicking, one of the muligs started yelling at its companions and started to try to move, but ice was forming on and through the water. The muligs found themselves stuck in the ice. They began to hack away at it, but as soon as they thought they had broken it enough to break free, water flowed into the holes and instantly refroze.

Trapped in the ice, the muligs cried out in pain and fear. Now that they had standstill targets, the archers picked them off one by one. On the corners of the settlement, trolls, goblins, and other muligs tried to move to that side to reinforce their trapped compadres, but the ice caused them to slip and fall and many found themselves also trapped in it as they tried to force their way. After several minutes, the monsters stopped trying to retake that lost ground. Orinus put the gemstone back in the pouch and stood still for several minutes, collecting his strength and energy. He felt the waves of exhaustion that using magic caused within him pass, and he turned to direct most of the archers to the other walls where they were now needed. As he moved to follow, he glanced over the wall and smiled in satisfaction. That spell, he thought, should last until sunset.

"Can one blame the driving fear of another when all hope seems to be lost? How quickly one sells his soul. One sacrifices all they thought they held dear when the choice is their life over another's. Yet can one truly blame them? Not all creatures are born courageous. That is why only the courageous, those rare few, become the heroes of our legends."
~ Meri the Green, Witch of the Lakes

13

*T*ristal stood outside the magistrate's office and took a deep breath. Staring at a thick tapestry that appeared to be rather old, she noted the imagery: creatures of myth and lore bounded across an open field while larger creatures she knew from stories to be dragons dominated the sky. The scene was strange and yet comforting, a child's story come to life, yet deep within her, she felt as though she were looking at a history. She sighed at her childish wishing and adjusted her thoughts to the present.

She sensed something was off with the magistrate, but she couldn't put her finger on it. She looked around the settlement and took count of the members of her unit. She accounted for each of them to include Orinus, who was moving off the southern wall toward the eastern wall. She started off in that direction when a woman with flaming red hair stopped her. "You are from Wargate?" the woman asked.

Tristal nodded. "Yes, though Magistrate Geraldt is not exactly happy to see us."

The woman frowned. "Will you follow me?"

Tristal remained still. "You are?"

The woman laughed sharply. "Oh. Sorry. I am Meri. I am the one that asked Wargate for help."

Tristal relaxed and nodded for Meri to lead the way.

As they walked toward the eastern wall, Meri spoke lowly. "I asked you to come for the obvious reason, but I believe there is a threat within these very walls. I have suspicions, but I don't know how to go about learning the truth."

Tristal waited for her to continue.

Meri looked back the way they had come and then leaned in to Tristal, "I believe Geraldt has somehow caused this."

Tristal was careful not to let her face betray her feelings, but she nodded, "Go on."

"Well, he is a new magistrate. He only moved here a year ago. Since then, he moved very quickly to gain favor with our previous magistrate who was well-loved and trusted. But a couple months ago, Magistrate Pakt fell suddenly ill. I was not here, or I might have been able to help in some way, but our healers were confounded by his illness. After he passed away, Geraldt simply moved in and took over. When we all protested because we have a way of choosing our magistrates, he killed the most vocal of us in front of the entire town and then challenged the rest of us. Of course, we backed down."

Tristal interrupted, "Okay, so he is power hungry, but what does that have to do with the horde surrounding you all?"

Meri sighed, "That is what I am unsure about. You see, the night before the monsters moved in, I was approached by the woman who cleans Geraldt's

119

home. She swears she heard him talking to himself in his office. She thought someone was there because she thought she heard another much deeper voice, but as she passed by the open door, Geraldt was staring into his looking glass, but no one else was there. I dismissed her observation, but the next morning, about a third of what you see out there now had arrived and were systematically trying to get through our gates."

Tristal nodded. "That is suspicious, but men do sometimes admire their own reflections, and monsters do sometimes attack settlements."

Meri put her hands on her hips and stared Tristal down. "Like this?"

Tristal did not argue, her own gut feeling of the current magistrate seeming to have a reason now. She touched Meri lightly on her arm.

"I will share what you told me with Orinus. Maybe the two of us can sort out what drew these monsters here and what the magistrate's intentions are. I hope they are simply the ambitions of a greedy man. Those men are easily dealt with."

"If not?"

Tristal shrugged dismissively. "Still easily dealt with but typically can be a lot messier."

Meri said nothing but followed Tristal up the ladder onto the wall where she found and joined Orinus. After telling him what Meri had said, the two left the wall together and sought out the magistrate.

Orinus pushed the door to the magistrate's home open and stepped inside, closely followed by Tristal. Orinus did not waste energy on silence spells or anything else to hide their presence. He suspected he might need to call on his reserves and saved his energy for any confrontation he might have with the magistrate.

Tristal stepped around him and led the way to the office where she had sat with the magistrate. She put her ear to the closed door but heard nothing, so she slowly opened it and peered in through the small crack. She saw the magistrate sitting in his chair, staring right at her.

He waved her in.

Opening the door wide, Tristal and Orinus moved into the room.

"I was expecting you," the magistrate commented.

Tristal and Orinus cast suspicious glances at each other but said nothing.

"That nosey old housekeeper and that ridiculous mage are too much trouble. I should have done away with them both from the very beginning."

Tristal stared at the man, "Why?"

The man seemed unable to help himself, "They cause trouble. Always trouble. Now my neck is on the line. Yes. I should have killed them both. Then you would not have come and this wouldn't be an issue."

Orinus asked, "What wouldn't be an issue?"

Geraldt looked at Orinus and sneered, "He knows of you, you know. He knows of you, and he will be livid when he learns that you are still alive. I wish I could be the one…" he paused and pulled a small stone no bigger than a bean out of his pocket. "…no matter. What's done is done. I should have killed those two."

He locked eyes with Tristal as he stuffed the stone in his mouth. Orinus moved quickly across the room, but it was too late.

The moment Geraldt closed his mouth around the stone, he began to change. First, all the color from his skin began to wash away, turning him gray-blue from his hair to his hands. Then he dried out: his skin, his hair, even his clothing getting crackled and mottled. As Orinus reached him and stretched his arm out to touch the magistrate's shoulder, the man simply dissolved into dust.

Orinus turned to face Tristal, who was frozen in disbelief. Just as she started to say something to Orinus, a loud shout rose up from the settlement. Both cocked their heads to hear better and then dashed out of the magistrate's office and into the center of the settlement. They looked all around to see the settlers on the walls and gathered around the open areas crying, laughing, and celebrating.

Meri ran to them just as Tristal's unit gathered in front of her.

"What is going on?" Tristal asked.

Meri shrugged her shoulders and smiled widely. "We thought it was something you did."

"What?" responded Orinus.

Meri looked at both of them in surprise. "You didn't have anything to do with this?"

Tristal and Orinus looked at her and each other. "Do with what?" they both demanded.

Meri shook her head in confusion. "Come on. You better see for yourselves."

She led the way up a ladder to look out over the wall.

All around the settlement, the monsters were gone. Just gone. Not running away. Not dead on the ground. Just gone.

Orinus looked closer and saw piles of dust all around the marshy areas and the field that they had crossed to get inside. He glanced sideways at Tristal, who stared open-mouthed at the scene before her. Even the bodies of the monsters they had killed had turned to dust. She felt Orinus's stare and met it.

"The stone that he swallowed?"

Orinus nodded, making more sense of the purpose of the pebbles he had found on the monsters he had slain.

"But who..."

Orinus didn't let her finish. He knew exactly who.

"The White Lord," he replied.

Tristal didn't argue. Instead, she turned her gaze out over the landscape. She and Orinus stood staring out at it, both lost in their own thoughts, wondering what this revelation meant for Mythos, for Mythnium.

"Vengeance was not his sole motive. Death and destruction were not his motives. Somewhere in the deep dark recesses of his evil mind, he sought annihilation. Annihilation. He sought to destroy natural order, nature itself. To have such dark drive and motive. Gods! How terrifying this creature we call the White Lord."
~ King Aris of the Drow

14

A frightful din sent his handful of servants rushing out of the throne room. Screaming, roaring, and intense growling filled the room and carried out into the hallways, echoing throughout his fortress. Everyone within hearing distance trembled in fear. The White Lord was terrifying on a good day, but when he was in a rage, his anger made the very foundations of his fortress tremble.

The sounds of ultimate rage carried on for nearly thirty minutes as the White Lord raged about the throne room, picking up and throwing anything he could get in his hands. Shattered furniture littered the floor. Tapestries hung in ragged tatters from broken poles on the walls. Even some of the columns supporting a mezzanine that surrounded three sides of the throne room bore deep cracks, crumbles of rock falling away.

His rage subsided bit by bit as he paced the room, back and forth, back and forth, muttering to himself. Occasionally, he kicked out at the wreckage in the room sending splinters flying, talking to himself about all the things he wanted to do to the mage that had ruined his plans by seeking out help from Wargate. Then he ranted to himself about the ineptitude of Geraldt and how he should have taken care of the mage before she had been an issue. He picked up a goblet and crushed it in his hands, the pointy edges of it cutting deeply into his palm, causing him more anger.

He thought over the message Geraldt had sent him via the looking glass. The moron had not killed the female mage as he had been instructed. Instead, he had allowed her to live and inadvertently had allowed her to send a message to Wargate. Then instead of being sure his guards followed his orders, he let them do their own thing, which allowed a Wargate unit, plus Orinus…

He paused in his thoughts.

Orinus.

Damn that mage, he thought to himself.

Normally, human mages meant little to the White Lord. They were short-lived because they were human. Even out of those who showed a talent for harnessing the magic of Mythnium, few ever mastered it. The White Lord had spent his life keeping a tab on the few dwarf mages but mostly on the elf and Drow mages who had lifetimes nearly as long as his to master their craft. It often made him curious why the dwarves and elves did not more actively pursue mastery of the magical currents. Even among the self-proclaimed masters who sequestered themselves away at Farcaste Reach under the self-important proclamation that they were there to collect knowledge of magic to share and train others to use, there were only a handful that the White Lord thought might pose a threat.

Orinus, however, was a very different case. The White Lord had sensed Orinus's touch on the magical currents before he had been sent away to Farcaste Reach as a boy. Orinus appeared to have an intuitive grasp of the way the currents moved and flowed over Mythnium. The White Lord suspected that Orinus had a more natural grasp of magic than even he did; that unnerved him more than a little.

As Orinus's training and exploration of magic extended over the course of the time he was at Farcaste Reach, the White Lord grew ever more anxious by the ripples Orinus sent out every time he touched the currents. His power was incredible, and the White Lord could taste the emotions that often tinted those ripples even cast across an ocean on another continent. He could sense Orinus fight to control his emotions when touching the magical currents and knew that Orinus was afraid of his own power. The White Lord's attempt to kill Orinus had been a decision made out of a sense of self-preservation and had been encouraged by the White Lord's own god. If Orinus ever discovered how to use his emotions to add to the use of magic, he could become increasingly more powerful than even the White Lord.

To discover that the mage had not only survived but had somehow remained hidden from the White Lord for all these years was baffling and infuriating. How had Orinus been able to touch magic, to influence the currents without the White Lord being able to sense the ripples? It was impossible.

Unless.

The White Lord scowled upward toward the heavens at the gods he despised.

Unless, of course, the gods were working against him and his god. That made perfect sense.

Rage rising in him again, he threw what was left of the goblet across the room and through a window, shattering it completely.

He scowled at the room. He should have known. After all these years, he should have suspected when he never heard back from the mercenary. But when Orinus failed to reach Wargate, and no one had seen or heard from him since his sister was killed, it was easy to assume the mage had also been killed in the magical fire. He should have known better. He should have hired a better mercenary. He should have sent someone to confirm that the mercenary had completed his mission.

He roared in outrage at his own failure. Orinus was already proving to be troublesome. The disappearance of over a dozen of the groups he had dispatched across Mythos, all under the subtle but powerful control of the unremarkable enchanted pebbles, had stymied the White Lord. Now, however, those disappearances made complete sense. The additional fact that Orinus was now with this unknown unit from Wargate proved worrisome and also intriguing.

The White Lord paused in his pacing and wondered about the White Elf captain of the unit that Geraldt had mentioned. He had not heard of her before but was not overly surprised. She might just be young, or maybe she had not left Wargate often, but her unit's arrival at Middleton was unexpected. He should have foreseen something like this.

Middleton had been a critical stepping stone in the White Lord's plans. The settlement sat in the middle of the other Syan Lake settlements, hence its name, and it sat at the southernmost end of the Mythos Road, which extended all the way north to Watercastle. He had planned to secure Middleton and the other settlements. With the help of the maps that Geraldt had shared of the trade routes and trails that led through the Alisyan Mountains to Syan Lake, the White Lord had been certain he could use Middleton to gain a solid foothold on the southeastern side of Mythos. From there, his plans were intricate and long-term, but they all hinged on capturing and controlling those settlements and the south end of the most utilized road on all of Mythos.

That he had not foreseen this interference from Wargate made him angry all over again. That his spies within Wargate had not alerted him infuriated him, and he made a mental note to deliver heavy consequences on the lot. That his god, Naga, had not seen Wargate's interference not only made him angry but also made him pause and wonder. This was not the first time his god had failed to either see or divulge a pertinent piece of information that ended up being crucial to some plan or staging some military strike. The tiniest doubt regarding the power of his deity glimmered. He pondered the relationship he had with Naga.

From the beginning when Naga had revealed himself to the White Lord, calling him by his true name, the White Lord had been skeptical. Naga, the god of the Heridon, had called to the White Lord nearly a century after the Cataclysm and had done so through one of the White Lord's dreams. When Naga had appeared in his dreams, the White Lord instinctively reacted in suspicion and fear and tried to fight the strange manifestation that had appeared, which was as an ethereal and mighty looking

Heridon. Cautious, even in his dreams, still learning his own mastery of the magical currents and still mentally unbalanced and confused, the White Lord had tried ignoring the god's intrusions.

Over time, however, Naga showed the White Lord things in his dreams that spoke of things going on throughout the rest of Mythnium, and that began a shared desire to spread beyond his domain on Mygras. As time moved forward, Naga continued to reveal information that was useful to the White Lord and had even helped him piece together portions of his past immediately following the Cataclysm. Those tiny remnants fueled the White Lord's rage and quest for revenge. Still, he could not help but accept that Naga, like every other god, was using him for his own purposes. Long after swearing oaths of worship to Naga, the White Lord often found himself frustrated with what he perceived to be limitations in the abilities of his god. He swore that he would only allow himself to be a tool for the god so long as it benefited him. Recently, he had begun to feel that the time might have come for him to risk the god's wrath by setting about on his own path to achieve his goals.

For nearly an hour, the White Lord ranged from thoughtful to outraged to thoughtful again. The only piece of furniture or decoration in the entire room that remained unscathed was his throne. He finally walked to it and sat down in a huff. He let his rage wash over and through him. He clung to it, using it to bolster his resolve. He admitted to himself grudgingly that he might have to adjust his plans a little, but there were other settlements along the south. The maps Geraldt had shared had shown the White Lord a great many alternatives, but they would take time to scout. Finding other people he could coerce to do his bidding would take careful planning and manipulation. He closed his eyes in resignation.

Just as he reclined back into the large throne, he heard the heavy tapping sound of Libitina's claws on the stone stairs leading to the throne room. He opened his eyes and leaned forward to watch her approach. In a flash, his anger was replaced by grim excitement for in Libitina's toothy maw gently rested an incredible sapphire-colored egg.

"Considering the things we don't know, we must listen. We must observe. We must ask questions. When we cannot listen, observe, or ask questions, we must slow our desire to act. We must restrain ourselves and hold on to patience, even the patience of the elves, for action in ignorance undoubtedly results in folly rife with regret."
~ Orinus, *The Memoir of a Mage*

15

Curtains of the finest silks blew inward, and the letters and missives scattered about the table fluttered under the heaviness of flat rocks and weights. Wisps of his long hair, free from the confines of his ceremonial braids, flew into his face, causing him to brush them to the side or try to tuck them behind his ears.

Nearly silent steps behind him caused him to turn to the door, and he smiled invitingly to the old elf pausing in the entryway. Without waiting for a verbal invite, the old elf, burdened with an armful of scrolls and books, responded to the smile and bowed sharply before stepping into the room and depositing his load onto the table with no care for the papers already there.

"Hello, Uncle Bartholomew," the first elf greeted.

"We have word from Olphara, but her news will have to wait because we also have word from Farcaste Reach," stated the older elf without preamble as he sat heavily on a cushioned stool by the table and rubbed his elbows in an effort to relieve the soreness from carrying so much so far.

King Mronas did not reply. Instead, he moved to the entry and carefully slid the door shut before he turned back to face his aging uncle. His uncle had long left court to fill a role in the libraries of Elmnas. Located within the palace, it was still far removed from the halls where the king and queen lived and held court. King Mronas noted the way his uncle rubbed his elbows. He turned away, moving to the open window overlooking a section of Elmnas below, allowing his uncle to rub away the pain and relax before continuing their conversation.

He stared out over Elmnas and commented, "What is the news of the Reach?"

"They have been attacked."

King Mronas spun on his heel and stared at his uncle. "Can you repeat that?"

Bartholomew nodded. "The White Lord attacked the Reach. He has grown increasingly stronger. He opened a portal large enough to allow his armies through…"

"But the Reach has withstood so much: The Cataclysm itself…"

"Indeed, further testament to the White Lord's growing strength. May I continue with this report?"

King Mronas stood rigid where he was, the implications of what he was hearing washing over him with cold dread. Finally, he nodded for his uncle to continue.

"The White Lord focused his attack on the tower. Once he was able to breach the walls of the Reach, he marched directly to the tower, and with the help of… well, we are all certain it was merely more use of his own magic, but the report says a dragon… He breached the tower, kidnapping several students and historians."

Mronas frowned, "Did you say he used a dragon?"

Bartholomew nodded but also shrugged. "We are not sure how sane the writer of this message was following that attack. The report insists that a dragon was seen flying over the Reach burning, eating, or destroying everything that got in its way. But we know the White Lord loves to use misdirection and magical phantoms to manipulate those he attacks. We believe that is all this was. After all, if he had the ability to portal his armies across the sea, it makes sense that he would have the ability to blast the tower's doors."

King Mronas paced a few steps in thought. "Did the report say what the White Lord was after? Who he took?"

Bartholomew glanced at the parchment in his hands. "They didn't say they had any idea what the White Lord was after, but among those he captured was Pruzin, the Willow historian."

Mronas nodded. He was familiar with the old elf. "I don't suppose there is anything we can do to assist?"

"We can send help, food, and supplies to the Reach. I am certain the people of the Reach would be grateful as they begin rebuilding. If you mean help for Pruzin – we suspect the old historian is dead. He would not easily divulge any information to the White Lord, and when he doesn't, well…"

Mronas continued pacing. Then taking a deep breath, he refocused his thoughts. He wondered what news Olphara had for them. He thought of the few messages that had come from her over the last ten years. The elation he had felt when he realized his niece had been found alive and well but then dismay when he got word that she wanted no part of the life she had been born into. He had longed to fetch her and bring her to Elmnas and force her into becoming the woman her people needed her to be, but it was his uncle who had talked him out of it. He still regretted that decision in many ways, but he had not been idle.

While he sincerely hoped Aldrina would change her mind, he continued on with his own plans that he had set in motion long before he ever knew that she was alive. He took a deep breath. This was something he needed to discuss with his uncle whose opinion he valued above nearly everyone else. He turned to face him as he sat relaxed on the stool, waiting patiently for him to respond to his announcement.

"You said we have word from Olphara."

"Yes. It appears there have been some developments that will have some effect not only on you and your plans for the Ebony Isles but also on our relations with the Silver Dwarves."

King Mronas raised an eyebrow, and moved to a stool next to his uncle. "Pray. Tell me."

"Let me start with the Silver Dwarves."

"Very well."

"Olphara has had a visit from a group of Silver Dwarves who were traveling from Farcaste Reach. It appears that they have a young woman who has inherited a talent with shaping metal."

"Oh, yes!" perked up Mronas. "Didn't my father commission a dagger made by a Dwarven woman who was able to see within the metal? To shape it and imbue it with magic? I thought she was the last…"

"I gather so did the dwarves. Since that woman passed, it was not inherent in her daughter or granddaughter. Much was forgotten, so they decided to send this young woman to Mythos to visit various libraries and to Farcaste Reach to learn more about her skill."

"I see. What does that have to do with us?"

"It appears we are next on the intended stops for this young dwarf and her brother, who is also a talented blacksmith. They are coming with a small retinue led by one of their elders."

"Very good. We'll be sure to greet them with all the honor our treaty calls for and be the best of hosts. I imagine she will want to spend some time learning from our own smiths?"

Mronas stopped when his uncle raised a hand.

"Olphara made a point of naming the elder. She speculated you might want notice in case other arrangements might need to be made."

Mronas frowned. "Why would I want to make other arrange…" He paused and leaned toward his uncle; his eyes wide. "No. No, they would not send him. After the fiasco at my wedding?"

Mronas's uncle merely smiled wanly and nodded. "Martan is indeed the one leading this group."

Mronas sat back and rubbed his chin in thought. "I will decide what to do about this news later. What else does Olphara have to say? Anything about Aldrina?"

Bartholomew paused, looking beyond his nephew and out the window as though something caught his attention. The king waited. While his uncle was still of sound mind as he grew older, he found it harder and harder to bring his thoughts to the surface. Conversations with him grew increasingly longer as the old elf worked carefully to say exactly what he meant so that there was never any confusion. Finally, Bartholomew took a deep breath and refocused his gaze on the king.

"She says that Aldrina has become a healer with some talent. However, Aldrina has broken with their customs and has had a token created that will help her with her healing abilities. As a result, Olphara has had to ask her to leave their clan."

Mronas stood abruptly and stared down at his uncle. "That will not do! Send a unit immediately to find Aldrina and bring her here…"

"That is not necessary..."

"Of course it's necessary! She can't be alone in the wilds of the mountains, or the gods only know where...!"

"Mronas. Sit down."

Mronas peered at his uncle, taking note of the sharp tone to his command, and he slowly sat back down.

"Aldrina will be fine, I think. She has befriended the young dwarf woman, and the dwarves invited her to travel with them. Since they are coming here, Aldrina is also coming here."

Mronas leaned back and crossed his arms on his chest with a small smile of satisfaction playing at the corners of his mouth. "Aldrina is coming here."

"It appears so. Olphara does not know if Aldrina is coming here to pursue her rightful place among our people or if she is simply traveling with the dwarves who she has befriended. However, the party will be leaving Olphara's protection and be on their way here; she expects they will arrive within fourteen sunrises.

Mronas smiled widely at his uncle. "Well, that changes things."

Bartholomew nodded. "I expected so."

"I will have to contact Rackas. I believe that man would've raised Aldrina as his own had he had the opportunity. Sad really. But he has been useful to us, and now, gods willing, he will be useful to Aldrina too.

I will inform him to set things in motion there. Our timetable will have to move up quite a bit, but can you see that our contacts are informed? Will we be ready to sail within three months?"

The older elf rose to his feet and nodded at his nephew.

"I will see that we are ready. Though will you still proceed regardless of Aldrina's decision? She does still have a choice, does she not?"

Mronas frowned up at his uncle. He was slightly irritated to have his plans and orders called into question though he knew his uncle only had the best intentions, which was that the king always keep his people at the forefront of his decision making.

"Yes, Uncle Bartholomew, Aldrina still has a choice. And yes, I will proceed regardless because you see, no matter what Aldrina decides, no one on the Isles will know one way or the other beyond what we tell them. Knowing she is alive. Believing she is returning. Having hope of a queen on the throne versus that tyrant. The people there will do more to aid us than our own troops. We are simply going to help them along. Once General Duwo is deposed, then we can set about setting the island country right."

Bartholomew nodded. He disagreed with this course of action in general but agreed with the need that was driving it. Regardless, he trusted his nephew to set things right and knew that with the help of his advisors, Mronas would continue to be as balanced and equitable a ruler as he could be.

Mronas rose beside his uncle and wrapped an arm around the older elf's shoulder. They walked to look out the window together.

"Will you also ask Valero and Colna to come to me? With the events at the Reach and with Aldrina coming home, it is time my daughter comes home as well. She will have a part to play in these unfolding events no matter what Aldrina decides."

Bartholomew nodded. He smiled to himself as he stood next to his nephew. He longed to see the king's daughter for she had long been one of his favorite young elves. She had been absent for too long, and now was the right time. He could feel it in his old bones.

"The warrior within seeks peace above all. In seeking peace, the warrior realizes that violence must occur in order to protect or secure peace. The warrior, thus, is ever at war within himself, for peace and war must go hand in hand, and yet one always strives to overtake the other."
~ Dwarven Proverb

16

The swordsman stood tall beside the archer as they waited outside the throne room to see King Mronas, king of the Forest Elves. Neither said a word to the other. Over the years, they had become so attuned to each other that it wasn't a matter of finishing the other's sentences. They simply could tell by the way the other stood, twitched, or laughed what the other was feeling. From the tone of their voice or the tension in their body, they knew what the other was trying to convey. United in marriage for nearly forty years and friends for over a century, the two still preferred the company of the other over that of anyone else.

The swordsman was tall for a Forest Elf, and incredibly broad-shouldered. When he was younger, a captain of the King's Guard, he had worn his hair long with braids that changed with rank and experience. Now he wore his hair shaved short. That was still a sign of his rank of general and military advisor to the king. He was well-loved by the people of Elmnas for his heroics and his loyalty to his people. A warrior that rarely lost a battle, he was committed to his troops, sometimes even above his commitment to his king. It was for that reason the king trusted and respected him. He might be a fierce warrior, but the tall elf was committed to life and its preservation if he could manage it.

The archer at his side was a head shorter, the average height for her people. She was quite a bit younger than the swordsman, but she had been part of his unit for many years. They had formed a strong bond fighting side by side that had turned into a partnership and a bond that then turned into sincere and time-tested love.

In her own right, she was a hero among their people. She had exceptional eyesight, even among the elves who were known for being long-sighted. Her sight made her one of the best archers the elves had ever known. Much like her lover, she had an incredible appreciation for life but had a special affinity to the cycles of life. She held an almost religious fascination with the natural order of the world around her, which often displayed itself as childlike wonder.

An Elven guard stepped out of the throne room and motioned for the two to enter. They walked side by side, equals and complements to the other, completely confident in themselves and in each other. They approached the throne where King Mronas sat in his favorite riding apparel, his hair braided intricately around the delicate crown that sat on his head, looking at leisure, but his furrowed brow betrayed the worries he carried.

The throne beside his, belonging to his queen, sat empty. Queen Myralli was often absent from the throne room in recent years. Her personal concerns kept her from sharing the ruling duties she once shared with King Mronas. Rumor and speculation surrounded her noted absence, but their people loved her. No matter the reasoning, there was no unrest as a result, simply sincere worry for their queen.

Both warrior elves put their hands to their chest. Together they greeted their king, solemnly saying, "With hearts as one." They bowed deeply before their king and waited for him to speak.

"Rise, my friends," said King Mronas, and he waved for them to be at ease before him.

"Valero. Colna. I have need of you of you both."

Valero and Colna nodded but said nothing, waiting for their king to elaborate.

King Mronas ran his hands along the arms of his throne. The throne itself was a rather humble wooden chair with delicately carved patterns of trees, vines, and forest creatures that moved along the arms and onto the back of the chair. This one had only recently replaced the heavy stone throne that had stood in their ancient throne room for centuries. As he traced the patterns at his fingertips, appreciating the delicate designs, a testament to the mission of the Forest Elves to protect life, the elves before him sensed an inner struggle within their king.

Finally, he looked up at them. "I need you to find Grazina and bring her home."

Colna resisted looking at Valero in surprise. Grazina, King Mronas's only daughter, had left the palace several years before after a devastating accident that left her physically and emotionally marred. Since her disappearance, no word of her whereabouts had ever reached Elmnas, the city of the Forest Elves centered in the thickest part of the Deep Forest. Valero felt Colna's reaction, which he too felt, but he also resisted expressing surprise.

King Mronas watched their faces. They were among his best warriors for a reason. While he could see the spark of surprise in their eyes, nothing else gave them away. He sighed deeply.

"I know I said that I would not seek her out and pressure her to return, but things have come to my attention that need to be addressed. She needs to be part of the decisions that we, the council and I, find ourselves needing to make. These things will affect our people. Her people. Her duty now is here with her people."

Valero spoke up, "Things, my Lord?"

King Mronas nodded. "I know you both have long been convinced that the White Lord is on the move again. Planning something, moving his pieces, and so on. I am certain that my lack of outward concern over your reports has caused you both some dismay, but I can assure you I never took your reports lightly. In fact, just the opposite. Your reports, combined with the reports of other troops, travelers, caravans, and missives from the largely human settlements all along the southern edge of Mythos have caused me to look much closer."

He stood up, agitated, and moved to stand stiffly on the bottom step of the dais the throne sat upon.

"Today," he said quietly so the Elven guards and passersby could not overhear, "we received word from Farcaste Reach. The White Lord has attacked it, captured some of their historians, and has already retreated back to Croglinke. We also received word from the Willows regarding my niece. It appears she is on her way to Elmnas in the company of dwarves. While that is exciting and well-received news, we have also gotten more concerning words from Wargate. They had been asked for help from a mage at a southern settlement on Syan Lake. Middleton, I believe is the name. They sent a unit, and have not yet heard back, but they were sending that unit to help Middleton fight off what was called a 'horde' of monsters."

Colna frowned, "They called it a horde?"

King Mronas met Colna's clear gaze and nodded.

"Yes. Now, that said, I have had my own discreet methods of trying to keep tabs on my daughter. The last I had gotten word of a sighting of her, she was supposed to be not far from Syan Lake. Sadly, that is all I know. Knowing that is the last place she was supposed to be, combined with this alarming news… You understand why I'd like her brought home. I need my very best to track her, find her, protect her, and bring her home."

Valero and Colna both crossed their arms over their chest in a sign of honor and respect as they bowed to King Mronas.

In unison, they replied, "We'll see it done."

They remained bowed until they heard the king's footsteps vanish into another room, then they stood up, gave each other a long hard look, and turned to set about their travel arrangements.

"The end of an adventure is proof of courage one had to muster in order to take that first step toward an unknown outcome. For no matter the known destination, every journey is a series of choices, decisions, influences, and consequences the adventurer can never know for certain prior to that single first step, which in and of itself sets forth its own series of outcomes."
~ *Journeys: Notes Gathered from the Willow Clans*

17

Colna sat tall in her saddle, her bow hanging by her left leg so she could easily reach it if needed, her quiver strapped to the saddle. She scanned the low hills dotted with large rocks and stubby trees from where she sat under the shade of the Deep Forest. There weren't many settlements along the edges of the Deep Forest. The Forest Elves were protective of their forest, and the people that lived outside of it tended to live closer to the coastlines or along the rivers and lakes that dotted the countryside. As expected, there was nothing to see along the road that led out of the forest and into the low hills ahead of them.

She turned her horse and trotted back to where Valero and three other elves waited in the shade of the trees. "Nothing significant to report."

Valero responded. "Good. As it is, it will take another three or four days to reach Syan Lake. We'll stop at Middleton and try to learn what we can. We might need to visit some of the other settlements as well. Then again, if that party from Wargate has not taken care of the threat they were dispatched for, we may have the opportunity to offer our assistance."

He directed his attention to the three other elves. "One of you will ride ahead and act as a scout. One of you will ride behind as our rear guard. The open fields all around us will give us more time to respond to any threat, but the hills, boulders, and low trees also offer places to hide for small parties or lone monsters. I'd rather we were not ambushed along the way."

One of the elves, a younger female, her light brown hair braided in dozens of tiny braids and held in place with a thick leather tie, kicked her horse gently and directed it out ahead of the group.

Colna called after her, "Listen as well as you watch, Layni!"

Layni waved back in response and rode off.

Just as she rode off, Brax, one of Valero's original unit and one of his closest friends, moved his horse beside Valero's. "I will wait till you crest that first hill before following." Without waiting for Valero's response, he turned his horse and trotted a short distance away.

Valero watched him ride away before he turned to face the third elf. "That will leave you to ride with us, Emrys."

Emrys sighed. "Please tell me my uncle didn't give you some order to keep me safe or some such nonsense. I have been trained just as well as you and have been on my fair share of forays into the forest."

Valero smirked at the younger elf who was not yet a century old. "No, Emrys. Your uncle didn't give us any orders to treat you special. Colna and I have just not had the opportunity to get to know you or to serve with you. Since this will be a long journey, and there is nothing to do but talk or sit in silence, we would like to talk. If that is okay with you."

Emrys glanced from one to the other. They were the king's most trusted warriors and often among his advisors. For that reason alone, Emrys was nervous to share too much with them. He knew they held loyalty to the king. While he was no threat and had no desires for power, he also knew he often dismayed his uncle who was the king's chief advisor. He was not the picture of an obedient elf. His antics often caused him to stand before the king or the council as they admonished him for what they perceived to be causing poor reflection on the royal house. He found their rigidness typically annoying, but he was honest every time when he admitted he had no intention of being the black sheep of the family. He simply wanted to have fun.

Colna sensed Emrys's unease. She leaned toward him as the three of them moved their horses into a brisk walk. "We aren't trying to pry or learn your secrets or fears or anything like that. We simply know you are important to your uncle, and we would like to become more than the strangers that we actually are."

Emrys faced Colna and found her gaze clear and honest. Glancing at Valero, he found his gaze less friendly, but nothing was there that alarmed Emrys.

Shrugging, he replied, "What do you want to know?'

Colna smiled, "Well, for starters, we'd really love to hear how it was that you got the king's crown all the way up on the top spire of the sanctuary."

Emrys laughed. "Well…" he began, and as he worked into his story, the Elven party made their way out of the Deep Forest toward Middleton and Syan Lake.

Layni signaled the others early on the fourth day. Valero in turn signaled Brax, who rode just out of sight behind them. The three days' ride had been mostly uneventful with the exception of a group of traveling rana, a race of amphibious fish people loosely related to the merpeople of the oceans and seas. Rana rarely move away from the coastal areas since their lives depended on access to non-stagnant water. To meet them so far inland caused the three veteran elves concern, so they stopped to get news from the group. After learning that the group were actually from one of the other settlements on Syan Lake, Valero hoped that they might learn of news of Grazina but quickly discerned that the rana had no knowledge of her. They did, however, offer disturbing news of monsters attacking the settlements along the lake's shores in strangely unified ways. Their own home had been destroyed and most of the people there killed. The dozen or so that remained were hoping to find a place to rebuild among the rana who lived in the river delta that surrounded Watercastle.

After the rana had moved on, Valero pushed his small unit to move faster, forgoing long meals or long periods of rest. On the fourth morning, he saw Layni's signal that meant they had reached Syan Lake. Sure enough, as they joined her on a small rise overlooking the land that gently sloped down to the lake, they were glad they had rushed. Before them all along the lake's shores, wisps of smoke rose into the air from settlements either under siege or on fire from battle. Valero looked to Colna for her vision was far superior to his.

She closed her eyes tightly to refresh them and then reopened them, gazing first at one settlement then another. She could not see them clearly enough to see how the fighting was going, but her gaze settled on the one that the road ended before. The area outside the settlement seemed gray, almost scorched, and the settlement itself still had solid gates. But the wisps of smoke from it appeared to be coming from the chimneys of the buildings within rather than the buildings or walls themselves.

She pointed to it. "That settlement there in front of us is Middleton. It appears to either have won against the monsters or has not yet been attacked. I think we should hurry to see if the unit from Wargate has arrived and what news there is."

Valero grimly surveyed the panorama before him. "Can you tell the nature of the beasts attacking the other settlements?"

Colna frowned, "I can't be sure from this distance, but it looked like a mix of creatures."

Valero shot her a look. "I hope you're wrong."

Brax muttered from behind, "Me too, but that would coincide with the rana's tale."

The five stared before them, each lost in their own thoughts.

Finally, Valero kicked his horse into a trot, calling out to the others. "Let's get to that settlement quickly. If we can help any of them, I'd like to get to it before the day fades away too much."

"The ability of us all to touch the currents of magic lies mostly dormant. Those few of us who touch the currents, who work with them, who learn to draw them in, to shape them – those few will be the ones to admire and to fear."
~ Olphara, High Chieftain of the Willow Clans

18

*T*he gate opened outward, and the Forest Elves found themselves looking at a Wargate military unit with a tiny White Elf leading them. Valero took them in and understanding washed over him. He got off his horse, motioning the others to do the same, and together they led their horses into the settlement. He glanced around, quickly taking stock of his surroundings. Their walls were damaged severely in spots, and many of the buildings close to the walls were smoldering, but overall, the structures themselves seemed sound. He returned his gaze to the White Elf.

Bowing to her in respect for her standing, he greeted, "I am General Valero Ald-Bric, general and advisor to King Elmnas."

Tristal stepped toward the tall strangely muscular elf, and bowed in return. "Greetings. I'm Captain Tristal White Stone. We were requested by the town's mage, Meri." She nodded in Meri's direction.

Valero nodded at her, but then his attention fell on the imposing figure of Orinus. He could feel the power emanating from the human mage.

Orinus returned the curious stare of the elf but felt no need to introduce himself. Instead, he nodded in respect and turned his attention to the rest of Valero's unit.

One by one, the others presented themselves to Tristal, and then Tristal's unit did the same.

Once the introductions were done, Tristal spoke, "General, we have some dire suspicions. While my people see that yours are given a meal and a place to rest, will you come with me? I have already sent word to Wargate, but I think your king will want to know as well."

Valero waved at Colna and the others to follow Tristal's group, and he followed Tristal into the magistrate's home where she, Meri, and Orinus had been working to decide what to do next as monsters still attacked other settlements up and down the lake's shores.

Tristal turned to close the door to the room they were meeting in, but Orinus stopped her as he stepped into the room as well. She cocked an eyebrow at him, not failing to notice he had not introduced himself to Valero, but she let him pass by her with no objection.

Valero regarded the human mage with respect and mild curiosity, but his own inane sense of magic told him the man was no threat to him. He turned his back on the man and walked around the small room, which was lined with books and scrolls. He looked at the maps laid out on the table and saw they were maps of trails and trade routes that webbed all across the southern side of Mythos and included routes most considered too dangerous as they led though the Alisyan Mountains to the southern seas.

He turned toward Tristal and Orinus and leaned against the table, his hands casually held before him.

Taking her cue, Tristal told Valero of everything her unit had done to help save the settlement. She also admitted that they didn't actually save the settlement but that the suicide of the magistrate had. She told him of the strange stone he had put in his mouth and the mysterious and sudden obliteration of the monsters all around the settlement. And she told him about their suspicions regarding the White Lord.

When she was done, Valero moved to sit down. He ignored the presence of the other two as he considered what Tristal told him. After several long minutes, causing Tristal to shift her weight from one foot to the other impatiently, Valero rose to his feet. Orinus smirked at her impatience.

Before he could speak, Orinus stepped forward. "The magistrate committed suicide by swallowing a stone similar to one of these." He held out the handful of pebbles he had collected, and Valero took them and looked at them closely.

"Why these are summoning stones. And you say the magistrate died and the monsters simply turned to dust?"

Tristal and Orinus both nodded.

"I will send Emrys back to Elmnas right away." He looked to Orinus. "I trust you can offer a spell or talisman that can help him reach King Mronas quickly and safely?"

Orinus nodded in the affirmative but waited for Valero to continue.

Valero continued, "My unit is on orders to find someone. With this news, that mission is even more important. I had hoped that we could spend some time here to help the settlements, but we must move on."

Tristal asked, "Who are you searching for?"

"King Mronas's daughter."

"The… You mean Grazina Ald-Mronas?" Orinus asked, realizing immediately that, of course, that was who Valero meant.

Valero nodded. "You know her or have heard of her?"

"I have heard of her disappearance and the speculation that surrounds it, but no, I have not seen her or heard any rumors regarding her whereabouts."

Tristal replied, "Meri might know something."

Valero nodded. "I need to ask her. Regardless, as Emrys heads north, my unit will head east and search for her along the way."

Valero left the room, and Tristal and Orinus hung back.

"I think we should go with them," Orinus said.

"What?" Tristal objected, "No. No. Now that this settlement is helped, we should move to help the other ones."

Orinus sighed. "Is that your decision to make? Or do you need to consult with Wargate?"

Tristal bristled under Orinus's direct question. She knew he was right.

"Fine. I will contact Wargate immediately."

Orinus nodded at the looking glass. "Use that. It's faster. If they want us to assist Valero, then we need to know before they leave, not after."

Tristal grumbled under her breath about know-it-all mages, but she nodded that he was right as she moved to face the looking glass.

*"Never underestimate the least of us.
We learn early on to be sly, quick-witted,
and swift to attack lest the greatest of us
have the opportunity to overcome them."*
~ Unknown

19

*H*e stood in the shadows behind a stack of goods that had been offloaded from a merchant ship and watched as two men conversed animatedly. He couldn't hear what the men were saying. But it was obvious that the smaller man was afraid, not of the larger more dominating figure of the second man but of something altogether different. Intrigued, Rackas slid behind the stack of goods. Sticking tightly to the shadows, he inched his way down a row until he could hear the two men though his new position hindered his ability to see them.

"I was promised much more than this!" the second man sneered to the first. Rackas grimaced as General Duwo's resonant voice echoed off the crates and boxes he stood among.

A small whiny voice, shaking with dread. responded, "He told me to tell you that you have not given him what he demanded, and so you will not get any more payment until you have met the agreed upon terms."

The smaller man sniffled and coughed then cleared his throat, "He told me to remind you of the part he played in helping you dethrone the prince and his Elven whore. If it weren't for his help…"

Rackas heard a sudden gasp for air. Daring to peek around a lump of something wrapped in canvas, he saw that the general had shoved the smaller man up against a crate, lifting him easily off the ground. His feet dangled as he pushed for purchase against the crate behind him, and his face was ashen from lack of air.

"I have not forgotten, you worm."

The general held the smaller man for a few more seconds then stepped back and released him to fall on the ground. The smaller man hit the ground with a grunt, but Rackas saw him glare up at the general as he retook his footing.

"You would do well to treat me with more respect," sneered the man from the ground.

Rackas could not see the general's face, but he could imagine the scowl he was directing at the smaller man. Rackas wondered at the little man's bravado. Did he not know just how dangerous and deadly the general was? Rackas crouched low as lights flickered behind the general, and a soldier holding a torch stepped into view.

General Duwo turned to the new arrival. "Get this warehouse cleared out. You know where to take it. Then see to it that the goods going with this man are loaded onto his ship immediately. Get it done before dawn. Do you understand?"

The soldier didn't even respond. He simply turned on his heel and rushed back the way he came, leaving the general and the unknown man glaring at each other in the dim light.

"Seems I have no choice but to take what the White Lord will give me," said the general. He stepped toward the smaller man and poked him in the chest. "But I tell you this right now. I'll not tolerate

154

the likes of you in my presence again. See to it that the next person the White Lord sends to do business is…" he paused to think of the right word. "Be sure the next person is not a sniveling idiot."

The small man stood tall and puffed out his chest at the general, newfound confidence emanating from him even as he sniffled and wheezed. "You'll deal with whomever the White Lord wishes you to deal with. Even me. If you don't want it to be me and think he will send someone more to your level, you might want to rethink that. He might send you one of his White Guard."

The general snorted in reply, and Rackas felt a shudder go down his spine. Clearly, the general thought the smaller man was bluffing, but Rackas had seen the handiwork of the White Guard. They were killing machines the White Lord often sent to deal with his minions who he felt failed him in some way. People that could cause him trouble but not so much that he felt the need to deal with them himself. It was rumored that the members of his White Guard were reanimated warriors from the White Lord's own armies. Fallen soldiers filled with new life, soulless and full of powerful magic with only one purpose: to utterly destroy whomever the White Lord deemed needed destroying. The one saving grace appeared to be that it took a lot of magical binding to control them, so the White Lord did not send them often. Rackas surmised that was why the general did not put much stock in the smaller man's threat.

Rackas watched the smaller man bow up even more to the general and heard him hiss, "You think I'm making a hollow threat. I assure you, General Duwo, ruler of the Ebony Isles, given into your hands at the White Lord's pleasure, he sent me to you this trip because he is already contemplating sending his White Guard."

Rackas's eyes opened wide in disbelief to see that the smaller man's words had a visible effect on the general. The general hunched his shoulders and nodded, almost submissively, to the smaller man.

"I hear you, Irgus." The general paused as though seeking the right words to say. "I will do all in my power to see that the next shipment for your master is to his exact specifications. You will pass this on to him, I hope?"

Rackas made note of the smaller man's name: Irgus. He had never heard it before, but the fact he was a messenger from the White Lord confirmed his suspicions. All at once, Rackas was eager to be on his way home to get a message back to Bartholomew and King Mronas, but he forced himself to crouch in silence as Irgus responded to the general's sudden show of deference.

Irgus grinned evilly up at the general, tilted his head to the side, and rubbed his neck where the man had held him up against the crates.

"I will pass on your message, General. I will pass on your message and your promise as well as a thorough report of what I have endured and observed while visiting these beautiful isles."

Rackas watched the general stiffen his stance but mused as he remained quiet even though the telltale twitch in his cheeks betrayed the words he was biting back. The man was truly afraid of the White Lord. Rackas pondered what that might mean even now. It had been many years since the general had conducted his coupe that had killed the prince and sent his wife and daughter fleeing for their lives.

Finally, the general could take no more. He shook his head as though to clear his mind. "I take it we are done here then?"

Irgus yawned widely, sniffled some more, and nodded. "We are done for now, General. Just for now."

Without another word, the general turned on his heel and marched off in the direction his soldier had gone. Rackas watched Irgus stare after the general before he spat at the ground in obvious anger. But then Rackas watched in surprise as Irgus sank to the ground, shaking uncontrollably. He could hear the small man whimpering to himself. "Oh, no. Oh, no. The White Lord is going to kill me. Oh, no…"

Rackas felt a spark of pity for the small man but quickly shut it down. Minions of the White Lord deserved no pity as far as Rackas was concerned. He watched the small man cower, shaking and weeping there in the middle of the crates and goods, then he silently crept away from Irgus until he reached the sea-facing wall of the warehouse. Finding the small hole he had carefully cut out where the warehouse met some sharp rocks that led down to the water, he moved the netting that covered it, and crept out in the deep darkness of night just before the dawn.

He had a report that he needed to get to Elmnas as fast as he could.

*"Beware the solitary Drow. Beware the eyes
that glow from the deepest recesses of Mythnium.
Beware the ferocity of those who sequester deep
within the bowels of Netherland, who hold tightly to
their own ways so different from ours, we who
lavish under the glow of our suns, moon, and
stars."*
~ *Ancient Dwarven Text*

20

She lifted a hand to shield her eyes as she stepped toward the mouth of the cave. Even waiting until a few hours after nightfall, the light of the surface night was immensely greater than the lightest areas of Netherland. Keeping her hand over her eyes, she stepped beyond the cave and stared at the ground until her eyes more fully adjusted to the light. Once she could stare at her feet for a few minutes without squinting, she raised her eyes little by little until she looked up at the night sky and saw the millions of stars reflecting down on her. She never tired of looking at the stars, and she smiled slightly to herself. It had been nearly ten years since she had been to the surface. While she was more comfortable in the vast cave systems that webbed their way through Netherland, there was a sense of freedom to being on the surface that always refreshed her.

She had to admit she had been more than ready to leave Netherland. Recently, her role as a warden had become even more dangerous, and the fear that was beginning to take hold of her people was stifling. The tension in the heavy air of Netherland was growing more and more and was resulting in disputes, battles, and violence over the top even for the Drow. She could not help but be distressed by it.

As a warden to her people, she was expected to act as a messenger and emissary between the distant cities and settlements that dotted the caves and burrows. She had been chosen to fill the role because of her skill as a warrior and also her ability to react to things with more restraint than her people were known for. It was true that the Drow were a warlike race, more apt to tear each other apart than to try and find resolution, but since the Great Cataclysm, the Drow had felt a shift in ideologies, a shift toward self-preservation.

While the Drow had not been as affected as the surface races, the effects on them trickled down to the Drow. They found themselves cut off from the surface, suddenly despised and feared. Many of the avenues that had been used as trade routes between Netherland and the surface had been destroyed by the Cataclysm itself or by surface people who feared every shadow in the time directly following the event. As a result, the Drow had to work to rebuild trade relations with the surface. Emissaries who reacted in deadly anger over the tiniest perceived slight had failed to re-establish communication and trade that the Drow relied on.

The wardens were created by King Aris. He sought out Drow who had no familial or political ties. He often chose those who had been orphaned in city or settlement disputes. She had been one of them. When she had been found, she had been a gutter rat. She was quick and smart. She had become one of the stealthiest thieves in Ervenhall and had eluded merchants and soldiers for decades before she was caught. Thinking for sure she was going to be either exiled to the deepest depths of Netherland or executed, she prayed for execution. She had been suspicious when she was taken before the king himself and told by him that he wanted to train her and enlist her in this new guard.

Despite her suspicions, she had excelled at the training, which was more than learning how to be a better fighter. She was taught surface languages. She was taught the basics of the surface races and cultures. She was taught diplomacy, and she was expected to seek peaceful resolution with every mission at all costs, the exact opposite of the natural tendencies of the Drow.

The last decade she had returned to Ervenhall with grim tidings from the surface. Her mission had only been to scout old trade routes and try to gain information of cities or settlements that would be willing to trade. In light of her report, King Aris had called on her to stay in Netherland to act as his main emissary to the scattered Drow in order to make them all aware of what was going on above their heads.

She had come out high in the Alisyan Mountains. Her ultimate goal as commanded by the king was to gather information of the events happening on the surface. The priests and sorcerers of her Drow people were foretelling, sensing further unrest that could affect them again even as far removed as they were. Their best defense was to know the source of the unrest. She had been told that her king's most trusted priest had foreseen the White Lord moving again, but more concerning than that was a shadow of something stirring in the far east, which was suspected to be even more powerful than the White Lord.

Virconia had been tasked with trying to discern what that shadow was, to try to determine the nature of that shadow. She frowned as the weight of the task settled on her. Foresight was dangerous, and the predictions by priests who lived largely isolated from the rest of their own often proved to be most dangerous to try to discern and act upon.

She continued to stare up at the night sky as she thought of the scale of her task. A flare of light caught her attention. She shifted her focus and saw a distant campfire burning on a nearby slope. Curious, she adjusted the pack on her back and moved in the direction of the fire.

"Enduring companionship, be it friends, soldiers at arms, families, or clans, is made firm and strong under the duress of shared hardship."
~ Igma – Goddess of Wisdom

21

*E*stryl laughed loudly at another of Stranick's jokes. She glanced at Aldrina who stood leaning against a wagon wheel and staring into the fire, clearly not paying any attention. Estryl sighed. Her new friend was taking being cast out of the Willow Elf community hard. She understood but wished there were a way to help her friend. Stranick and Elder Martan started to speak of the route they were taking the following day, believing it would lead them out of the steep mountains within a few days. They hoped to gain the low hills and fields that led to Syan Lake by the end of the week.

Not needing to be part of that decision making, Estryl moved to Aldrina's side and looked up at her. "Why don't you rest?"

Aldrina looked down and met Estryl's gaze. She had a sadness about her that clouded her eyes and darkened her face. "I wonder if I did the right thing," she said, absently rubbing the amulet that hung around her neck.

"I get that it went against their belief system, but you're not a Willow Elf, Aldrina. You are not expected to have the same inherent talents they do with healing magic. I think the fact that you chose to be a healer and are learning to hone your skills defines who you are. The amulet is not who you are, but it helps you be better at what you want to do. I know you will miss Olphara and the way her people have become like family to you. Trust me, they will miss you even more."

Aldrina sighed heavily. "I never had a family. Not that I remember at any rate."

Estryl gently hit Aldrina on the arm. "Well, you have two now. You will always be part of Olphara's people even if you cannot be among them. And now you have me, Stranick, and Martan."

Aldrina smiled warmly at the Silver Dwarf. "The gods do work in wonderful ways."

Estryl grinned. "Don't they?"

A slide of rocks on the slope above them caused them to quiet. On alert, they swung in the direction of the sound. Aldrina was no fighter, but she was poised to move away from any danger, while Estryl, also not trained to fight, moved toward the sound instead of away from it. In an instant, Stranick was at her side, a heavy hammer in his hand, while Elder Martan moved to Aldrina's side with his own weapon in his hands.

All four gasped as a pair of red eyes materialized just beyond the light of the campfire. They all braced for an attack and nearly reacted violently when the red eyes moved into the light, revealing they belonged to a lithe, beautiful, and deadly Drow woman.

She stood with her hands up, no weapons within reach. She said nothing as she watched the three dwarves and the human woman in front of her. She immediately sensed Estryl's magic as she simultaneously took in the weapons the dwarves carried, the amulet around the human's neck, and sensed a couple of heavily armed dwarves who were obviously on guard and alerted to her presence.

After several tense seconds, Elder Martan stepped forward. He took a closer look at the Drow woman, noting that she wore the sigils of a Drow warrior. If she had intended to harm them, she would have made short work of them before they ever realized she was there. Still, he knew better than to trust a Drow. He hefted his ax so that its blade rested against his shoulder, both hands still tight on the handle so he could swing it easily if need be.

"What do you want?" he asked in his abrupt manner.

The Drow bowed her head ever so slightly in deference and acknowledgment that she was speaking to an elder. "Might I warm myself by your fire?"

Estryl glanced at her brother. She had never seen a Drow before, but she knew their reputation. Stranick stared at the Drow, but something about the woman seemed rather benign, and he visibly relaxed. Taking her cue from her brother, Estryl also relaxed and motioned for the guards who were still standing outside the light of the fire to be at ease.

Elder Martan, however, remained tense and ready. "Why would we allow one of your kind to come into our camp?"

Virconia bowed deeply, her arms stretched out to either side. "By the gods of the surface, I intend you no harm. I'm alone and just arrived to the surface this night. I am in search of information and nothing more. I'd dishonor myself by harming anyone who might offer me a direction in which I can gain this information."

164

Elder Martan frowned. "What is this information you seek?"

Aldrina moved past Elder Martan. "Come. You are welcome to sit at our fire. Warm yourself first, then we can proceed with asking questions of one another."

Virconia stood tall and met the human woman's clear gaze. She sensed the woman was more than she seemed but also sensed only genuine kindness in her. Nodding her thanks and glancing warily at Elder Martan, she gingerly made her way to the fire.

Elder Martan barked at her back, "Leave your pack by the wagon. And your weapons too."

As Virconia complied without argument, he turned to Aldrina and in a harsh whisper reprimanded her, "She is a warrior. Do you not see the sigils on her belt and within the tattoos on her face?"

Aldrina looked where Martan indicated. She had seen the sigils but did not know what they indicated.

Martan realized the woman was ignorant. "By the gods, we have a lot to teach you about this world, don't we?"

Aldrina bristled at the suggestion that she was naïve, but she bit back her retort out of respect for the old dwarf.

Estryl moved to her side. "Never fear. You will learn."

Together, Estryl, Aldrina, and Elder Martan moved to join the Drow at the fire while Stranick remained standing at Elder Martan's signal.

Virconia spread her hands toward the fire. In reality, she was not cold at all, but she knew that sharing a fire with surface dwellers went a long way in helping to gain their trust. It was around such a campfire that she had made her first friends among the surface dwellers – a ragtag group of dwarves, two elves, and a couple of humans. She did not entertain the idea that this group might also become friends to her, but she did think she might gain their trust enough to at least help her determine where her journey should continue from that point forward.

She met Estryl's gaze, assuming that her magic made her the leader of the group. "I'm Virconia of Ervenhall. I am acting as a liaison for my king, King Aris. I was tasked to gather information regarding the White Lord…"

"The White Lord?" interrupted Estryl.

Virconia ignored the interruption, and continued, "… because we have seen some disturbing occurrences among the monsters of the deep."

Estryl interrupted again, "The monsters of the deep? What kind of occurrences?"

Virconia looked at the dwarf. She could tell that Estryl was young by Dwarven standards, and there appeared to be an eagerness about her that belied her own experience on the surface compared to the relative safety of the caves, mines, and underground fortresses of the Silver Dwarves. Rather than be annoyed by the impatient nature of the female dwarf, Virconia raised a hand for the dwarf to let her continue.

"Oh. Oh. Of course," replied Estryl as she clamped her mouth shut but leaned in toward Virconia in extreme curiosity.

Virconia nearly smiled, but kept her face emotionless. "The monsters have grown bolder. We are used to bands of goblins, golems, worms, and other monsters causing trouble from time to time. But over the past several years, they have moved closer to our cities. Recently, they have started working in concert with each other. I have never seen anything like it, and the eldest among my people have not either."

She looked around then to Elder Martan, "You can, of course, understand our need to know if this is unusual just for Netherland or if the surface is seeing something similar."

Elder Martan gave nothing away, loathe to trust the woman before him with her red eyes boring into his.

Virconia realized the old dwarf would give nothing away, so she changed tactics. Shrugging, she said, "I can see you good people are on a journey of your own. If it will not put you out, may I stay in your camp for the night just so I can get my bearings? Then in the morning, I will be on my way as well?"

Aldrina nodded her okay. Estryl was exuberant in her permission though she looked to Martan for the final say. He didn't trust the Drow, but neither did he want to dismiss her and then have his throat slit in the middle of the night, so he grudgingly agreed, indicating she could spread her bedroll on the far side of the camp from Estryl's wagon.

Once Elder Martan was done laying his directives, he excused himself to go to sleep, admonishing the others to get rest as well so they could start early the next day. After he disappeared in the wagon he shared with Stranick, Estryl nearly jumped in her seat.

"Virconia, I am Estryl. Never mind Elder Martan; he means well. That one standing behind you is my brother, Stranick. This is Aldrina – she is a healer. And the two in the shadows are Gav and Tor."

Virconia nodded. "Thank you for showing me such kindness. I know it's hard to trust my people."

Estryl waved away her comment. "I've never met a Drow. I am very curious. Tell me about your people."

Virconia leaned back where she sat. "Where would you like me to start?"

Virconia heard the low rumble first, but in her sleep, it sounded like the low rumble of the earth that she was so used to in Netherland. Then it occurred to her where she was, and she shot up in a flash. She wasn't in Netherland, and that deep rumble in the earth on the surface meant something entirely different.

"Wake up!" she yelled as she turned and tried to see the location of the impending attack.

Just as her eyes, able to see so clearly in the dark, settled on the Rock Giant, a large boulder clipped her right arm, causing her to spin around. The boulder hit the wagon Estryl and Aldrina shared, splintering its front wheel and causing it to tip a little. Estryl quickly climbed out just as Elder Martan and Stranick climbed out of the other one. All three were ready for battle.

Elder Martan yelled, "Where are they?"

Virconia pointed beyond the light of the fire. "One is there to your left. Another is over here, directly in front of me, and a third is up the slope. That is the one lobbing boulders. Oh! He just tossed another – Aldrina!"

Aldrina flung herself out the back of the wagon just an instant before it was crushed under the weight of a boulder nearly the same size as the wagon.

Elder Martan and Stranick raced off to the left to fight that giant, while Estryl stood beside Aldrina, both unsure of what to do.

Virconia stared at them for a split second. "Don't just stand there! Use your magic."

Both women just sputtered at her, "That's not how our magic works!"

Virconia didn't have time to process their response as the giant that was in front of her moved into the light of the fire and swung its heavy club at her. Virconia easily sidestepped it and slashed her drawn blades across the top if its exposed hand. Not waiting for the giant to retaliate, she focused her attention on the hand holding the weapon and drove her blades into it as deep as she could. It's hand now useless, the giant dropped its club but, in a fury, tried to stomp on Virconia. She sidestepped it easily but stepped right into the path of another tossed boulder. This one caught her on her left shoulder and threw her into the air. She landed at Aldrina's feet in a crumpled heap, and she knew her arm, ribs, and shoulder were broken. Unable to catch her breath, she felt herself getting dizzy and didn't realize that in landing she had cracked her skull on a small rock. She heard Estryl shout in anger, just as Aldrina knelt beside her. As she started to pass out, she thought she heard the distinct war call of one of the White Elf clans. She hoped she was right, because this small band didn't stand a chance against three Rock Giants on their own.

"She's waking up," called an unfamiliar voice as Virconia blinked open her eyes. She was under a canvas tent of some sort, but it was clearly daytime. Her head hurt immensely as did her entire body, but she sighed inwardly. Somehow, she was alive. She didn't dare try to move yet. Just lying still was incredibly painful so she only let her eyes move. Staring down at her from a safe distance was one of the guard dwarves, but he moved out of sight as Aldrina stepped to her side. Beyond Aldrina, Virconia could see a group of White Elves armed to the teeth standing about, obviously pleased with themselves.

"We nearly lost you," Aldrina stated as she leaned over Virconia. Virconia noted that Aldrina looked exhausted as though she had been awake for days on end. Fearing the worst, Virconia waited for Aldrina to go on.

"I had to use my amulet to help me heal your body. I am sorry for your pain. Once I was finished setting your bones, healing the internal bleeding, and healing your head and neck, I just didn't have enough in me to help you ease the pain. However, now that you're awake, I can make you some tea with herbs that will help a great deal."

Virconia grabbed Aldrina's arm as she turned to leave for the tea. "I should have died."

Aldrina stopped dead in her tracks. She slowly turned to face Virconia and nodded. "You nearly died fighting to save us all."

At that moment, Virconia remembered everything. "How...?"

Aldrina smiled. "Let me get that tea for you first. I can sense the pain you are in."

Virconia didn't bother replying. Instead, she let go of Aldrina and closed her eyes, willing her body to continue to heal, but she could barely handle the pain. She realized in that moment that she must have been a wreck for she had been in many fights and battles. While she had endured many wounds, some nearly fatal, she could not recall ever hurting as bad as she did in that moment.

She lay with her eyes closed and listened to the movement around camp. It sounded like there were many more people moving around and talking. She wondered if maybe they had moved on down the mountain pass and were at a settlement of some sort. In the middle of her wondering, Aldrina returned.

"Here you go," she said and leaned down to help Virconia raise her head.

Shooting pain ran down Virconia's spine and into her head, making it feel as though it were being split open, but she forced herself to take the cup from Aldrina's other hand and drank it completely. Within seconds, warmth spread through her, and she felt the pain diminish greatly though not completely.

Meeting Aldrina's eyes, Virconia said, "You saved my life."

Aldrina shrugged it off. "I'm a healer. I hope to save many lives if I can."

Virconia shook her head slightly. "No, you gave more than you should have to save me. I cannot repay you for that. I owe you a debt."

Aldrina's eyes grew wide. "No. No. None of that. You don't know us. I don't know of any complete strangers that would just risk their lives like you did for us. That matters. I knew I had a duty to do everything I could to heal you."

Virconia sensed there was more to it than that. She could see it in the exhaustion that Aldrina was trying to hide. "Still," she replied, "I am bound to you because of all you have done for me."

Aldrina didn't know what to say. She didn't know what Virconia meant, and she was afraid to ask. The very appearance of Virconia unsettled Aldrina. Virconia, before her massive injuries, had been a beautiful woman to behold. Her ebony skin was so black it almost appeared blue, and her red eyes intense and unusual. Her tattoos were outlined in white in contrast with her dark skin. Her build, small compared to humans, was strong and lithe, the body of a warrior that was confirmed with a large array of scars from cuts, stabs, and arrow wounds. But looking back into Virconia's red eyes, Aldrina saw honor and a sense of duty. She didn't see a heart thirsty for blood as was so rumored of the Drow. Aldrina couldn't help but wonder if Virconia was a testament of what her race was really like. Or was she an outcast because she was different than them?

Virconia continued to stare at Aldrina. "As is custom among my people, because you saved my life, I'm bound to you until the day I die or you die. In whatever capacity I can serve you, I shall do it." Exhausted from the effort and fierceness of her proclamation, the Dark Elf drifted off to some much-needed sleep.

Caught off guard at this new development, Aldrina gripped her amulet. She could still sense a great deal of pain in the Dark Elf, so she held the amulet over Virconia. Moving it slowly along

Virconia's body, Aldrina recited a prayer for healing that Olphara had taught her. By the time she reached Virconia's feet, she was so drained she collapsed into a chair to the side of the tent and drifted off into a fitful sleep of her own. Outside, the dwarves and the elves ate, drank, and celebrated a victory.

*"The fiercest protector is
the one who lives selflessly."*
~ Peran – God of War

22

Olphara was roused from her slumber with a start, hands shaking her roughly. Someone was calling her name with an urgency laced with terror. She blinked her eyes, realizing it was still dark outside. Light flickered across the canvas of her tent, telling her instantly that more was burning than merely the campfires they had staggered throughout the camp. Instantly, she shoved aside the young elf that was sent to wake her.

"Who is attacking us, child?" she asked in a raspy whisper still sluggish from sleep.

"One of the guards said it was the White Lord!"

Olphara looked at the child in surprise.

"Surely not," she replied but grabbed a small blade, clipped on her cloak, and gathered a small pouch that held the only valuables she dared keep with her as her tribe moved about on their nomadic path through the mountains. Dressed and ready to go in under a minute, she moved to the entrance of her tent and gently moved it a bit to the side so she could peer out and get her bearings.

What met her gaze was one of horror as she watched only a handful of the White Lord's soldiers move through her camp ripping into tents, smashing, burning, and killing everything that stood in their path. With a thud of realization and a chill of terror, she noted the white armor catching the light of the flames that raged all about them.

The White Lord had sent his White Guard.

Questions racing through her mind, Olphara sprang into action. She turned back into her tent. Guiding the child before her, she rushed to the back. Quickly, she cut a large slit in the canvas and peered through to make sure it was clear. Seeing nothing except still untouched tents, she pushed the child before her and stepped out into the chill air of the night. Cries for help sounded from around the camp and only a few yells of defiance rang out as metal clashed on metal.

Her heart sank knowing most of the people of her camp would be slaughtered before the White Guard. Her tribe only had a few guards who kept watch, and they mainly served to put up a warning or to defend so that the Willows and any patients among them could try to escape whatever was attacking them. They were not prepared for a fight, most definitely not prepared for the likes of the White Guard.

She glanced about her and picked a path to lead the child to the edge of the camp where a narrow trail led to the many caverns that dotted the mountains. Rushing the child ahead of her, she tried to determine if anyone else was heading that way as well. She saw no one running in her direction, and the cries and screams behind her went silent. In an instant, Olphara sank to the ground in a low crouch, the child gathered to her side, breathing heavily but thankfully silent. Olphara could not understand the instant silence and suspected someone must be manipulating the magical currents. She glanced behind her but saw no one in pursuit, so she kept low and continued to move toward the trail.

As she reached the edge of the camp, the trail before her, she heard a low rumble rise up behind her and then a voice that seemed to reverberate through her body and into her soul.

"Olphara."

She didn't stop. Instead, she gave up trying to hide and be stealthy and led the child to the trail. Once they vanished around a rocky outcropping, she kneeled before the child. Even as her name sounded out behind her, she knew the caller to be the White Lord himself.

She took the child's face in her hands and made the child focus on her. "You know where the closest cavern is, yes?"

The child nodded, his blue eyes wide in fright, his teeth chattering in terror even as his body trembled.

"Good. You run there as fast as you can. You go inside and push the metal plate on the left side of the entrance. The entrance will shut behind you. Only open the entrance if you hear me say your name. Do you understand me?"

The child nodded.

Olphara hugged the boy and then turned him toward the rocky trail and shoved him down it. "Hurry, child. Hurry."

She watched the boy disappear into the dark and prayed he would reach the cavern safely. Then she turned and peered around the rocks toward the camp. Backlit by the fires of the camp stood the White Lord. At his side stood two of the White Guard, each holding the arm of someone who hung limply between them.

The White Lord stepped forward. Even though he was not looking in exactly her direction, his voice cut into her.

176

"Olphara. Your people are decimated. You have many who need your healing touch."

Fire and ice burned within Olphara. She battled with anger at the pain she knew any survivors must be feeling and dread as she tried to understand what the White Lord could possibly want with her. She was just an old Willow. Just a healer. Then it hit her. She was also Keeper of the Histories. The realization hit her hard, and she felt dread like she had never known before, but she remained where she was.

She watched the White Lord step toward the edge of the camp.

"I know you're there, healer. I can sense you even if I cannot see you. I have someone who would benefit greatly from your abilities. Someone you know, I think. Maybe an old friend? I'm not sure. I don't know how you Willows keep track of each other. Still, I know he knows who you are, so I assume you must know who he is."

He nodded to the guards and motioned them forward.

Olphara gasped in spite of herself.

There between the guards was Pruzin, the historian from Farcaste Reach. Even in the darkness with only the light of the fires reflecting off the rocks, she could see how broken his body was.

"Olphara, come. Come out. Come see to old Pruzin here. Do you know him? I am certain you must. After all, he is a historian, and you are a Keeper of the Histories. You two must have crossed paths. Come. Come see to his wounds. I fear I have been a bit too zealous in my conversations with him."

Olphara sat rigid and then started as she heard someone step behind her.

177

"Shhh," came a frantic whisper, and a rough hand touched her bare arm. She turned and breathed a sigh of relief to see it was one of her guards. She looked beyond him and was happily surprised to see the camp's entire guard and several of the other healers gathered behind her.

"How?" she mouthed silently.

The guard leaned in to whisper in her ear. "A few of us tried to keep the White Lord's Guard busy while the rest of us cut people out of their tents. Most of us were already in the cavern when the child came in. Boy gave one of the healers such a fright she passed out."

The guard glanced out at the White Lord. "What does he want?"

Olphara pointed at Pruzin. "Me. Something he thinks I know. Or just access to the histories. Something he thinks may be in the scrolls and books. I don't know what."

The guard nodded. "I don't think that old elf is going to survive the night…"

Olphara gripped the guard's hand. "He must. We must find a way to get him away from the White Lord."

"We can't. It's impossible."

Olphara shook her head and stood up. As she stepped out of the shadows of the rocks and into the light where the White Lord could see her, she whispered over her shoulder. "Get the healers to the cavern and get them ready to get to work. You and the guards get ready to seal the entrance behind me."

The guard stared up at her, his face in the shadows of the rock, but she knew he must think her mad.

"Olphara! No!" he whispered loudly as she took a step away from the shelter of the rock.

She watched as the White Lord turned his gaze toward her, and she sucked in her breath. Breathing slowly and deeply, she forced herself to stay calm despite the terror she felt running in her veins.

"Ah! There you are. You are Olphara?"

Olphara met the White Lord's gaze and wondered how powerful he really was. Could he sense truth versus lies?

Testing a theory, she responded in a shaky voice, allowing her real fear to make her body cower and shake. "No. Olphara is dead. Your brutes killed her."

She looked over at Pruzin who hung limply between the White Guards, but he made eye contact with her. He was fully aware of where he was and who she was.

She grimaced at the White Lord and made to move toward Pruzin. "I can help him! Let me help him!"

Without waiting for the White Lord to respond, she rushed to the old elf's side and started making a big show of looking him over.

"Olphara is dead, you say? Now that is inconvenient," the White Lord commented. "I assume you are her second?"

Olphara shook her head, denying his question. "No, she is visiting another tribe."

The White Lord grunted and took a step toward her. Olphara could feel anger and frustration rolling off him in waves. She looked at Pruzin and stood between him and the White Lord. Turning her head downward so the tall White Guards could not see her, she mouthed to Pruzin, "Can you walk?"

Pruzin blinked in response, and Olphara smiled slightly.

She turned to the White Lord. "You monster! I need to help this elf right away! Tell your men to let him go. I can lay him down there and begin my work."

The White Lord stared at her, caught off guard by her boldness, but he had dealt with Willows before and knew them to be fierce protectors of the wounded and sickly. Suspicious, but not thinking the old Willow capable of anything that could cause him or his men harm, he nodded to his men.

They released Pruzin and he started to sink to his knees, but Olphara whispered to him as she pretended to try to catch him, "Now! To the trail behind me!"

As he lunged forward, spry on his feet despite the torment he had endured, Olphara dashed an ampoule of liquid on the ground, causing a thick smoke to rise up around her. She turned after Pruzin as the White Lord shouted commands. The ground shook under her feet as the White Guard took chase after them.

Around the bend the old Willows rushed, their bodies belying their age, and for Pruzin, his incredible pain. Still the pair dashed along the trail as fast as they could, hoping the cover of darkness would help them. Olphara felt a sting in her shoulder and realized one of the White Guards had thrown a blade at her. She felt its burn in her shoulder and in her lungs and realized it had punctured deep. She gasped for breath but then saw two of her guards standing on either side of the cavern. They rushed forward to help the healer and the historian. They pushed the two older Willows ahead of them and then shoved them inside even as one of them yelled, "Close it!"

Olphara and Pruzin fell to the ground of the cavern in a heap as complete darkness shut in around them and the entrance sealed shut.

Olphara screamed out in protest as she realized the guards had sacrificed themselves in order to save her. "No!" she cried, but then a soft glow emanated from deeper in the cavern, and gentle hands lifted her off the ground and began to carry her toward the light. She looked to the side and saw that the others had lifted Pruzin as well. Their eyes met and they smiled grimly at each other.

"Hello, old friend," she said to Pruzin.

He started to respond, but instead began to cough sharply, his body doubling up on itself, making it hard for his bearers to carry him. She lost sight of him as they set him down. As she was carried deeper into the cavern, she allowed her body to fall into a deep trance so that her healers could begin work on the stab wound in her shoulder.

Olphara leaned against a staff and stared down the trail that led deeper into the maze of caverns. Staggered along the trail was the occasional torch, and the survivors of her tribe walked in a line along the trail in solemn and sad silence. Beside her, Pruzin leaned heavily on a staff as well though another healer had a firm grip on his arm just in case.

"You say the White Lord is after…"

Pruzin sighed and whispered, his voice raspy still from screaming at the hands of the White Lord and his careful torture, "A Silver Dwarf."

Olphara glanced sideways at Pruzin. "How much was he able to learn about the dwarf?"

Pruzin grinned at his old friend. "Not her name or where she is going. But he is no idiot. Now that he knows she is not with you, he will likely figure out that she is on her way to the Forest Elves."

"Why does he want her?"

Pruzin frowned. "I believe he wanted her to exploit her abilities and the histories to further his search. He is searching for something beyond the dragons."

Olphara huffed. "Dragons…"

"He has one, Olphara."

Olphara saw the healer opposite her gasp.

She looked at Pruzin closely, not believing him, but he was not lying.

Pruzin continued, "He has a Red Dragon. He calls her Libitina, and she helped him attack Farcaste Reach. He only captured me because she was able to break down the doors of the tower."

Olphara looked away from Pruzin and stared at the backs of the elves ahead of her. She tried to imagine the size and power of a beast capable of breaking into the tower. She shook her head as she realized the tables were turning to favor the White Lord. Whatever his goals, with the might of a dragon long thought to be more legend than fact, keeping him at bay would be much more difficult.

She sighed and then made a decision.

"If that is the case, then we must make our way to Elmnas as well. Word will spread to the Forest Elves before we even reach them, but maybe we can catch up to the Silver Dwarves, warn them, and we can all seek sanctuary and knowledge with King Mronas."

Pruzin nodded in agreement then looked at Olphara. "We have to walk the whole way?"

Olphara glanced at Pruzin and then at the staffs they were both clutching. She smiled lightly, "Yes, we will have to walk the whole way, but you know what sort of tricks we have up our sleeves for healing. We have a few too that might help us move along a bit faster."

Pruzin nodded. "Well then, let's get on with it!"

"The magic that was plays against the magic that is. These creatures, these races I have created set about on a path that disrespected the old magic and proved to be their near demise. They pray to me asking me why I allowed it all. I tell them if they pause to listen to search the magic. The answers are in the currents that flow like rivers all about them. The answers to the past that nearly destroyed them and the answers to a future that could save them – they are all there. Will these creatures have the will and the fortitude to search the currents? If they do, will they have the courage to do what those answers demand?"
~ Siki – Father Creator

23

*T*ristal groaned in the saddle. She hated riding horses. Her smaller body was not made for riding horseback day after day. Orinus, riding beside her, offered her a pouch of herbs.

"Take a pinch. It will help."

"Help with what?" she retorted grumpily.

"Just take some. I grow tired of your moaning and groaning."

Tristal snatched the pouch from the mage, took a pinch, and stuffed it into her mouth. She chewed it, savoring the spicy sweet flavor of it before she swallowed. She handed the pouch back but was not ready to say thank you. After a few minutes, she felt her muscles loosen and the pain in her legs and back slowly subside.

Orinus smiled to himself. He knew how effective the herbs were, but Tristal was prickly with all of them after her communication with Wargate went exactly opposite of how she hoped. Apparently, King Mronas had been in contact with Wargate as well, asking for their help in tracking his daughter. It was fortuitous, per Wargate's leadership, that Tristal's unit was there and already with Valero and Colna. They directed her to accompany General Valero on his quest to find Grazina. Of course, Tristal argued against it, but no amount of arguing changed their minds, and orders were orders.

Valero knew and agreed with Tristal's desire to help the other settlements, so he directed Brax to remain with two of Tristal's unit to organize a group from Middleton and move to the next town to help turn the tide if they could. Brax, Meri, Tristal's men, and a dozen people from the settlement had left before they had. By reports from Meri to Orinus, they had helped win back the closest settlement and were preparing to add to their numbers to move on to the next, moving westward.

Now as their party—consisting of himself, Colna, Layni, Tristal, Orinus, and the remaining four of Tristal's unit—moved southeast and away from Middleton and the eastern settlements by Syan Lake, Valero hoped they were actually moving closer to wherever Grazina might be. Most of the smaller villages and settlements they passed through on their way had been abandoned or razed to the ground. The handful of people that remained knew nothing of the Elven princess, most wishing nothing to do at all with the diverse group on horseback asking about her.

Valero let himself fall back from the lead and fell between Tristal and Orinus. Orinus finally allowed his identity be known to Valero and Colna. They were both surprised but agreed not to give him away to even their king because he still hoped to remain incognito as much as he could.

"Can you track people you have never met?" Valero asked Orinus.

"Do you have anything that they may have used with magic?"

Valero shook his head. "No. She has innate magical abilities as do most of royal blood, but she mostly avoided using them. Plus, I didn't think to bring anything she may have used before she left Elmnas."

Tristal glanced at Valero. "Why did your princess leave?"

Valero shrugged. "I know she left her parents explaining why, but that was not something they divulged to me. Whatever it was, it was enough that they let her go without immediately bringing her back."

Tristal shook her head, "I don't get it. What person would leave a life of luxury to just disappear? Disappearing is hard. She had to have completely forsaken all that she is in order to be able to blend in and not be recognized. She's likely led a very hard life since leaving."

Valero agreed. "I hate to imagine what she may have endured in order to remain hidden."

Tristal asked, "So why now?"

Valero cocked his head. "Why now what?"

"Why are you seeking her out now after all these years?"

Valero did not answer.

Instead, Orinus answered, "Because what we have seen at Syan Lake is happening more and more all

186

over Mythos. I imagine that means King Mronas believes the princess to be in mortal danger or believes she may be needed for whatever is coming."

Valero nodded at Orinus's evaluation while Tristal leaned forward in her saddle to see Orinus on the other side of Valero. "What do you think is coming?"

Orinus looked at Tristal. "I don't have to tell you. You know exactly what—who—I think is coming."

Tristal sat back in her saddle and complained. "I should be helping at Syan Lake or be at Wargate helping make preparations if they are even making them."

All at once, Orinus stopped his horse. He turned in his saddle and looked back to the west.

Valero stopped too, but Tristal kept moving forward with the rest of the band. "What is it?" Valero asked.

Orinus closed his eyes and let his magic flow outward from him. He sensed another magic. He tried to determine what it was, where it was, who it belonged to, but he couldn't understand it. He looked at Valero.

"I sense a magic unlike anything I have ever encountered before. It's old. Very old."

Valero looked behind them.

"Is it following us? Should we be concerned?"

Orinus closed his eyes again and pushed outward as far as he could. Whatever it was, it just barely touched his own but was nearly as powerful as his. He tried to reach out to it, but everything was strange about it. Finally, he opened his eyes and stared at Valero.

"I think it is Dwarven," he said, doubting it as he said it. Dwarves hadn't had any powerful mages or

187

magic in so long that it was thought that dwarves were losing their hold on magic.

Valero glanced backward again. "I heard rumor of a Silver Dwarf blacksmith who was going to Farcaste Reach because he was touched by an ancient magic. Maybe the rumor is true?"

Orinus looked at Valero with wide eyes. "Silver Dwarves at Farcaste Reach?"

Valero nodded. "So the rumor goes. I don't know how much stock I would put in it. We had a caravan come through with a couple blacksmiths from the Silver Isles, but they were obviously merchants and nothing more."

Orinus stared at Valero. "Are you very sensitive to magic?"

Valero shrugged, "I guess, but maybe only certain kinds of magic. I think I notice it more if I am looking for it."

Orinus grunted. "I see."

He kicked his horse forward, but the strange touch of magic intrigued him. He looked back over his shoulder. "I wonder if I should go…"

Valero saw the sudden internal turmoil in the mage. "If it doesn't appear dangerous, shouldn't we keep going?"

Orinus looked at Valero then at the backs of Colna and Tristal and at the others who rode before and behind him. He hated being out in the open, and he hated even more to be part of a group with so many elves, so many people in general. It made him uncomfortable and vulnerable. Part of him wanted to turn his horse around and make a wild dash toward the strange magic beckoning him, but he had made a commitment to help.

With a heavy sigh, he responded, "You're right."

Realizing that Orinus was finished talking for the moment, Valero spurred his horse forward to check in with the other people in their group.

"The coin having two sides is a poor support for any argument. Rather a ball. A ball, in its circumference, better portrays all the different aspects and sides of various perspectives from different angles, from different trajectories. There are never simply two sides to a story. There is the perspective of one person against the perspective of another person, but in reality, there is also the perspective of the person observing, the person directly affected, the person indirectly affected, the person who has yet to stumble onto the scene, and every person who will ever become involved in the argument."
~ *Unknown*

24

On the morning of the fourth day just after they had broken camp and begun to journey farther east, they smelled the salt of the ocean and the mustiness of the vast swamps that still lay between them and that ocean. They only traveled a few hours when the fields and hills to either side gave way to shallow ponds, marshes, and bogs with the road built-up to keep from disappearing into the mud. Occasionally, the wide road was widened even more to allow travelers to stop and rest or to allow caravans to pass unhindered. At one of the wide areas, they noted a human sitting alone on a wagon. He was leaning forward so far that at first glance they thought he was dead. However, as they approached, they must have aroused him from sleep for he suddenly sat up and shouted at them to keep their distance.

"Stay away! I warn you! I'm cursed!" he cried at them.

The group shared uneasy glances, and their senses heightened for any threat. Orinus rode up to the man.

"Stay away, I tell you! Don't come any closer!" the man shrieked in anger and despair.

"I am a mage, sir. I have wards that protect me from a great many things. Now please, tell me. How are you cursed? Are you alone?"

The man covered his face with his hands and moaned bitterly as though he were in great pain. "It was that elf witch. Blast her with the god's own fire!"

Orinus glanced at Valero quizzically. "Elf witch?" he prompted.

"Oh, yeah. I don't mind elves so much, you know. Oh, but this one. Oh. She's an evil whore of a devil. I needed help you see. I didn't have anyone else to turn to, and the rana said she could help. So I went to her."

Orinus waited, but the man seemed overcome again in some pain although Orinus could not see any sort of wound or outward ailment. After a few minutes with Valero and Colna shifting nervously in their saddles and Tristal irritated with the beleaguered man, he took a deep breath and regained his composure.

"That witch. I asked her for a potion to help me get revenge on the rana who killed my wife. She told me she wasn't a witch. Oh, she protested over and over, but I saw all the dried plants around her hut. I saw the jars and vials. I saw her ugly face. It was a witch's face I tell you. She was so lovely on one side of her face. You could fall in love with a creature that beautiful, but when I saw the other side of her face, I knew. Yet she kept telling me she couldn't help me."

Orinus heard Colna gasp audibly at the description of the elf woman and then heard Colna and Valero whispering in hushed tones. Focusing back on the man, he leaned in. "This witch cursed you instead of helping you?"

The man shook his head vehemently. "I just got so frustrated. I needed her help. How come she wouldn't help me? So I got mad and tried to force her. As I reached for her, she said something in a language I didn't understand. I was blown off my feet and ran for my wagon. She cursed me! Her spell, she did something to me. I can't breathe and I feel like my gut is turning to stone!"

He bent over in agony but then reached out to Orinus. "You... You look like a good man. Will you kill the witch for me? Will you get revenge on her for this?"

Orinus refrained from taking the man's hand. He surmised that the elf woman merely cast a repulsion spell to keep the man from harming her. In doing so, the man must have landed on something that broke his ribs. His curse was internal injuries that likely led to a collapsed lung and internal bleeding. Regardless, Orinus knew the man was past saving. Taking pity on the miserable soul, he whispered a chant and the man fell into a deep sleep that Orinus knew he would never wake from, but at least the man would know no more pain.

He turned his horse and rejoined the others.

Tristal stared at him. "You killed him?"

Orinus frowned. "I put him to sleep. He won't wake up from it, but no, I didn't kill him. I relieved him of his pain."

Valero and Colna sat tense and alert. "We must go. She must be nearby. He said the rana directed him to her. We must ask the them at once," said Valero. Without waiting, he spurred his horse toward a grouping of huts that spread out a short distance ahead of them.

The group reached the rana village, and Valero jumped from his saddle as members of the community left their short huts to approach him. While Valero exchanged pleasantries, Tristal observed the fish people's community. She had seen rana before but had never been among so many, let alone been in one of their villages.

These strange fish-like people distantly related to the merpeople of the oceans were often beautiful if not strange in appearance. They had long faces with wide mouths and big lips. Their eyes, very similar to those of fish, were large, bulbous, and spread wide on their faces. They had no noses but breathed through strange gills that were often hidden by their hair that looked like sea grass. They were humanoid, but their hands and feet were webbed, and they had the most beautiful colored scales covering their bodies from their necks to their feet. It was said that the scales could change color to reflect their emotions and moods, but Tristal did not know if that were true as she stared at some whose scales ranged the colors of the rainbow. Because of their relation to merpeople and fish creatures, they could not survive far from fresh or salty water, which they drew their nourishment from.

It was also said that rana were telepathic to some degree. They shared emotions if not thoughts. Because of this ability, they very rarely were seen apart from their communities called schools. Their united minds made them one of the most peaceful of the races with rarely any crime or social problems. It was only the rare member that broke away from its community, usually to reconnect with another school somewhere, but it was not unheard of to see a lone rana who chose a life of disconnect and solitude.

Tristal observed the village and noted that all the little huts appeared to open both to the road and also to the strips of water that ran through the swamps. She heard and saw rana children splashing about in the water while older ones went about different occupations within their small village.

After a while, Valero walked back to them. "The witch the man spoke of is most definitely Grazina."

Colna whispered harshly, "But she's no witch... How do you know?"

Valero held out a small ring with a green gemstone, and Colna gasped when she saw it. "She traded this with the rana some years ago in exchange for their help to find a secluded place in the swamp where she could live in peace and solitude. She rarely came to the village but came often enough over the years that they consider her a friend to them."

Valero stared at the ring.

"So where do we find her?" asked Tristal.

"She's gone."

"What? Where?" asked Tristal and Colna at the same time.

Orinus reached out to Valero and motioned at the ring. "May I?" he asked.

Valero nodded and handed it to him.

Orinus closed his eyes as he held the ring tightly in his hand. He could sense Grazina's innate power still on the ring even after the passing of time. He

194

could also sense the grandmother who owned the ring before her, and the elf who owned it before her. He honed in on Grazina's power and sensed a thin wave off to the north. He turned in that direction and felt it grow stronger. He opened his eyes and pointed the way. "It appears the princess is headed that way."

Valero hopped in his saddle. "She is returning home on her own then. Come. If we hurry, we can meet her along the way and protect her the rest of the way."

Orinus looked at Valero, "I think the princess has proven that after all this time on her own, she is quite capable of protecting herself."

Valero agreed but responded, "Be that as it is, her protection is our mission. If she is going home and beats us there, that is fine. We need to be back there anyway. The king and queen will need us."

"Fan the flames of war with a single well-planned assassination of a beloved leader. Fan the flames of chaos itself with a single assassination of someone that well-loved leader loves."
~ *Mute Scribe Archives* at Croglinke

25

On the southern continent, the White Lord paced the large yard where his men trained outside the fortress at Croglinke. He had much to do and was impatient to get started, just as he was impatient for the unhatched dragon to make its appearance. He had feared that they would have to wait for another celestial event to be able to hatch the egg, but Libitina informed him that it hadn't been needed to get her to hatch. Why the White Lord had bought into the superstitious foolery of the high priest amused the Red Dragon, but she kept her amusement to herself. She did tell him what she needed to do, and he made sure she was kept provided for in the massive hollow he had carved out for her so she could wrap her long body around the egg and brood on it until it woke and hatched.

The White Lord was impatient for another dragon to join his ranks, but Libitina insisted that hatching an egg could not be rushed and had already been sequestered in her hollow for days. He frowned. On one hand, he was thrilled Libitina was able to draw on her telepathy to seek out the dragon egg. But while that was a success, his plans on Mythos seemed to be thwarted at every turn. He turned on his heel and paced the other direction but then stopped as he spotted a rana peering at him from a door in the wall to the training yard.

"What is it?" the White Lord demanded.

The rana wrung his webbed hands nervously and stepped into the yard. His large eyes darted all about and his mouth opened and closed as though he were gasping for air. Bowing before the White Lord, he reached out a hand with a small scrap of paper in it.

The White Lord snatched it from the lone rana, a strangely greedy creature for one of his race and just as strangely a loner. The rana, who called himself Derk, was easy to lure into his plans with promises of money and power, the creature never suspecting that the White Lord might not keep his word. Derk had now been with the White Lord for decades, working as a messenger and spy throughout southern Mythos. It had been Derk who had coerced Magistrate Geraldt and many other leaders among the Syan Lake settlements.

The White Lord ignored the shaking fish man and unrolled the paper. Immediately, he roared, not in rage but in enthusiasm, as he read news that told him that the Forest Elf princess was alive and her destination now known.

The White Lord looked at Derk, who cowered before his direct stare. "You have finally brought me some good news."

Derk attempted to smile but was shaking so badly that it came across as a painful grimace.

The White Lord continued, "Now your work really begins."

Derk nodded, "Whatever you command."

The White Lord paced around Derk, taking in his smell of fear and reveling in it. "Go to Mythos. Gather as many monsters, exiles, sellswords, whatever you can easily control, and find and kill Mronas's daughter."

"My Lord?"

"Kill her. She must not reach her parents. They must have no heir. When I am ready to make my move, the kingdom of the Forest Elves must be in disarray. Killing their daughter will help us along very nicely."

Derk did not respond in any way. He simply waited to be dismissed.

The White Lord stood behind Derk and leaned in to whisper in his ear, causing Derk to quiver in fear. "Do not fail. Or you will be dragged out to the Ercrog and left for the desert worms to feed on."

Derk nearly fainted from the threat. He stammered," I will not fail, my Lord."

The White Lord nearly laughed out loud. "Be gone. You have a long journey."

Without waiting to be told again, Derk dashed out of the training yard, just as several men and women of various races moved in and began sparring with one another. The White Lord moved through his growing army of rogues, sellswords, outcasts, and criminals. He paid them no heed at all, his thoughts now on the dragon in the egg.

I cannot force him to hatch, Libitina told the White Lord.

He slapped his own leg in frustration. "By the gods, this is taking too long. What is the hold up?"

Libitina stretched and moved so that the White Lord could see the egg nestled in the tight curve of her body.

As I told you before – he must hatch in his own time.

The White Lord stared hard at the egg, "Is there something wrong with it?"

Libitina moved her head and pressed her snout to the egg. Reaching out, she made a mental connection with the unhatched dragon. While it did not communicate with her, she could sense that it was aware, listening, and cautious. Libitina wondered if the dragon would remember it's prehatch cognition for she did not recall being aware of anything until the high priest had poured the White Lord's blood into her shell, and then it was as though she was jarred awake from a nightmare. She tried to discern more from the dragon but could not.

She huffed as she moved to meet the White Lord's gaze.

I don't know how long it will take. He is cautious, this one. I will have to take my time and draw him out.

Still staring at the egg and trying to mentally impose his own power over the dragon in the shell, the White Lord heard Libitina, but he also sensed the dragon within. He mentally yelled at it, and he and Libitina both felt the dragon's mind recoil.

Libitina glared at the White Lord.

What do you think you're doing? she demanded, her mental intrusion in the White Lord's mind so loud, it nearly shattered his mental blocks.

He met her glare with one of his own. His eyes flashed in rage and impatience.

"You find a way to get it to hatch. Quickly."

Without another glance, he turned and stormed out of the hollow.

Libitina stared after him. Disappointment and anger grew within her. She was not used to being the subject of the White Lord's anger. Despite her own ferocity, she felt the weight of his anger, and it unsettled her for the first time in her life.

She cleared her mind and returned her focus on the unhatched dragon.

Come out. Come out, she called to it mentally.

She felt its essence stir and respond to her call, but then as though it sensed something else, it recoiled back far away from her.

She laid her head on her feet and gnawed at a talon as she tried to figure out a way to coax the little dragon out. As she did so, she could sense its own curiosity. It appeared to be searching outward and away from her. As it did, she was able to follow it in a way, and then she raised her head in sudden astonishment.

There were others. More dragons! It felt as though there were hundreds of them! She nearly roared from the exciting revelation. More dragons to find and bring to the White Lord to hatch and grow! Then just as suddenly as she felt them all, a door slammed in her mind, and the connection to them disappeared.

She tried to reach out again to the dragon in the egg but to no avail. It may as well be dead for she could not sense its essence at all anymore. She certainly could not determine where the other eggs were.

Still, the knowledge that there was a huge cache of eggs somewhere out there, that she was one of a multitude that just needed to be revived, gave her such joy she could barely restrain herself. But her commitment to making the egg hatch won over. As much as she wanted to tell the White Lord the news, something deep inside her begged her not to.

"Our gods don't care who we are, just that we worship and obey them. This makes it easy to follow the one god who fits our individual ideologies, to justify the course of action we simply desire to take. Certainly, a violent warmonger will not worship or commune with Asuna any more than a teacher or a healer would worship Peran. The two gods are diametrically opposed to one another in ideology and method."
~ *Lessons in Theology*, Farcaste Reach

26

Staring across Croglinke to the ocean beyond the cliffs, he thought of the paths that lay before him. With Libitina nursing the egg, he had thought he was well on his way to his ultimate goal. Now though he reflected on the loss of Pruzin, the failed capture of Olphara, the news of the dwarf and the song magic, the mission he had set Derk upon to kill Grazina – there were so many things going on at once. Overwhelmed and also a bit out of touch with the course of events, he wanted to be part of the action.

There was nothing he could do to help the egg hatch. Libitina's fierce rebuke proved that much. Oh, the power of her intrusion in his mind when she got angry. The power made him pause. Had he underestimated her? Was she truly his to control? Doubt, a new feeling to him, made him flex his hands in agitation.

There was also nothing he could do about the loss of Pruzin and the escape of Olphara. He had put great effort into her capture, and she had slipped through his fingers while he was right there! His own failure consumed him with rage that burned deep within him, barely held in control. He wanted those histories. He knew there was critical knowledge in those ancient texts that would reveal something he knew was missing. It added to his frustration that he could not resolve that mystery.

And the dwarf… It occurred to him that he should have set Derk on to find the dwarf as well.

I can send a missive, he thought. Derk can handle both the dwarf and the princess while he is that far north. With the resources at his disposal, there should be no problem there.

Then he thought of the Elven princess, and he grinned to himself as he watched the ships coming and going to Croglinke. As the sounds of Croglinke wafted up to him on the wind, he turned his attention to his immediate domain spread out around him. He watched people moving along the streets and through the markets. Each one was small and insignificant alone, but he noted the number of them. Together, once he gathered them, they would make a formidable force to take to Mythos.

Inspiration struck and he left the high balcony and entered his chamber where a guard stood ready for the White Lord's command.

"I wish to commune with my god," he told the guard tersely and watched in satisfaction as the guard moved immediately to see that an acolyte be brought to him.

While the guard left in a hurry to see the preparations were made, the White Lord moved to a side chamber where a large tub of water sat waiting for his use. Disrobing, he slipped into the tub and scrubbed himself clean from head to toe until his scales appeared to shine with an iridescent luster so similar to the luster of the beloved pearls gathered from the shallows. After he washed, he stood before a mirror and noted that following the communion with his god, his scales would no longer be white, but would be various hues of red. The pearlescence would be gone, replaced by the sticky residue of the blood of his sacrifice. He marveled over the transformation he was about to undergo and the beauty he found in the result of the sacrifice. He hoped that the result would give him the answers he sought.

The guards silently removed the body of the acolyte to prepare for display among the others in the dining hall while the White Lord sat in the middle of the floor with his legs crossed and his arms resting on his knees.

"My Lord Naga, I pray you accept this sacrifice. I pray you join me in communion, a joining of spirits, that I may see your glory, and that you may give me insight into the path I should take."

Like a resonant drum in his mind, he felt the essence of his god wash over him.

I am with you, Akrach Zoor'Ysand. Your sacrifice, your offering, it pleases me. So humble.

The White Lord noted the mocking tone, and he leaned forward with his head bowed low. "She was pure, my Lord. That is very rare; this you know. Especially here. Maybe if you blessed an excursion to Mythos…"

You are not ready to return to Mythos. After your failure? You think I will offer my blessing on another foolish mission?

The White Lord grimaced under the mental onslaught from his god. Still, he also felt his frustration building rather than receding. Why was his god not supporting him? They both reveled in the chaos of war, the promise of victory and subjugation.

Unable to stop himself, he asked, "Has my god tired of the revelry within the chaos?"

You dare try to assume my motives?

"No, my Lord, I'm simply trying to understand why you withhold your power and your blessings. I do not understand why we continue to wait. The dwarf, the princess, our two dragons... Oh, Naga, my Lord, we are on the cusp. I can feel it. Share your knowledge with me. If now is not the time to move, then please help me understand so that I can make plans and become better prepared for the time when it does come."

He waited for an answer but was met with silence. After several long minutes, the White Lord took a deep breath and asked, "Have I fallen out of favor with you, my Lord?"

Chuckling resonated throughout his mind as his god laughed heartily.

There are so many currents in the magic and in the weave of time that you cannot begin to fathom, Akrach, whom I named White Lord. I have given you every blessing you need in order to achieve your ultimate desires, yet you allow your impatience to rise up within you? Now? When by your own admission things are falling into place? Threads are coming unraveled while others are being knit as though by Siki and Cria themselves? I withhold

205

nothing from you, my faithful servant. Your failure distresses me. Your impatience irritates me. Your questions sadden me.

The White Lord noted the increase in resonance and feeling to Naga's probing into his mind. Without thinking about it, he fought back. A sudden sharp pain struck his mind, and the White Lord threw himself to the floor. Lying on his stomach, he whimpered at the pain in his mind. The shock of the mental attack was something he had never felt from his god before.

You dare fight me too?

"My God. Naga, my Lord. Please. I beg your forgiveness."

The pain receded, replaced by a whisper as though from across the room, but it was still in his mind.

Do not ask for miracles and signs, shows of my power, increases to the blessings I have already bestowed. Now it is time for you to use all you have been given to prove to me your worth. Now I call on you, my most faithful servant, to prove to me that this lifetime I have invested in you and your goals will bring me honor and glory.

The White Lord grimaced, but replied, "As you wish, my Lord. I will prove my loyalty to you."

He felt the power of his god recede from his mind, leaving him with more doubts and questions than ever before. He rested his head on the blood-covered floor and allowed himself to dwell on his communion with Naga. Never before had Naga lost patience with him. Why now? Was his failure to capture Olphara and the histories that bad?

As he lay there thinking, he wondered over the pain of the mental intrusion. That was something new although there was something very familiar to it. As it dawned on him why it felt familiar, he felt his body stiffen. His god was keeping something from him. He didn't know what it was, but for the first time in all his years of worship, the White Lord came to a new conclusion: His own god could not be trusted.

He did not know why, but he sensed that the answer was just out of reach.

As he pushed himself up off the floor with the realization of lost trust building within him and adding to new rage, he promised himself that he was going to find out what his god was keeping from him and why.

*"A life well-lived is simply moving
from one hardship to another
with hope leading the way."*
~ Dwarven Proverb

27

Feeling completely healed after Aldrina's careful ministrations, Virconia stood beside Aldrina and Estryl as they looked down the last leg of the mountain road that led along Syan Lake with its many small settlements. Thick smoke rose from many of them. Most of the fields spreading away from them belied the fights that had been fought there. Aldrina feared what they would find along the road, but there was no other way to get to the main road that led north the way they wanted to go. Beside her, Estryl recalled the view being very different from the first time she had traversed it on her way to Farcaste Reach. Virconia simply stared. Dread filled her for she not only saw the evidence of battles, but she could smell death on the air.

Stranick and Elder Martan remained at the head of their wagon. Elder Martan looked at the scene before them through a spyglass while Stranick scowled at the thought that there would be more fighting and danger to his sister.

Estryl looked up to Elder Martan. "What do you see?"

The old dwarf kept the glass to his eye as he spoke, Virconia's own incredible sight confirming a great deal of what the dwarf shared. "All the settlements on this side of the lake look as though they have been abandoned. The walls are all burned or torn down. The structures are mostly burnt husks. I don't see any bodies though. Not out in the fields either. Very unusual. You'd think there would be bodies or fresh graves."

Virconia replied, "Can you see the fourth settlement with that contraption?"

Elder Martan lowered the glass and offered it to the Dark Elf. "It is blurry for me, but maybe your eyes can better see."

Virconia heard the derision in the elder's voice. He had most certainly not accepted her among their party. She didn't blame him, but she didn't appreciate it either.

She took the spyglass and lifted it to her eyes. Looking through it, she found the fourth settlement and two of the ones beyond it, all of them, like the ones closest to them, nestled closely to the banks of the large lake. Moving back to the fourth one, she clearly saw the walls burned but intact. The buildings within the walls were largely unscathed as well. She saw motion on the walls and within the settlement.

Handing the glass back to the dwarf, she looked at him. "There is nothing between us and the fourth settlement, which is still inhabited."

Glancing at Estryl, Elder Martan shrugged his shoulders in question.

Estryl frowned in thought before responding. "We need to replenish our supplies…"

Aldrina interrupted, "And I sense a need for a healer…"

Estryl finished, "… we will head there and see if they have things for trade or if they need help. Then we will decide what needs to be done from there."

Elder Martan grunted in reply.

The three women moved to the second wagon that had needed a lot of repairs made before they were able to continue down the mountains after the giants' attack. Now an uncovered wagon with cobbled-together wheels that shook and shuddered as though they were about to fall off, it held all their supplies. The lead wagon was kept as a cabin on wheels that the women could sleep in at night.

Martan clicked his tongue at the horses, and they jolted the wagon forward. The second wagon followed behind with Estryl driving the horses. Aldrina sat next to her, her eyes closed as she rested in preparation for any healing she might have to do when they reached the settlement. Next to the wagon, Virconia walked, her hands on her weapons, her eyes always moving, and listening for the sounds of anything that could pose a threat.

Asked to leave their wagons outside the walls, Elder Martan and Virconia remained with them while the rest of the party moved inside the walls to meet with a mage named Meri.

She smiled widely at the unusual group. "We are so glad to see you. We haven't seen anyone come down out of the mountains for months. What news?"

Aldrina relayed the news of their journey since leaving Olphara's clan deep in the Alisyan Mountains but quickly moved to their observations of the settlements.

Meri looked all around her, torn between grief and elation. "The hordes moved in about two weeks ago.

We lost a few of the settlements but only after we fought with everything we had. I reached out to Wargate, who sent a unit to help us. When they arrived, they had a powerful mage with them. With their help we were able to win the fight for our settlement. Then we moved outward and tried to help the others. Those toward the mountains we could not win back, so we did what we could to evacuate survivors. The ones to the east, we were able to help defend."

Estryl interrupted, "Where are all the bodies?"

Meri repeated, "Bodies?"

"Yeah. Your dead. Or the dead creatures? We didn't see a single dead body."

Meri sighed. "We burn our dead. So that is why you have not seen any of our dead, but the monsters... That is something confounding. We first saw it here. When our magistrate was revealed to be working under the orders of the White Lord, he committed suicide. The instant he died, all the monsters surrounding us just turned to dust. When we evacuated the other settlements and turned the tides for the eastward ones, the same thing happened. They were there one second, snarling and hissing and hurling threats and weapons, and then they were dust blowing in the wind."

Aldrina's eyes grew wide. "Really?"

Meri nodded in affirmation. "The mage that was here thought it was directly related to the White Lord's magic, but he was confused by it as well. As he said, it seems extremely wasteful of resources."

Estryl commented, "You said they turned to dust that blew away?"

Meri nodded.

"I think Elder Martan might know more, but I think I read at Farcaste Reach of a spell that moved troops from one spot to another by simply blowing them from one area to another."

Meri stared at the short dwarf. "That never occurred to me… Could that be what happened?"

She was silent as she thought. "If that is true and the White Lord simply relocated his forces, where do you think he'd send them from here?"

Aldrina commented, "Let's hope he drew them back to Mygras."

The group gathered nodded in agreement. And hoped.

Aldrina stood up from where she bent over a small child that had been burned during the attack and smiled down at the now sleeping child. According to the child's mother, the poor girl was in so much pain she had been unable to get any rest. Now the mother lay next to her child, asleep as well, as she held her child's small hand. The little girl had a peaceful smile on her face. She was the last of nearly a dozen people that Aldrina had been able to help that day. Weariness washed over her. Sadly, that dozen people were the only injured still alive. Not having a healer among their people, Meri had done what she could with magic, but most of the injured succumbed to those injuries, leaving only those with outer burns, broken bones, and mild head injuries for Aldrina to heal.

As she left the small home, she walked to where Estryl sat on the edge of a well. She plopped down beside her friend and leaned against her shoulder.

"Are you okay?" Estryl asked.

Aldrina sighed heavily. "Just tired and sad. These people have lost so much. With winter coming soon, they have no fields to harvest, and the lake will soon be frozen over. They still have a tough road ahead of them."

"Yes, but they are alive, and from what I see, they are full of hope. That group from Wargate and that mage gave them something to believe in. I think that is powerful."

"You're right. These are a resilient people. That much is certain."

Estryl stood up and waved to Stranick and the guards, who were sharing some of their supplies with Meri and her people. It was time for them to get back on the road. Estryl didn't know why, but she felt drawn onward, and she suddenly felt in a hurry to get to Elmnas.

Aldrina sensed Estryl's sudden unrest, and she rose to her feet as well. She touched the amulet hanging on her chest, and again, she wondered about the nature of Estryl's magic. It was something unique and very special. How did this magic influence Estryl? Or did Estryl influence it?

Estryl felt her friend's gaze and asked, "What is it?"

Aldrina smiled. "Nothing. I'm just thankful that the gods brought us together."

Estryl smiled widely, mirth touching her eyes. "Me as well."

She strode to Meri. "I hope these things will last you until more help can come."

Meri smiled down at Estryl. "You have helped us more than you know." She looked at Aldrina pointedly. "I guess you will be leaving now. Are you sure you won't at least stay the remainder of the day? Nights out there might be dangerous."

Estryl laughed loudly. "You haven't met our Drow. Heaven help the fiends that try to take us. That woman is a single-person army!"

Meri smiled uncomfortably at the mention of the Dark Elf just outside the walls. "Well, I hope she is as trustworthy as you say…"

Aldrina stepped forward. "She is."

Meri nodded mutely, and Estryl stretched out her hand.

As the two women shook hands, Estryl promised to send help if they could.

The group left Meri and her people, climbed into their wagons, and turned the wagons north. Finally, they were on the Mythos Road, the main road that stretched north and south from the southern edge of Mythos, east of the Deep Forest. The road touched the western edge of The Spikes where Wargate sat, went up through Watercastle, and ended up in the frozen barrens of the extreme north. Though they were only a third of the way to where they wanted to be, they were hopeful that the next leg of the journey would be easier going along the well-traveled road among more even terrain. They hoped.

"Power is taking careful pains to control how you respond to the situations beyond your control."
~ Orinus, *The Memoir of a Mage*

28

*E*lder Martan slowed his wagon to a stop and stared at the two figures that stood in the road blocking the way. A young man and a young woman stood before him. He could tell immediately that they were siblings; they looked so much alike. "Get out of the road," he called to them.

The two glanced at each other but did not answer and did not move.

Elder Martan looked at Stranick who just stared at the two humans with his hand ready on his weapon. Behind them, they heard Estryl call out, "What's the hold up?"

Before Martan could respond, he saw Virconia in his peripheral vision moving alongside the wagon to see what was stopping them. He turned to watch her as she visibly stiffened. Her face was hidden under her heavy cloak, but she relaxed her hands and her shoulders.

She moved to stand in front of the wagon and threw her hood back so the humans could see her face. "Well met, young ones."

The human siblings gasped. "Virconia?" the young man called out.

She nodded and bowed slightly. "Hello, Sid. Greetings, Rona."

She turned back to look at Elder Martan who simply stared with his mouth hanging open in disbelief as this Dark Elf unnerved him once again. She ignored his gaping expression. "We are okay. I know and vouch for these two."

Turning back to the young people, who were now walking toward her, she bowed again to each of them. Rona smiled at Virconia, but Sid grabbed the Dark Elf in a tight hug. He stepped back and met her blood-red eyes with a sincere smile. "I knew we would meet again."

Virconia, uncomfortable at the physical display of affection, stepped back and carefully lifted her hood back over her head, noting that the others had left the wagons and were coming to meet the twins.

Once everyone gathered, she introduced the siblings, indicating they were twins. She had traveled with their group when the twins were younger.

Estryl immediately liked the young humans, guessing they had to be in their mid to late twenties, so young compared to everyone else in their party. As she watched them interact with each other, she noted how they seemed to speak as one, and she picked up on a sort of telepathy that they obviously shared. She wondered if they had other skills.

After a few minutes, Elder Martan spoke up. "This is a wonderful reunion, I am sure, but we have to be on our way." He moved back to the lead wagon and waited pointedly for the group to follow suit.

Estryl turned to the twins. "Will you join us?"

Sid looked at Rona. "Well, we would love to, but we think we are going in opposite directions."

Virconia frowned. "Would you join us just for the evening then? Come with us and share our campfire tonight?"

Rona took her brother's hand, but he responded. "Yes. We aren't in a hurry. Taking a bit of a rest would be a nice reprieve. Sadly, we have nothing to share in the way of food or supplies. We were hoping to purchase some from you if we could."

Estryl looked to Virconia, who remained silent. "Well, I don't know how much we can spare, but we can certainly share our meal with you tonight."

"Very well," replied Sid.

Virconia stood to the side of the road with Sid and Rona while everyone else got back up on the wagons. "I think I will walk with you both if I may."

Rona met Virconia's gaze. "We would like that a lot."

Falling into step behind the wagons, the three spent the time catching up since they had departed so many years ago.

Once they reached a wide spot in the road, a large clearing in the small grouping of trees, they stopped to help set up camp. As they reclined on bedrolls around the fire, Virconia asked about the scarred elf woman that had been with their group at the time.

Sid grimaced, and Rona replied, "We parted ways."

Virconia asked, "On bad terms?"

"Not on the best of terms," Sid said. "You remember the dwarves that were with us? Dagon and Frip?"

Virconia nodded that she did.

"We were set upon by a group of people who had obviously been through a great ordeal. They were hungry, tired, and frightened. Rather than let us learn what had happened to them or try to help them, they insisted on trying to fight us. Grazina tried hard to reason with them, but they reacted badly to her appearance and attacked us. Through it all, Grazina tried to stop the fighting, but in the end, Frip and

Dagon, Rona and I, had killed all of them except one old woman. She cursed at us and disappeared into the forest. We knew she was wounded, but we could not find her."

"Why would there be hard feelings about defending yourselves from those people?"

Rona sighed heavily and Sid turned red, tears welling in his eyes. "In the fight, several of the women were carrying small children in harnesses on their bodies. We had no idea. The children were hidden under their cloaks and coats. We had killed everyone. We had killed innocent children."

Virconia and the rest of the group stared at the twins in silence, not knowing what words to say in response.

Rona continued, "Grazina was horrified. She went on and on about innocence needing to be protected. We spent most of that night trying to console her, but we couldn't even console ourselves. At some point, we all passed out in fitful exhaustion, and when we woke in the morning, she was gone. She didn't leave a trace."

Sid finished. "And not ten days after that, Frip and Dagon left as well."

Virconia stared at the two. "You have been on your own ever since?"

Sid shrugged. "Well, we were near to Farcaste Reach at that point, so we simply traveled on and got there with no trouble. In general, though, yes. We have been on our own ever since."

Estryl leaned toward the two. "We just left Farcaste Reach. Now we are traveling to Elmnas. Where are you both going?"

Rona looked up at the stars, "I've had a vision. We learned a bit while we were at the mage's school.

218

For me, I learned how to better discern what my visions mean, while Sid learned how to use his skills to be a more intuitive fighter. But this vision…" She hesitated. "I cannot tell if the vision is of times past or times to come, but it is so intense that I have been having it for weeks now. I need to return to the school and consult with the mage's circle."

Estryl couldn't resist asking. "What is your vision?"

Rona blanched and lowered her gaze. "I saw a Red Dragon full of fury and hate and murder. At the edges, I think I saw the White Lord. I certainly felt evil like I have never felt before. But the vision is of a creature long disappeared now combined with the White Lord. Nothing in the vision changes or gives me more clues, so I just can't make sense of it."

Estryl considered the vision. "Your visions have always come true?"

Rona shook her head. "No. I mean yes. I have seen things from the past. Things that have happened. It's as though I can see them and they help me understand events as they happened or why they happened. So, yes, those have come true, just in the past tense. But visions I have of the future? Some have. I think some still have yet to come true. I think some have not because circumstances have changed, or someone made an unexpected decision."

Elder Martan stoked the fire and asked, "Can you give us an example?"

Rona looked at Virconia. "I knew Virconia would meet us again. I saw it. I didn't know the exact place or time, but I saw her standing before us in a road. I could sense in the vision that she was with others but could not see who. So today, seeing her again was as though experiencing déjà vu."

219

Elder Martan was not impressed. In his mind, it very well could have been nothing more than déjà vu, but he did not press the case.

Rona sensed his skepticism, so she continued. "I saw you too."

He stared at her.

"I saw you holding a shield unlike any other you had ever held. I could feel your hope and also your dread because it could mean someone you care about could be manipulated. I could feel your inner turmoil." She paused, then asked, "How did that turn out?"

Estryl spoke for him. "I made that shield. I'm the reason he is here."

Rona looked back at Elder Martan. "Is that example good enough for you?"

The old dwarf merely nodded, embarrassed in front of the younger dwarves who had no idea he cared for them as if they had been his own children. He rose to his feet and walked away from the camp.

The rest stared after him.

Aldrina, who had sat content to listen and observe, stood up and stretched. "Well, it's been a long day. If you will excuse me." And she moved to the covered wagon to sleep.

*"Fierce and mighty Peran, my deliverer, heed
me in my time of need. Guide my sword so I might
repel the evil forces that gather about. Empower me
with your divine bloodlust that I may enjoy victory
over my enemies."*
~ *Warrior's Prayer to Peran, God of War*

29

Dust rose up in the air all around them as the fight wore on. The suns were high in the sky adding heat to the already brittle air, making it hard to breathe.

Tristal staggered under the heavy blow the troll landed on her shoulder. She stepped back and to the side to try to get beyond its reach, but the pain was so great, she was seeing stars and unsure on her feet. As she tried to move out of the way, the fighting clamored all around her, making her head spin. Shaking her head fiercely to regain focus, she heard arrows zipping all around her as Colna let one after the other fly, nearly all of them finding homes in the eyes, ears, and mouths of the large group of trolls.

Behind her, Valero swung his sword back and forth, often switching hands and stance with ease causing the trolls around him to be unsure of where his next thrust or stab would land. He moved with such fluid movements—turning, ducking, twisting this way and that—it was impossible to know where his next attack would come from. For all his movement, however, he did not stray outside the protective circle the group had created in order to better defend themselves and each other. He cut several down when he noted a gap in the rush of

221

monsters. Catching his breath and taking stock of the group, he was relieved to see everyone was still standing though he noted the group had spread out farther than he would have liked.

He started to call for everyone to step back toward each other when he felt a sharp sting in his neck. Reaching up with one hand, he pulled out a small dart. Gasping at the pain that burned in his neck and spread like fire down his arms, into his chest, and into his head, he tried to cry out for help, but couldn't find his voice. Willing his legs to move, he spun around and glanced at Orinus, who was in the midst of casting spells even as he fought off trolls with his staff. Orinus felt Valero's stare and met the elf's shocked gaze. In slow motion, he saw the elf's mouth move in a silent but desperate plea for help. Cutting his casting short after an instant observation that Colna and the others were fighting frantically, Orinus instead blasted the trolls immediately surrounding him. Then he dashed for Valero, catching the muscular elf as he fell. As he lowered Valero to the ground, he shouted out above the din of battle.

"Darts!"

Colna and Tristal glanced toward Orinus even as they continued to fight. Colna saw her lover on the ground and she cried out, letting more arrows loose and stabbing at nearby trolls with the ends of her bow as she pushed her way toward him. Tristal, pushing her pain down, was suddenly at her side, and the two fought together as one, moving in a circle to get to Orinus and Valero and protect them.

Meanwhile, Layni signaled to the others to keep fighting but waved them into a tighter circle to try to help Tristal and Colna. They fought bravely, trying hard not to think about their fallen commander.

Orinus held Valero and chanted, trying to force the poison from the dart out of him. But as Valero started to cough and sputter, his skin turning blueish as he gasped for air, Orinus realized there was nothing he could do. Colna reached them and threw herself at Valero, crying and screaming at the same time. She saw the dread on Orinus's face and realized her mate was dying. She grabbed Valero and pulled him onto her lap while Orinus regained his feet and stared about them.

He felt dread slip into his gut as he realized they were about to be overrun. He saw Tristal, wounded but still fighting, her strength running out. Her left arm hung useless by her side. Her eyes were glazing over with pain even though she kept shaking her head to try to clear the cobwebs. He saw Layni, terror in her eyes, fighting desperately just to stay alive. The young elf was distracted. She kept glancing behind her toward Colna and Valero. The trolls' stabs and slashes were getting closer and closer to her. Her parries were becoming rushed and instinctive, and he knew it was just a matter of time before one of the trolls landed a cut on her that would kill her. He looked for the rest of the group and could not see them. The others had all fallen from wounds, and he was unsure if they were alive or dead.

He looked at the trolls. There was a madness behind their eyes, an inexplicable rage that was beyond even that of their volatile race. He saw a mad rage within them that he knew very well. It was one he worked very hard to keep under control. He bowed his head, realizing with a lump in his gut that if he did not act, they would all die at the hands of these crazed trolls. He allowed his carefully placed walls to fall and felt the ever-present rage spring forward within him. Gripping his staff so tight his fingers turned white, he used it to help him focus the explosive rage, which he worked to combine with the strongest magical currents. He took a deep breath as hot determination flooded through him. Hoping he wasn't too late, he lifted his head and whispered a few words into the air.

Blinding lights and flashes of heat so intense it caused his own party to instantly pass out, spread out and rolled away from him in several waves of flashes and fires. It burned the flesh off the trolls, burned into them and through them. As their bodies burned and melted into the desert sands they stood on, the trolls' rage turned to shock and horror. Wave after wave rolled out from him, each wave less fierce than the one before it but still effective. After several long minutes, the fury within him dissipated.

Realizing he had fallen to his knees, he closed his eyes and worked to control his breathing. In. Out. Inhale. Exhale. Calm. Exhaustion washed over him with every breath, but he refused to give in to it, unsure if he had succeeded in saving the party. After what felt like an eternity, he gulped in another breath of air. He lifted his head, and blinked rapidly in the dust of the settling desert sands. His senses all on edge, he could feel the magical currents around him like a static charge. They were brittle and frayed. The air smelled as though lightning was about to strike. His heart rate back to normal, he forced himself to stand, and he saw clearly all around him. With his group in the center, he stared in shock at the results of his rage: the trolls were gone. There was no trace of them at all. They were simply wiped away in the heat of his furious outburst. The desert sands they stood upon had turned to black glasslike obsidian in a near perfect circle all around them.

Remembering Valero, Orinus spun on his heel and turned to see the group passed out but otherwise unharmed by his casting. He stepped to Colna and Valero, and knelt beside them. He reached out and shook Colna. Slowly, Colna woke. She stared up at Orinus with confusion in her eyes and then remembrance. She sat up quickly and her cries rang out in the brittle air as she instinctively felt for her mate. She touched his face and looked for breath, but there was none.

"No. No. No," she cried out, her voice cracking with her broken heart. "Don't leave me, my love."

She laid her head on his chest and wept uncontrollably while Orinus moved to the rest of the party and woke them up. As they all recovered from his magical blast, they stared in shock at the devastation all around them, unable to comprehend what they were seeing and unable to come to terms with the loss of their valiant leader.

"Why in Peran's name didn't you use your magic sooner?" Tristal demanded, searching Orinus's eyes. He didn't answer her as he wrapped her arm and shoulder tightly. She grabbed his shirt with her other hand and shook him, forcing him to meet her eyes. "Answer me, mage!"

Orinus leaned away from Tristal, forcing her to let go of his shirt. Staring into her eyes, his rage simmering once more, he saw the same rage matched in the White Elf's lavender eyes. "I have trained all my life to keep my emotions in check when touching the magical currents. While you were using your training to fight with your blades, I was using my training to fight with magic."

Tristal shook her head in anger. "No, that's not an answer. You were afraid. You could have ended the fight long before Valero…" She trailed off, her gaze flickering to where Colna sat with Valero's body.

"You're right. Damn you. I was afraid. I am afraid. Every time I touch the currents, I'm afraid my emotions will get the best of me. You have no idea the toll using magic takes on me."

Tristal glared. "I see the toll. I'm not blind to its effects on you."

Orinus resumed wrapping the bandage and tightened until Tristal winced.

"The physical toll, the exhaustion, the fatigue… That is nothing. Nothing. I am talking about the toll it takes when I allow my emotions into the casting. I lose a piece of me. My soul. Do you understand?"

Tristal frowned. "No. I think you're making excuses because despite all your power, you are nothing but a coward."

Orinus sat back on his heels and stared at Tristal for several seconds until she squirmed under his stare.

His voice low like a steel edge, sharp and without room for response, he replied, "I may be a coward about certain things, Captain, but I would never confuse cowardice with wisdom and caution. My soul is everything to me. It is the only thing of value I have left in this life."

Orinus finished helping Tristal into a sling for her arm, and he left her to ponder his words while he moved across the camp to where Colna sat. She sat cross-legged beside the body, her head in her hands as sobs shook her. Her bow and quiver lay on the ground next to her, ready to be used in a moment. Orinus knelt beside her, unexpected grief of his own touching him. He laid a hand on the dead elf's body hoping to feel some sort of energy still within, hoping against hope that he could call Valero back from the dead. Orinus had never dealt with necromancy, but he had learned a great deal about it while he was training. In order for him to bring someone back without turning them into the undead, he'd have to sacrifice his own life force. In that moment, Orinus realized he would. His short time in the warrior elf's presence had taught him many things about himself. He searched, but as he felt and sensed that no energy at all remained in Valero's body, he sank into himself, wondering if Tristal was more right about him than he cared to admit.

He whispered to Colna, "I am so sorry. Maybe I could have gotten to him sooner…"

Colna turned her head to face Orinus. Her bright green eyes red from crying, and her dusty face streaked with tear stains, she stared into the human mage's eyes. She saw sincere grief in his eyes, and she warmed toward him.

"There was nothing you could have done. The poison these trolls use in their darts acts so fast. I wonder why they didn't use them on all of us. It would have made short work of us." Her voice cracked, and she choked back a sob. "I promise you, there was nothing you could have done for him."

She looked back at Valero's body, and Orinus started to rise to his feet.

Colna reached out suddenly, stopping Orinus. "You saved our lives, mage. Remember that above all. I can sense it was hard for you to do, but you did it. Whatever it cost you, you did it to save us. I know that. But look at us. We are wounded, bleeding, and broken, but…" she paused to gather her composure, "…we are all alive. Thank you."

Without another word, fighting to keep her tears at bay, she let him go.

Orinus finished rising to his feet and stared at the back of Colna's head for several minutes, overcome with a rush of emotions he was not used to. He had let his emotions take control although he had sworn years before never to allow that to happen again. Yet as he looked around from Colna, to Layni, to Tristal, and the others who had injuries of varying degrees but would live, he felt different this time. The first time he had let his emotions loose, he had felt shame for the slaughter he committed following his sister's murder. This time, he felt relief that they were still alive. He glanced at Valero's body and grimaced inwardly. How he wished they were all still alive.

"Continuing to live on after lives around you are lost takes more courage following a battle than the fight in the battle itself. Had I known the way I could never find joy in anything ever again, I would have heeded my father's advice. I would have trained to be a scribe or a teacher. I would never have picked up the sword."
~ *Letters to Elmnas, The Unnamed Soldier*

30

*L*ayni cried out in her sleep, waking the rest of the group. Colna moved to the younger elf's side and tried to soothe her, but Layni was too shaken.

"I see them," she told Colna, her eyes wide with fear bordering on madness.

Colna looked at the elf curiously, noting Layni's skin was flushed, the hairs on her arms standing on end, goosebumps everywhere.

"Who do you see?"

"The trolls. They're still here. All around us. Can't you see them?" She pointed around the camp and whimpered in fear. "They want to kill us all."

Colna looked everywhere Layni pointed, but she saw and sensed nothing.

She leaned in to look Layni in the eyes and saw terror reflected in them. "There is nothing there. It is just us here."

Layni started to protest, her body taut, but Colna laid a hand on her arm to calm her. "I will sit with you until you sleep. I'll make sure you're okay."

Layni kept staring beyond Colna, beyond the circle of the fire. Seeing things in the shadows of the desert, she bit her lip till she drew blood. Colna took her chin in one hand and forced her to look back at her. "Layni. It's okay."

Layni slapped at Colna's hand. "How can you say that? How? You? Valero is dead! Dead, Colna. The strongest of us. The best of us. It's not okay. It will never be okay. Never."

Colna held Layni's angry stare and simply nodded, her eyes welling up with tears for she could not dispute Layni's outburst. Blinking the tears back, she nodded. "You're right. I'm sorry. You're right. But we all need rest. You need rest. Please, lie down."

Layni realized the pain she had inflicted on her mentor, and she lowered her head in shame. Without a word, she nodded and Colna helped her lie back down. Colna promised she would move her own bedroll closer after she checked on Tristal, who sat on her bedroll just staring at them. Colna noted that Orinus and the others were already back asleep.

Squatting in front of Tristal, who held her arm gingerly as she sat, Colna noted the White Elf's discomfort.

"What was that all about?" Tristal asked.

Colna frowned. "Night terrors maybe. She is shaken up. We have fought other battles against goblins or single trolls, but nothing like what we faced at the settlement or today. This level of brutality is new to her."

"Will she be okay?"

Colna didn't know how to answer that, so she shrugged in reply as she reached out and touched Tristal's damaged arm and shoulder gingerly. "How are you? Do you need something for the pain?"

Tristal shook her head. "No. I'm fine. It hurts a great deal, but those herbs and concoctions diminish my senses."

Colna commented, "So does excessive pain."

Tristal smiled grimly. "I suppose it can, but now the worst has passed. I want to be as alert as I can, especially now that I am injured." She glanced sideways and commented, "Especially since we can't seem to count on some to carry their weight…"

Colna interrupted, "You know that is unfair."

Tristal snapped her gaze back to Colna, anger flashing in her eyes.

Colna continued, "We were overwhelmed. You know that as well as I do. If he hadn't acted when he did, we'd all be…"

"That is my point! He could have ended it before it began."

Colna shook her head. "I don't think he could have. I think it is a lot more complicated to use magic the way he does. Could you not feel the tingle in the air afterward?"

Tristal cocked her head to the side. "Like before a storm. So?"

"I can't be certain, but I think he still held something back, and I am glad he did. Somehow he obliterated the trolls but just knocked us out? How is that possible? Have you asked yourself that? The power is evident in this glass rock we are camping on. How can he be doing something like this, but still keep us safe in the process?"

Tristal shrugged, her stubborn anger not allowing her to concede.

Colna sighed, "You do him a great disservice by not trying to understand the efforts he is making. If you need something, just ask."

Tristal nodded shortly, not liking being spoken to like a child. No matter, she still respected Colna. Colna noted the White Elf's frustration but knew there was nothing more to say, so she stood up and moved to get her bedroll to move it closer to Layni when she felt someone staring at her. She looked to the side and saw Orinus lying on his side, watching her. She ignored him as she gathered her bedroll, but as she headed toward Layni, she stopped and knelt beside him. "Something on your mind?"

Orinus looked soul weary, his internal struggles still raging within him.

He started to speak, but Colna stopped him. "You need rest, mage. I don't know how you were able to do what you did today, but I am sure it was taxing. We may have need of your abilities again sooner than we like, so please, if you think you need to apologize to me: Don't. I don't blame you. I'm not angry with you. You don't owe me, or anyone here, an apology, or," with a glance over her shoulder at Tristal," an explanation. As I said before, you saved us, and we owe you our thanks. Please. Get some rest."

Orinus smiled thinly, "I was just going to say that I know an easy incantation that might help Layni sleep with no dreams if you think it would help."

Colna's eyes grew wide, and she nearly laughed. "Oh. I see. I will ask her."

Orinus nodded and watched the Elven archer move to Layni. The two women exchanged a few words, but Colna turned to him and shook her head no. Sighing inwardly, knowing the elves likely distrusted his magic despite being thankful for it, he nodded, rolled onto his back, and cast the incantation on himself. He barely finished before he drifted off into blissful, dreamless sleep.

The following morning, Orinus lifted the corpse onto Valero's horse and strapped it tightly down. Colna had collected all of Valero's personal belongings. She kept a few things for herself in honor and remembrance of her mate, but the rest she distributed among the others. Orinus felt Valero's sword hanging heavily between his shoulders. Colna insisted Valero would want Orinus to have it, which Orinus disagreed with, but he had kept his disagreement to himself. Orinus had taken the sword reluctantly. Strong, broad, and sharp, it had been crafted by a master smith. For its size, it was in fact very lightweight. The heaviness he felt wearing it belonged more to the fact that Valero had been a fierce and brave warrior, large shoes for Orinus to fill, at least in his mind. Part of him resolved to return it to Colna once they were safely in Elmnas for he was convinced he had no right to the sword.

He climbed into his saddle after tying Valero's steed to his own, and he looked to the others. They all watched him in silence, and he realized in surprise and dread that they were looking to him to lead them onward. He bowed his head in consternation as he tried to think. He didn't want them to follow him nor did he deserve their trust. They should be looking to Colna. Or to Tristal since she was a captain from Wargate. He felt the words rising to object, but then the weight of the sword at his back caused the words to stick in his throat. After several long minutes, he finally raised his head and addressed the elves.

"I think we should continue to search for Grazina as we move toward Elmnas." He said it begrudgingly because he could still feel the strange and strong magic that was unknown to him. He had wanted to go off on his own in search of the source, but now… Now that Valero was dead, now that even Colna looked to him, he felt a strange weight of responsibility to Valero's mission and to this odd group.

The others nodded in agreement, and they directed their horses to a trot in the direction they had been traveling the day before. He watched them ride ahead of him for a few minutes as he tested the magical currents all around him. He could still feel that dwarf-tinted magic. He started and sat upright as he realized it was ahead of him in the very direction they were traveling. Excited, he spurred his own horse to catch up to the others. Maybe they would find the source and the princess all at once. If the gods were kind.

He nearly laughed out loud.

If the gods were kind, indeed. He imagined that they cared not at all.

"The awakening occurred when he began searching the currents to track the movement of his enemies and found that he was being tracked in turn. The awakening truly began when he realized he'd been betrayed even though he did not yet know who the betrayer was."
~ King Mronas, <u>Interviews of Elven Kings</u>, Vol 3

31

*H*e sat in a state of deep meditation considering the troubling thoughts following his communion with Naga as he stretched his senses outward toward Mythos. He replayed over and over the conversation with his god, and it left him more and more confused, which in turn left him more and more frustrated. But in that frustration, something played at the back of his mind. That familiar blast that was new from his god yet familiar in some strange way.

He shook his head. He needed to focus. He wanted to monitor the move of the currents over Mythos. Even from so far away, he could feel the magical currents ebbing and flowing through the world around him. It was how he had originally learned of Orinus and partly how he found Libitina's egg.

While everyone living on Mythnium was indeed part of the magical currents and most could use it if they so desired, only a few among the intelligent races willingly drew it in in order to influence the flow and utilize it. Most who used magic routinely were considered mages. Though in general, everyone knew they had innate abilities.

In his case, the White Lord had practiced using magic from his earliest remembered years. Among those who were now living, he was very likely the most proficient if not the most powerful mage. He was especially dangerous though because he held nothing back when he used it. He had no compunctions regarding side effects or collateral damage. In fact, in most cases, he welcomed the chaos that using magic left in its wake.

The magical blast rooted in rage had touched the White Lord outside of his meditation and forced him to leave everything to focus on what it was. As he sat in the middle of the room, he felt Orinus moving away from him, heading north on Mythos. He sensed excitement fighting with deep frustration in the aura surrounding the mage and grew curious. The reason Orinus had acted out in rage the day before must have been due to something tragic. The shift in aura was reason to explore. The White Lord followed the magical currents north, away from Orinus, searching though he did not know what he was searching for. Suddenly, he felt it, and he knew.

Orinus was seeking the dwarf just as he was. The White Lord observed the magic. Observing it, even from so far away, was different than simply learning of its existence. It was old yet was strangely familiar, but in its oldness, it was also frustratingly hard to trace. The user was young and unsure but noble in heart. The White Lord thought on his plan to sway the young dwarf to his own devices. As he continued to sense it, he realized that the dwarf had a rudimentary mastery of the elemental shaping magic that drew on the magical currents which flowed through objects rather than around them.

236

As he focused his attention on the way the currents interacted with the dwarf, he admitted to himself that he was not surprised that the dwarves had rediscovered one of their links to elemental magic. The person who was so gifted must be a blacksmith or stone mason of incredible talent and of a particular lineage. He thought back hundreds of years to the last of the elemental users. The last one he was aware of had been a mason who had used his skills to help different races of elves build structures that could withstand the changing of the forest or the geological changes of the mountains where they housed their precious history and tomes, like the magical doors that effectively blocked his chase after Olphara and Pruzin.

Refocusing on his meditation, he closed his eyes and redirected his focus back on Orinus. The mage truly bothered him. He suspected that the mage knew he was behind the attack on his life and wondered if he had any designs on retaliation. The emotional turmoil that surrounded the mage, affecting the magical currents around him, were hard to read. The White Lord tried to focus and push inward to try to determine more of the drive behind the mage when he felt a shift in the currents that he could not ignore.

The push in the currents was steady and very strong, at least as strong as him. Something very old, older than him. It was masterful, touching on something ancient. Turning his attention toward it, he allowed its push on the currents to bend his own manipulation of the currents. As the power rolled over him, he took a moment to revel in the incredibleness for it was familiar like a favorite blanket. Then memory and realization hit him, causing him to snap out of his mediation, making him jump to his feet with a roar of defiance.

"No!" he screamed to the air. "No!"

But then just as quickly, he calmed and started to smile a wide evil grin. His surprise and shock turned to malice as long unrequited rage built up inside him. This change in the currents meant he would need to change his plans and work faster. He'd also have to be incredibly careful to guard his mind and his intentions. He thought of his communion with Naga then of Libitina and the unhatched egg.

Yes, he'd have to be on guard.

Libitina felt the White Lord's blast of rage before she heard him roar in anger. Still tightly wound around the egg so that it was fully encompassed and sheltered by her body, she raised her head and looked in the direction of the White Lord. She sent out a probing question.

Is everything okay?

Even though they were not in the same room, the White Lord heard her mental question clearly. He immediately sheltered his thoughts and calmed himself.

I felt the dwarf that is using the old song magic.

Libitina perked up, and the White Lord could feel her interest.

Really? You can locate the creature? Do you wish me to bring the creature here?

He lied, *That is not necessary, my dear. I have one of my pawns in search of it. Besides I cannot pinpoint it to a specific location, just a general direction. However, the mage is also trying to track it.*

He could feel the dragon frown in disappointment.

Do not underestimate my pawn. He seems a weak sniveling thing, but he craves my approval as much as he craves the power that he thinks he will gain once he receives my approval.

Yes, the dragon countered, *but you gave the fool two tasks. Is he capable of delivering on both of them?*

I can assure you with the ability to control the mulig, he will have no trouble unless he is more inept than I judged. He knows the risk. If he fails me, he will spend the rest of his life in my dungeons feeding the cravings of myself and my men.

This mage – he is quite powerful, yes? The dragon asked suspecting the answer before she asked.

He is, but he keeps his power contained and limited. He fears his abilities. He is afraid of touching the currents in a way that he can experience their raw magic.

Mentally shrugging, Libitina replied, *Raw magic is so much more exciting.*

The White Lord did not disagree, and in thinking of raw magical power, he thought of his discovery.

There is something else, she prodded.

In answer, the White Lord shut her out, causing her to blink in surprise at the mental door slam. These mental blocks between the two of them were happening more and more often, and they were beginning to frustrate her. He was keeping things from her but was also making no effort to hide the fact that he was keeping her at a distance, which made her reflect on the true nature of their relationship.

It made her wonder. Had he been hiding things from her all along?

She put her nose to the egg and breathed lightly on it, sensing its soul once more. Again, it was cringing away from her. She felt sudden sadness. She didn't want the unhatched dragon to fear her. She wanted it to unite with her. It was after all her kind. They were alike.

No, not alike, came a tiny intrusion, and she realized it was from the egg.

She drew her head back and stared at the egg.

Will you come out? she threw at it.

Instead of answering her, she felt it withdraw once again, and her sadness grew. Confused by its single comment for the first time since she had been brooding over it, she wondered what it meant. Of course they were alike. They were both dragons. They were both creatures of heat and fire. Of war. Of blood.

As she thought that, the little soul touched her mind again, *You have it twisted.*

Libitina stared at the egg. *Twisted?*

Once again, infuriatingly, the soul retreated.

Libitina laid her head on her front feet. Troubled, she thought of the White Lord and his distancing from her. She thought of the stubborn little dragon refusing to hatch. She thought of how alone she suddenly felt, and she realized that she didn't like it one bit. She also realized that the White Lord no longer appeared to trust her, and that made her realize that she could not trust him.

"Those who are prepared for here and now, for the future as unpredictable and uncertain as it is, are always those very same who learned how to look to the past without dwelling so long in it that they forgot how to live."
~ General Valero Ald-Bric, *The Lost Conversations*

32

*T*he gaunt, unhealthy-looking but well-dressed rana stood at the edge of the forest and waited patiently for the group to come into view.

"How long do we wait, Derk?" muttered a mulig behind him.

The man turned to that grotesque beast and sneered. "As long as it takes."

He flashed the mulig a quick glance at the pebble he held in his hands. Seeing the stone, the mulig reacted as though it were struck. Like the rest of his race, he was scared of magic and talismans, staffs and amulets. Anything that had to do with magic, he and his kind typically avoided.

The man watched with grim satisfaction as the creature moved back into the ranks that stood behind him, then he turned his attention back to the road. The White Lord had been quite clear about what he wanted done with this addition to his previous orders. The man and his enslaved muligs were to find and capture a particular dwarf that he would recognize with a dweomer sent to him to help detect a specific magical current. Once captured, he was to send the dwarf directly to Mygras to the White Lord and then continue on his main objective to kill the princess. The man smiled wickedly to himself. He had never been tasked to capture a Silver Dwarf before. His fingers tapped impatiently on his belt as he waited.

Before long, he saw the caravan he was told to attack come into sight. Rather than move into the forest where the muligs were waiting, he stepped toward the road. Bending over, he grabbed a handful of dirt and rubbed it into his face, grasslike hair, and on his clothes. Trusting that he looked as though he'd been on his own for a while and counting on his naturally haggard appearance to aid in the illusion, he waved laboriously at the caravan.

As the first wagon moved up to him, he took mental note of the male dwarves driving it. A female dwarf and a human woman were driving the second, and a cloaked warrior stood near the old dwarf. Two dwarf guards walked alongside the wagons. He worked hard not to stare at the female dwarf who was engulfed in the magical currents he was looking for.

The younger male dwarf pulled the wagon to a halt, and the man looked up at him. "If you please, sir, help an old soul?"

Stranick stared at the rana, and then he glanced at Elder Martan for direction. Elder Martan stared at the fish-man, but his hesitation gave the stranger time to call upon the muligs. With a hand signal behind his back, he alerted them and they bolted through the edge of the forest and toward the unsuspecting caravan.

Stranick and Martan immediately responded while Aldrina and Estryl both leapt from their respective sides of the wagon to join the guards and the cloaked figure.

Derk pulled out dangerous twin blades and moved to his target, the female dwarf. His mission to capture her was clear. But as he stepped toward her, fighting all around him, the young male dwarf stepped between him and his prey.

The male dwarf held a heavy hammer in his hands. Derk could see the tension in the dwarf's arms and shoulders sending ripples along his muscles. He rushed the dwarf, hoping to use his speed to disarm him.

Stranick took a solid slash from one of the rana's blades with stoic resolve. In turn, his hammer made solid contact with the rana's other hand and knocked the blade out of his hands. Turning into the Derk's embrace, he grabbed his hammer with both hands and slammed the head of the hammer into the rana's chest, crushing his sternum and ribs and dropping him to the ground.

Meanwhile, Elder Martan and the cloaked figure moved to fight alongside the inexperienced Aldrina. Muligs brandishing heavy clubs of wood surrounded the trio, spitting at them to try to blind them. Elder Martan stepped toward the amphibious humanoids with his axe in hand. Swinging the axe over his head, he swung it out before him and dispatched two muligs in one blow, but the heaviness of the axe threw him off balance. He staggered forward into the middle of the group and away from Aldrina.

A large mulig, acting as the leader of the group, stepped toward the human woman, thinking her easy prey. He pulled up short as he caught the glint of red eyes glowering at him from under the hood of the cloaked figure.

A Dark Elf? He had not been told of a Dark Elf. Fear ran up and down his spine, but he pushed it

243

down and brandished his studded club before him throwing himself at the Drow.

Virconia met the mulig's club with her own and easily pushed back, causing him to adjust his stance and pause to take her measure.

Aldrina cried out in alarm. Holding a thin sword in both hands, she hated that she could not better defend herself. A wickedly grinning mulig stepped toward her, muttering something she could not understand. Backing up, she felt the wagon. She desperately lashed out at the creature, forcing it to back up a step, then she dashed under the wagon, hoping she could defend herself better where the creatures couldn't reach her.

Once Aldrina disappeared under the wagon, the muligs refocused their attention on Elder Martan, who had recovered his balance. A horrified Aldrina watched as the muligs landed blow after blow with their clubs on the sturdy dwarf. He got hit in the head, in his face, all over his body. She couldn't understand how he was still standing. But fight on he did. He killed one mulig and then hacked at another, but there were simply too many and he knew it. He turned toward the wagon and tried to reach it so that the wagon would be at his back, but as he made the move, one of the mulig clubs crashed down on his head so forcefully Aldrina saw his eyes bulge outward. He hit the ground heavily, and Aldrina screamed as she saw the life leave the old dwarf's eyes.

Virconia reacted with deadly swiftness, hacking at one and then another mulig, forcing them away from the wagon. But after a bit, she found herself surrounded and lost sight of Aldrina.

On the other side of the wagons, Stranick and Estryl fought furiously. Estryl had not noticed that the rana had clearly tried to get to her. Her only thought was to remain by her brother's side. She was no great fighter, but she was familiar with weapons and was fierce. She parried blows easily but was not experienced enough to land any blows on the ugly creatures. Stranick, on the other hand, landed blow after blow. One by one, the muligs began to fall before him. Realizing he was a serious threat to them, the mulig turned to Estryl to take out the weaker opponent. Estryl tried to parry, but they were wearing her down. Even though Stranick was so close, he could not stop them from getting to her.

Seeing his sister standing alone, Stranick fought his way through the muligs even harder. One by one, his hammer struck home and he stepped closer to his sister. His only thought to save her, he smashed one after another until he stood by her side. Growing tired and hurting from several heavy blows that they landed on him, he prayed to his gods that they would ease his pain and lend him strength to keep fighting.

On the other side, Virconia fought against the pain of yet another heavy blow, and she grinned in satisfaction as she fell the mulig that landed the blow. She glanced about her and saw the fallen body of Elder Martan, and she gritted her teeth in determination to reach the wagons and keep Aldrina safe. In her distraction, another hard hit gained her attention and nearly made her knees buckle. She fought through the pain and swung her blade before finding purchase in another mulig and then another. She fought for every step that finally got her to the wagon. She then turned around and dared the muligs to advance on her.

Estryl looked around and realized that the guards were dead. As far as she knew, she and Stranick were the only ones left standing, and that wasn't saying much. Not knowing how much more she could take, she turned her attention back to the leering muligs in front of her and grabbed for the short blade on her belt.

An approaching horn sounded. The mulig, fearful and confused, stopped. The horn sounded again, and the mulig looked uncertain. One saw the man dead on the ground and he roared. Spitting in Estryl's direction one last time, he made a strange howl and the mulig made a hasty retreat into the trees.

Estryl and Stranick breathed sighs of relief, but both stood ready, not sure why the creatures suddenly left them when they were so close to killing them. As Estryl felt waves of exhaustion wash over her, she saw a hooded figure step out of the trees where the mulig had just been. The figure approached, throwing her hood back as she drew near. In her hands were a horn and a slender sword.

Estryl heard a sudden intake of breath and turned to see Virconia standing at the back of the wagon peering at the figure. Virconia stepped toward the figure, an Elven woman with a horribly scarred face.

"Well met, Grazina." And she too pushed her hood back.

The elf's eyes grew wide in shock. "Virconia?"

The Drow nodded and then fell to her knees.

Grazina rushed to her side and helped her up. As the pair made it to the wagons, Virconia gasped in shock for Estryl was on the ground. Grazina tried to tend to Virconia, but she pushed her away.

"No. There is a human woman and an old dwarf. See that they are okay. I will watch over my friend and her brother here."

She crawled to Estryl and gently cradled the dwarf's head on her lap while she looked for what might have made her pass out. Stranick stared down at his sister, not knowing how to help. Barely had he registered that they were done fighting when he found himself unable to stand any longer. He felt his hammer fall to the ground. Blackness engulfed him as he too fell unconscious, completely unaware of the massive injuries he had sustained protecting Estryl.

Grazina saw the male dwarf fall but didn't wait or argue. Instead, she moved around the wagons, taking in the carnage as she went. The two dead guards had been beaten to bloody pulps, while a strange rana was dead with blood leaking out of his mouth.

On the other side of the wagon, she found nearly a dozen muligs cut down. Among them, she found the body of an old dwarf and obvious signs of Virconia's fighting techniques but no sign of a human woman. She was about to move away from the wagon to look for tracks when her keen hearing heard something shift under the wagon. Bending low, she made eye contact with the wide-eyed human woman who was laying on her stomach with a sword out before her.

Grazina gave a slight wave. "They have gone. You can come out now."

Aldrina inched forward cautiously. Finally, she stood up and gasped as she saw all around the wagons. She moved to Stranick. Seeing that he was breathing, she did a quick once-over on him. Believing him to be mostly okay, she ran over to

247

Elder Martan. She fell to her knees at his side and could not help crying over him.

Grazina stood behind her.

"He saved my life. If it weren't for him…"

Grazina responded by simply laying a hand on Aldrina's shoulder. She heard steps behind her and saw Virconia supporting the female dwarf.

Estryl threw herself to the ground beside the old dwarf. "No! No. No. No, please, no." she cried out.

Aldrina reached across Elder Martan's body and took one of Estryl's hands. Estryl looked up at her and saw the tears on her cheeks. She shed no tears of her own, but she felt as though her heart had been ripped out. She had never experienced grief like this, had never expected to have to fight her way along the surface just in search of knowledge. She cursed her talent and wished she were still safe in her forge in the Silver Isles. Grief changed to anger. Wiping her face angrily, she tried to stand up but realized she couldn't.

Aldrina noticed her pain immediately and wiped her own face as she realized she was needed. She looked to the scarred elf and rose to her feet. "Will you help get them to the wagons?"

Grazina nodded and started to ask Virconia for help but saw the Dark Elf grip her side and stagger. At once she moved to Virconia's side and helped her to the covered wagon.

"We need to move. Now," stated Virconia. "We can't stay here."

Grazina nodded. "I know where we can go where you can rest."

She helped Virconia up into the wagon and then turned to help Aldrina with Estryl, who was limping heavily. As Aldrina and Grazina moved to get Stranick, seeing he was still unconscious, Grazina told Aldrina what Virconia said.

"That is fine. I think she may be right. We were hit really hard. I can help heal them, but they will need rest to fully recover."

After they got Stranick up into the wagon with Estryl's help, the two women looked at the wagons. "Maybe we should just take the covered one."

Grazina agreed. "Let's move everything we can over and tie the horses to the back. But let's hurry. The signal I used the horn for won't mislead the muligs for long."

"What was that signal for?" Aldrina asked.

"A scouting party from Elmnas."

"But why would a group that size be afraid of a scouting party?"

Grazina smiled lightly. "Forest Elf scouts are deadly. One scouting party could easily handle a mulig party twice that size."

Aldrina looked at Grazina in surprise. "No way."

"Oh yes. The road here is close enough to the forest that the elves would have the trees to target the muligs from. For them it is almost too easy."

Aldrina shook her head. "I wish a scouting party had been near."

Grazina shrugged her shoulders. "You all did well for yourselves…"

Aldrina shot her a withering glance, and Grazina fell silent.

"We lost three of our group," she stated in anger.

"I am sorry. I didn't mean…"

Aldrina shook her head. "I know. Come on. We need to be on our way."

"The scars we carry reveal the outward hardships we survived. No. That is not all. Scars are windows or walls. If we allow them to be, they are windows into our most beautiful of places. Sadly, we most often use them as walls, intending for them to protect us from gaining more scars but then stopping the suns from illuminating those facets that make our soul so unique and glorious to behold."
~ *Healing Oracles of the Willow Elves*

33

Grazina steered the wagon down the road for a while before turning off onto an old trail so grown over few would even have known it was there. While Grazina drove the wagon, Aldrina remained in the back tending to her patients. Stranick did not wake, largely due to massive bumps on his head that were sure to cause him headaches for days and intense bruising that Aldrina was certain were broken bones that needed to be set. Estryl's knee had been smashed pretty badly, so Aldrina wrapped it, put an herbal poultice on it, and made Estryl promise not to walk on it for a few days.

It was Virconia that Aldrina fretted over. Virconia had not been fully recovered from her injuries on the mountain pass, and the blows from the muligs had aggravated those internal injuries that were life threatening. Despite Virconia's protests, Aldrina used her magic to help her sleep, and she begged Grazina to hurry to a place they could camp because she was worried she would need to cut into Virconia to alleviate some of the pressure from internal bleeding.

Finally, in the middle of the night, Grazina stopped the wagon and opened the flap. She saw Aldrina still awake. "We are here."

"Where is here?" Aldrina asked groggily.

Grazina flipped around on the bench and stepped into the wagon. She moved to Virconia's side. "Will she be okay?"

Aldrina nodded. "I think so. Now that we are stopped, I can continue to work on her. First, we need to move these two out of the wagon."

Grazina moved to the back of the wagon and hopped down. "I'll set up a tent for them and start a fire. Then we can move them."

Aldrina started to get to her feet to help, but Grazina motioned her to stay. "You stay there and close your eyes for a bit. I can do the tent and fire. When I am done, I'll help you move these two."

Aldrina watched the scarred elf leave the wagon and realized she didn't even know the elf's name. She didn't dwell on it though as she realized the elf was right: she needed to rest too. She leaned back against the side of the wagon and closed her eyes. It felt like she had just closed her eyes when Grazina shook her leg gently.

Without a word, they moved first Estryl and then Stranick to the tent where Grazina laid out bedrolls. On the fire, she had set a pot with water, and Aldrina could smell something cooking. "How long was I asleep?"

The elf smirked. "I checked Virconia while you were asleep. Her breathing was even, so I thought it would be okay to let you sleep a little longer."

In alarm, Aldrina glanced back at the wagon and saw the early morning light drifting through the trees. She rushed back to the wagon. Climbing inside, she found that the elf was right. Virconia was breathing easily. Using her magic, Aldrina felt along the Dark Elf's body sensing her broken bones and the internal injuries. She sighed as she realized it would take days to work on Virconia. Holding her amulet over the broken bones, she directed healing energy into the bones until she could feel them binding together. Then she moved to the internal injuries where she could feel blood and bile seeping out of organs and into connective tissue. She chanted over Virconia until the morning light shone into the open end of the wagon.

Exhausted but seeing that nothing more could be done for the moment, she left the wagon. The elf woman sat beside the fire and motioned for her to sit down. Aldrina sat near her, reaching out to accept a bowl of stew. She ate in silence, content to observe the elf woman. The severe scarring appeared to extend all along the woman's face and body, but only on one side. In stark contrast, the other side of her face and what she could see of her body was clear, unmarred, and beautiful.

Feeling her curious stare, the elf set her own bowl down and met the other woman's eyes. "In all the rush, I didn't get to introduce myself. I am Grazina."

Aldrina nearly choked on her food. "As in the missing...?"

Grazina nodded. "That was as I intended, but things have changed, and I'm returning home."

Aldrina cleared her throat. "You're going back to Elmnas?"

"That is the plan."

Aldrina smiled lightly. "We are also trying to make our way to Elmnas. Estryl, the dwarf, and her brother, Stranick, are on quest to learn more about Estryl's gift; she can shape metal by singing to it."

Grazina stared into the fire for a minute without reacting to Aldrina's response then asked, "How long do you need before your companions will be ready for travel?"

Aldrina thought. "I think Estryl and her brother will be ready in just a day or so. But Virconia…" she hesitated. "Today will really tell us more if she will survive. If today goes well, then she can likely travel in four or five days."

Grazina frowned. She rose to her feet and started to walk into the trees.

"Wait! Where are you going?" Aldrina called out after her.

"Just going to cast some warning spells so we aren't caught off guard if anyone comes too close."

Aldrina sighed deeply. Not for the first time, she asked herself what exactly she had gotten herself into by agreeing to travel with Estryl.

Back at the site where they were ambushed, light rain started to fall on the bodies of the rana and the mulig scattered about the road. One of the bodies started to cough and gasp for air. Slowly, he sat up and looked all about, taking in the dead creatures all around him. He grimaced in pain from where the dwarf's hammer had smashed into him, but he smiled inwardly for the dwarf had missed his vital organs.

Where a heart rested in most of the races' chests, his sat much farther to the right. Still, the injury hurt him a great deal. Tearing a long strip of cloth off his coat, he wound it around his chest and tied it tight. He'd have to find a healer to help him with the rest, but he could sense that he would be fine.

He rose to his feet and stared down the road in the direction he knew the dwarf and her friends had traveled. He frowned as he thought of his failure to capture that dwarf, but as he started down the road after them, he reassured himself that the talisman the White Lord had given him would be sufficient now that he knew the strength of the group.

"Sorrow no more.
Grieve only but a moment. Death is never final.
This you know. For long after the one you
cherished walks this land no more, the name on
your lips, the memory in your mind, the touch on
your soul
proves the immortality of their soul."
~ Sayki – God of Death

34

O rinus rode ahead of the group, preferring not to be caught up in the heightened emotions of the elves behind him. He understood Colna's grief. He understood Tristal's rage. He especially understood rage, but he needed to keep control of himself so he could track the magical current that intrigued him so.

After setting off to head back to Elmnas, they avoided all the roads and chose instead to simply follow compass bearings for a more direct route to Mythos Road, which would lead them to a more direct road to Elmnas.

After several days of travel, they had finally reached Mythos Road and were moving along at a brisk pace to the north. The magic that Orinus was tracking was growing ever closer, and he grew more and more excited at the prospect of meeting the dwarf blessed with that magic.

Without warning, he stopped his horse and signaled for the others to be quiet. He waited until they caught up to him and silently took in the grizzly scene before them. They moved ahead quietly until

Tristal moved her horse off the road and bounded from its back. "Over here," she cried out.

Orinus remained on his horse but moved it closer to see what Tristal had found among the remains of a large group of muligs. Lying on the ground, beaten to a bloody mess, was an old dwarf. Tristal searched the dwarf and found a clan ring on one hand, a thick gold chain around his neck that identified him as an elder, and a pouch at his waist that held stones and short missives clearly intended for his destinations.

She opened one missive and her eyes opened wide.

"What is it?" asked Colna who stood next to her.

Tristal handed her the missive and stood to show Orinus the jewelry and the pouch and its contents.

"This old dwarf was an elder of the Silver Dwarves. He was on his way to Elmnas in search of knowledge that could help a dwarf by the name of Estryl."

Orinus frowned. He closed his eyes and felt the currents around them. This fight had taken place days before and the tracks had long been washed away, but the Dwarven magic was still to the north.

He looked to Tristal and Colna and pointed to the north. "I would hazard a guess that his party didn't intend to leave him behind. Let's wrap him up and take him with us."

Colna started to object, but Orinus stopped her. "They were heading to Elmnas as are we. From what I can tell, their direction has not changed. We might catch up with them. We might not. But reuniting them with their elder may go a long way in…"

"In what?" queried Tristal.

"In finding allies."

Colna and Tristal looked at each other. "Allies?" they asked in unison.

Orinus rolled his eyes. For being such long-lived creatures, sometimes they really could not see the whole picture. He turned his gaze to the south, back the way they had come, and responded, "This is more evidence of the White Lord moving. We will need to ally the races if we hope to defend against him."

Tristal laughed, "He has never gained a foothold here."

Orinus looked at her sharply, "He hasn't yet."

Tristal shuddered at the implications of Orinus's flat statement. She turned her attention to the dead dwarf and directed Layni to help her wrap the body and secure it to the back of the horse that held Valero's body. Once they were done, they all remounted and followed Orinus farther north along Mythos Road.

"How can you tell where we are going?" complained Tristal, uneasy in the thick brush that grew taller than her horse. She couldn't see over it or through it, and it made her skin crawl to have no line of sight beyond Orinus's back.

Orinus looked over his shoulder at her and farther down the line where Colna rode leading Valero's horse and then Layni who brought up the rear.

"I'm following the magic."

Without any further explanation, he turned back to face forward, closing his eyes and directing his horse along the invisible current.

Tristal looked back at Colna, who merely shrugged her shoulders. Tristal worried about Colna. Since knowing the archer, Tristal had found Colna to be outgoing, warm, and lighthearted, but since Valero was struck down, Colna was much different. Tristal sensed incredible sadness and something else. She wasn't sure, but it was as though Colna lost her desire to live. That made Tristal worry.

And worry added to Tristal's internal rage. She clenched her fists on the reins and her horse shifted under her unease, sensing her mood. Even Orinus sensed it; he opened his eyes and looked back at her.

"We really need to talk about getting your emotions under control."

Tristal shot him an angry glare. "Mind your own damn…" she stopped suddenly as Orinus's horse stepped into a wide clearing where a wagon sat next to a campfire that was burning with a tent nearby. She stopped her horse next to Orinus's and looked around what appeared to be a hastily deserted camp.

She felt a blade at her throat and grimaced. She hadn't even heard her attacker move through the brush!

"Make any moves," said a low steady voice, "and this White Elf will eat my blade."

Orinus raised his hands, as did Colna and Layni following his lead. "We mean you no harm."

Orinus looked toward the woman who was holding the blade to Tristal's throat even as Colna exclaimed, "Your Highness!"

Shifting her attention but not her blade, the woman turned to look at Colna and then lowered her blade. "Colna?"

Colna leapt from her saddle and rushed to Grazina. The two met in a hug and then a ceremonial greeting reserved for only the closest of friends.

When they stepped apart, Grazina looked at the group. "My apologies. We were set upon by muligs led by a rana, and we are still recovering."

She pointed to a human woman who stood peeking out of the wagon, "That is Aldrina. She is a healer. The rest of our party are in the wagon or in that tent." She then pointed off to the side where they saw a rana sitting on the ground tied securely to a tree trunk.

"That one led the attack on us and then followed us. He should have been dead but was hit hard enough in the head that I heard him before he ever got close to our camp. Bumbling fool never saw me coming, but I wanted to interrogate him or take him to my father to be interrogated."

Colna appraised her friend with a respectful glance and then pointed to the horse she had been leading that had two wrapped bodies strapped across it.

"We found one of your party, I think."

Grazina moved to the bodies and lifted the wrappings. She gasped when she raised the first and saw the face of Valero. Turning to Colna with tears in her eyes, she whispered, "Oh, my dear friend. I am so very sorry." She bowed her head and touched her heart in a symbol of remembrance, then she kissed Valero's head and replaced the cloth covering.

She moved to the other body and lifted its covering to see the old dwarf. She nodded and replaced the blanket to cover him.

"I think Estryl and her brother will be relieved you found their elder."

She motioned for everyone to dismount and led them into the camp.

"Thoughts, though they remain hidden in the recesses of my mind, still influence every step I take, every path I decide upon. Therefore, I pray to the gods to keep my thoughts wholesome and good that every step I take be one that is beneficial to this world around me."
~ *Willow Prayer – Chant of the Acolyte*

35

O rinus moved from the tent where he introduced himself to the recumbent Stranick and Estryl, who were still resting and nursing their own wounds. From there, he walked to the wagon where the Dark Elf was still unconscious. He climbed in next to Aldrina. In silence, they sat side by side looking at Virconia.

After several long minutes, he broke the silence, "I can sense that you invested a lot of healing magic into the Drow. Is there anything I can do to help?"

Aldrina raised her heavy eyes to look at the mage and shook her head wearily. "I don't think so. If she were going to recover, she should have woken up by now. As it is, I have mended all her bones and internal injuries. The rest is up to her."

Orinus nodded. He trusted the healer, but he also sensed that she was rather new to it. On impulse, he reached out for her hand. "May I?"

Confused and suddenly shy, Aldrina nodded.

Orinus took her hand and lifted it over Virconia.

His eyes bore into Virconia as he held Aldrina's hand over the Drow's still body. "You can feel her vitality. Is that right?"

Aldrina nodded.

He moved her hand closer to Virconia's body, very slowly, methodically. "You can sense where there is injury, pain, and so on?"

Aldrina nodded.

"Okay. Let me see if I can enhance your healer's senses for just a moment. Maybe there is something you missed."

Aldrina sighed in resignation. She did suspect she was missing something, but she had searched and searched and found nothing. She feared what the others would think of her if this mage was able to do what she could not. But as she watched him, she sensed that he only intended to help her, to aid her in her own abilities. She could not help but ask herself why. What were his motivations? In all her experience with men, they left little doubt in her mind that they were only doing something that could bring them some benefit at some point. Internally, she shrugged. If he was after something from her or from her group, she would have to tackle that later because she was desperate to save her new friend's life. If this strange mage could help her, she was eager to take his help.

Orinus closed his eyes, and began chanting in a language Aldrina had never heard. As he chanted, she could feel his energy seeping into her.

"Now you move your hands over her as you would normally while I continue chanting."

Aldrina moved her hands slowly over Virconia's body starting at the top of her head, down to her neck, then to her shoulders, and along her chest. She moved down one arm, up the next, and then moved to Virconia's midsection. As she moved farther down Virconia's body with Orinus still chanting in a low voice beside her, she felt what she had missed the first dozen times. Even with Orinus's magic, it was just a tiny thing, but it was vital, and Aldrina gasped as she sensed a fracture to Virconia's pelvis that had somehow gone septic.

Gripping her amulet with one hand, she reached out to hold Orinus's hand with the other. She began chanting her own healing chants as taught to her by Olphara and the Willows. Drawing on the magical currents and Virconia's own natural healing force, Aldrina felt the difference in the way the currents moved to tie and bind, to suture and mend. Together, the healer and the mage sat over the Dark Elf for several hours until finally Aldrina could feel the bone knitting back together as it healed, and Virconia stirred for the first time in four days.

Aldrina let go of Orinus though she still gripped the amulet tightly; she leaned back with a relieved sigh. Without looking at the mage, she commented, "I could not have done that on my own. I don't know how to thank you."

Orinus leaned forward with his elbows on his knees and smiled, more to himself than anything.

"You're a new healer though you have been taught well. I can tell. You have talent, maybe due to your Elven blood though that matters little. Someday, sooner than you think maybe, you will be able to sense those wounds that you miss now. With experience and practice, you will far surpass what you sensed today. The magic I added to your abilities only enhanced your own ability. I suspect you will not need that beautiful amulet to aid you in time."

Aldrina glanced at the mage out of the corner of her eye, pondering his words. Was he right? Would she ever be able to heal without the amulet? Would she be able to sense things she wasn't certain even Olphara could?   As they sat in silence watching Virconia breathe with new ease, Aldrina felt a sudden kinship with the mage. She kept it to herself, but she hoped he and his party would stick around as they continued on to Elmnas.

"Torture is not the infliction of pain. Torture is the suggestion of pain worse than what was already delivered be it physical or mental. Torture used successfully is that suggestion of pain and then time for the victim to dwell on the promised delivery of that pain."
~ *Letters to Elmnas, The Unnamed Soldier*

36

While Orinus and Aldrina were working in the wagon, Tristal and Colna moved to interrogate the fish-man. He blamed the head injury from his failed attack on the caravan for the fact he had been caught. He stumbled onto the camp just that morning and had intended to wait till nightfall to sneak in to capture the dwarf. But in eavesdropping on the elf as she spoke to the healer in the wagon, he learned that the princess was that very elf who had come to the caravan's aid. He could not believe his luck that both his quarries were within reach. In his excitement, he had inadvertently turned too fast and snapped a twig on the tree he was standing next to. The elf had heard the tiny sound and reacted instantly. He didn't stand a chance against her in the state he was in, and he was easily captured and bound.

Tristal squatted in front of the rana, while Colna took out his gag. "We will start nicely, and if you cooperate, you may live. But I warn you, fish-man, if you try to play tough, refuse to answer, or lie to us, we will get rough, and you will surely die in the end."

From behind Tristal, a heavy step landed.

"He will die regardless."

Tristal looked over her shoulder to see the dwarf female leaning heavily on a crutch, her knee wrapped tightly, a grimace on her face as she glared at the rana.

Estryl moved to stand beside Tristal and glared down at the rana.

"You will talk."

The rana looked from the Forest Elf, to the White Elf, to the Silver Dwarf.

How on earth did I get into this mess, he thought. Part of him wanted to beg for mercy and tell them everything they wanted to know, but he knew if for some reason he lived once they were done with him, the White Lord would perform so much worse on him. He shuddered visibly and lowered his eyes to the ground before he closed them as though to sleep. If he was going to die, he would die here.

Estryl poked at the rana with her crutch. "Open your eyes!"

Tristal waved Estryl back, but she took a blade out and pulled up one of the Rana's pant legs to reveal his scaly skin underneath.

"I've heard it said," she began as she lightly traced her blade up and down his lower leg, "that rana can be descaled. Supposedly, it's incredibly painful, but it won't kill a rana. Even though it won't kill you, it will be raw and oozing and painful for the rest of your natural life."

She tucked the tip of her blade under one scale and barely lifted it, and the rana opened his eyes in sudden pain. He stared at first her then the blade. To him, it felt as though she had already torn off several scales, so sensitive was the flesh under the scales. He gritted his short teeth and tried not to cry out.

Tristal moved the blade just a tiny bit farther under the scale, which was roughly the size of rose petal. The rana reacted by jerking his leg, which sent her blade even farther under the scale, popping it off his body completely. Crying out in horror and intense pain, the rana opened his eyes and pleaded. "Please. Just kill me."

Tristal withdrew her blade and picked up the scale to look at it more closely. "These are actually quite pretty, you know?" She turned her attention to the rana. "Why should I just kill you?"

The rana gasped for breath in an effort to control the pain. "Please. The worst you can do to me is nothing compared to what he will do to me."

"Who?" pressed Tristal.

"Who do you think?" cried the rana.

"Back up. Let's not get ahead of ourselves." Colna knelt next to the rana. "First, tell us your name."

The rana looked from Colna to Tristal and then to Estryl who stood behind them. "Derk," he whispered.

Colna nodded encouragingly. "Derk." She looked to Tristal. Colna was not opposed to getting answers, but it hurt her to see any creature in pain. It bothered her a great deal that Tristal appeared to have absolutely no qualms about descaling the fish-man.

Tristal frowned at her but let Colna continue. "Derk, I am Colna. I'm from Elmnas. Where are you from?"

Derk looked confused. The line of questioning not at all what he expected. Suspicious, he lowered his eyelids halfway trying to read Colna's motives. Completely unsure, he shrugged internally. "Croglinke."

If any of the three women around him were surprised, they did not show it. That made him uncomfortable.

Tristal leaned in and tapped the newly uncovered flesh with her blade ever so lightly, but it sent waves of pain into the rana's body. "So you work for the White Lord."

It was a fact, not a question, and the pain nearly overwhelmed Derk, so he just nodded his head in reply.

"What does he want with you?"

Derk shook his head. "I can't tell you."

He looked at Estryl pointedly but then gasped as a hooded woman approached. She pushed back her hood revealing the incredible burn scars to one side of her face and neck.

"The princess," he gasped out loud in spite of himself.

Tristal and Colna turned to see Grazina standing next to Estryl.

Tristal turned back to the rana, suddenly impatient. She dug her blade under another scale and ripped it off without warning. Derk screamed loudly, drawing both Aldrina and Orinus from the wagon. They kept their distance, Aldrina watching in horror and Orinus in grim satisfaction.

Holding the second scale before Derk's eyes, Tristal asked, "What does the White Lord want with a dwarf and an elf?"

Derk, shaking in pain, shook his head. "I was to capture the dwarf and send her back to him. He has use for her abilities, but her," he looked to Grazina, "I was sent to kill her."

Colna leaned in and grabbed the rana's face. "What use could the White Lord have of a dwarf? And why would he want to kill the princess?"

Derk's eyes rolled in his head as he fought against the pain. "Something about ending the royal line, but I don't know about the dwarf. He didn't tell me. He just sent me directions to capture her."

Tristal looked at Colna. "Anything else we need to know from this cretin?"

Colna stood up and looked at Grazina, who shook her head no. She looked back at Tristal and sighed. "No. I think we know all we need to."

Without waiting for further reply, Tristal looked into the rana's eyes. "This is mercy." And she slit his throat so deeply, she cut his gills and ended his life instantly.

"The ability to communicate without speaking opens oneself to an intimacy not even experienced by most lovers. One must beware of that level of intimacy. It can be glorious, or it can be deadly."
~ Unknown

37

S he could feel his anger and frustration before he even entered the large arena where she had moved the dragon egg. In a rush, she moved to wrap herself around it, leaving her meal to bake in the tremendous heat of the suns.

The White Lord stomped through the large gate and glared up at her.

"This has gone on long enough. If it refuses to hatch, then drop it into the ocean. You are clearly wasting your time with it. You said there were others, so go find them. I will see this one is destroyed…"

Libitina roared in response, allowing smoke to exit her nostrils. She had never used her flames in response to the White Lord.

He stood his ground and continued to glare at her. "Enough!" he yelled at her, the power in his voice actually causing the stone tiers and walls surrounding them to shake.

She lowered her head so she could look him in the eyes, her wide maw just an arm's length from his chest.

For the last time, this cannot and will not be rushed. She stared deeply into his eyes, and she looked into his mind. *What is the rush all of a sudden?*

The White Lord grew furious at her probing and reacted by shoving her head aside with both of his hands, revealing his incredible physical strength.

She snatched her head back and shook away the feel of his claws on her scaly skin. In that moment, she realized their relationship had changed. He no longer respected her as his equal. Had he ever really respected her? The thought nagged at the back of her mind and echoed from the soul in the egg.

She moved the egg with her tail so that it was behind her and away from her feet, and she rose into a standing position looking down on the White Lord.

How dare you lay hands on me! she bellowed in his mind, and she let heat radiate off her as she prepared to expel fire at him should he move toward her again.

In reaction to her yelling in his brain, he staggered as though hit in the head, and she saw something she didn't understand. She gulped and swallowed the gases that would have incinerated him if she wanted. The impact of what she saw in his mind left her own mind reeling.

The White Lord stepped backward away from her, rage and sudden uncertainty in his eyes. But his mental blocks slid firmly back in place.

"That egg will hatch. Today. Or I will see it destroyed."

His threat left no room for argument, and he gave Libitina another withering glare as he left the arena.

Libitina watched him go and shook her head trying to recall what she saw more clearly.

She unconsciously moved the egg back to the center of her body where she curled around it. She too was impatient for the little dragon to hatch, but something deep inside her told her she was right not

271

to force it. She wanted to hatch the egg right. She wanted the dragon soul inside to be on her side, to be with her, to be her… friend?

She sighed. She would never call the White Lord her friend. They were allies, and that was all. He showed admiration in regard to her intelligence, her size, and her bloodlust, but beyond that, he showed her little interest. Now she began to suspect it was all simply a means to an end.

He was using her.

She admitted she knew that from the beginning. But at the beginning, she was the only one, and she didn't realize there were others. She fell in line with his plans to terrorize and take over not just Mygras but also Mythos. He sought revenge, she knew not what for, and she didn't think she cared.

Till now.

She laid her head on her front feet and stared out the gate at the White Lord's receding figure on his way back to his fortress. He had lost just a split second of control, and she saw past his mental blocks. Just an instant, but in that instant, she saw a piece that shook her to her core.

She watched him till he disappeared from sight and realized she had a choice to make. Now that choice seemed much more critical than she would have originally thought. She looked at the egg and nudged it with her muzzle.

Stay there, safe in your shell. I have to think.

The soul didn't respond though Libitina could have sworn it emanated more warmth for just a second.

As she lay there pondering what she had seen and the sudden strain on her relationship with the White Lord, she realized that he had to have been lying to her. She saw death and destruction, but she saw that within the plans he had revealed to her over the years, but this time was different.

This time, she saw not the death and destruction of the people on Mythos, but of her! And the dragon in the shell! She could have sworn she saw a wish for destruction of all dragons. But that didn't make sense. Everything she had grown up being told and taught during her time with the White Lord suddenly burned inside her and left a bitter taste in her mouth.

She had been lied to, but she could not fathom exactly what the lie was.

Was he out to destroy her?

After claiming to be her ally?

Was he having her search for dragon eggs to see them destroyed too?

That didn't make any sense. His sudden impatience to have another dragon join them in their quest implied there was something much deeper going on.

Libitina huffed smoke out of her nostrils in frustration.

One thing was for certain. This dragon soul was not ready to hatch, and as far as Libitina could tell, it was entirely because of things it was sensing in its environment.

A plan formed in her mind, and she smiled a toothy grin. She needed to know the truth about what she saw in the White Lord's thoughts. She also needed to satisfy this inherent need to see this dragon soul hatched properly. She knew she was not going to be able to find the truth or hatch the egg if she remained at Croglinke.

She let her mind travel outward and realized that there were only a few guards standing outside the gate. They were not there for her protection—this she knew. They were more like spies for the White Lord. They wouldn't be a problem.

She cast her thoughts into their minds, encouraging them to approach her in the arena. When the three stood in front of her, confusion on their faces at having been summoned by her, she didn't hesitate. In one quick snap, she collected the three in her mouth, their bodies hanging limp from her jaw. She crunched on them, making short work of their bodies, and trusted that their nourishment would be enough until she could adequately distance herself from the White Lord and his own telepathy.

She took the egg gingerly in her jaws and launched herself into the air with two mighty beats of her wings. One more powerful pump of her wings and she was above the arena walls. With the next mighty pumps of her wings, she directed her course east away from Croglinke and toward the Ercrog Desert, a mighty desert where only the crazy chose to live out their lives.

She thought grimly, I just might be crazy. He will come after me. Will I have enough time to know the truth? Will I want him to find me?

"Return.
Return to find a place you made so many
memories.
Return to find it has not changed.
Return to find that for all that has not changed,
beneath the surface, it has changed in ways you
never comprehended.
Return to find that you have been changed as
well.
Return to find that for all the ways you have
changed,
you are still essentially unchanged."
~ The Song of the Traveler

38

Aldrina saw to it that Estryl was seated with her leg propped up comfortably at the front of the wagon for the dwarf refused to sit in the back. Next to Estryl sat Stranick, his head still bandaged and one arm in a sling, but he looked remarkably better and was eager to be on the road again.

In the back of the wagon, forced to recline per Aldrina's strict demands as her healer, Virconia stared at the cloth covering of the wagon in frustration. She simmered inside with a sense of helplessness. She wanted to be out of the wagon, ready to fight and defend the group from whatever might be ahead of them.

The horse that carried Valero and Elder Martan was secured to the back of the wagon. Everyone sat on their own horse waiting for Aldrina to climb into the wagon where she could keep Virconia company while they traveled. She climbed up and nodded to Estryl at the front who nudged Stranick.

Stranick flicked the reins of the horses and started the wagon moving slowly out of the camp. Grazina rode to the front, leading the way along old trails that led to Elmnas rather than taking the more traveled roads. She thought it would be more prudent to take the longer, less traveled route in hopes they would attract less attention than if they traveled along the main road to Elmnas.

Orinus, Tristal, Colna, and Layni rode staggered behind the wagon. Now that they were with Grazina, it was natural for Colna and Layni to follow the princess's lead. Orinus was relieved. He did not want to lead. He still wasn't exactly sure he wanted to continue with this strange group although he was still intrigued by Estryl and had not had a chance to get to know her or learn more of what her use of magic was.

He had learned from Aldrina that Estryl was a blacksmith, and she had shown him the amulet that Estryl had crafted for her. He had been astonished by the flawless workmanship, considering Estryl was the youngest dwarf he had ever met. He would have expected craftmanship of her level to belong to that of a grizzled old dwarf who had hundreds of years of experience under their belt. Aldrina had told him that Estryl said that it was like singing a song, but that made no sense at all to Orinus. Intrigued by a magic he had never witnessed, he decided to stick with the group. After all, he told himself, he could just leave whenever he wanted. But then he looked back at Tristal, her arm fully healed with Aldrina's help, and realized he was lying to himself.

Tristal, riding next to Layni, saw Orinus glance back at her. She frowned in his direction, and he flashed her a sly smirk before turning back in his saddle to face the wagon, striking up a conversation with Colna next to him. She couldn't hear what they were saying, and she didn't care. She wanted to turn around and rejoin her unit at Syan Lake. She wondered how the people of the lakeside settlements were faring against the onslaught of creatures. Not knowing set her on edge, especially in light of the numerous skirmishes she had been part of ever since leaving Wargate. Before she left Wargate with her unit, it sounded as though these attacks were few and far between, a rare settlement here or there, mostly lone farms set off apart from others. But she realized that Wargate either did not know how bad it was truly getting, or they were downplaying it. In her mind, it didn't matter which. They needed to be told the truth, and they needed to get more units and patrols out to help the people of Mythos.

Beside her, Layni sat stiffly in the saddle. Since the fight in the desert, where Valero's group had come so close to defeat, she could not shake the fear that had settled deep within her. She flinched at every sound that she couldn't immediately identify. She kept her head on a swivel, on the verge of crying out with every unknown shadow she saw under the thick canopy of the trees of the Deep Forest. She barely slept, and while Colna knew it and had begged her to either have Orinus help her or at least ride in the wagon so she could rest, Layni took one look at the wagon and all she saw was a deathtrap waiting to happen. There was no way she was going to sit in it and wait for the inevitable.

Colna glanced back at Layni from time to time. She was genuinely concerned for the young elf. She had recommended her for the mission to find Grazina because Layni was quick-minded, good with a sword, and being groomed to join Colna's archers, the main protective guard for Elmnas. Colna had high hopes for her, but in the aftermath of this mission, she saw a broken woman; she knew that Layni would never join her archers. She sighed deeply in resignation as she continued her conversation with Orinus talking of random facts about the Deep Forest and its flora and fauna. Inwardly, she hoped that Layni could heal her internal wounds and find peace. She hoped she could as well.

Inside the wagon, Aldrina watched Virconia who had slipped off to sleep. Aldrina held her hand over her Dark Elf friend and felt for more internal bleeding. Feeling none, she checked Virconia's other wounds, which all seemed to be healing normally. Leaning back with a sigh of relief, she looked out the front of the wagon and stared at the back of the Elven princess. Aldrina recalled how Olphara had been able to sense her heritage, but could Grazina? Could Grazina possibly guess that they were in fact cousins? Aldrina felt dread hit her in the gut. She did not want to go to Elmnas, nor did she want everyone to know her secret. She felt certain if she revealed what they didn't know about her, she would be forced into a role, a political web that she wanted no part of. She just wanted to help people, and she wanted to continue to be a healer. Her thoughts went back to how Olphara had sensed her lineage, and she thought to herself, *Can Grazina sense it too? Will her parents?* The question nagged at her and nagged at her until she finally drifted off to sleep.

Grazina rode back toward the group and motioned for them to halt. Waving at Colna, she turned her horse and waited for her to catch up.

"Thank the gods this last part of our journey was uneventful," Colna commented upon reaching the princess's side.

Grazina nodded. She glanced back at the party as they waited. "I imagine they will still need to display their weapons?"

Colna shook her head. "No, with you and I leading them in and Layni at the back, we will be allowed in with little questioning."

Grazina raised an eyebrow at Colna. "Really?"

Colna nodded and Grazina turned her focus back to the way ahead where the old trail met with the Elmnas Road just outside the perimeter of Elmnas itself. "Will you go let them know we are about to enter Elmnas?"

"Yes, Your Grace," replied Colna and saw Grazina visibly wince.

"I guess I will have to get used to that again."

Colna smiled and laid a hand over her friend's hand. "I guess you will, but I can see you're capable of handling whatever awaits you, awaits us, now we are here at home."

Grazina cast a nervous glance back at the group. "Whatever will mother and father think about us coming home with dwarves, mages, and a Drow?"

Colna shrugged, "Who cares? We know them to be our friends and allies. Once, the king and queen realize we trust them, respect them, and accept them as such, they will as well. And the council and the others will all follow their example."

Grazina watched Colna ride up to the wagon and then to the trio at the back of the group. After she was done, she rode back to ride beside her princess.

"All set?" Colna asked, sensing nervousness in her friend.

Grazina turned her gaze to the path ahead and nodded firmly. "Let's go."

As they led the way out of the trees and into a giant clearing in the middle of the Deep Forest, she could not help but gasp in awe at the majesty and beauty of her home, the home to the Forest Elves. The clearing spread outward in a massive circle, but in the center of the clearing was an ancient tree that dwarfed all the trees of the Deep Forest, rising so high it appeared to touch the clouds. As she and Colna led the way, she heard the gasps and whispers from the others behind them. She continued to share their wonder as she also took in the home she had missed for so long.

The tree's canopy spread wide, casting perpetual shade over much of the clearing, and at the base of the tree extended its equally gigantic root system. Carved into its massive trunk was a magically created palace of twisting and winding branches that wrapped around the trunk with doors, windows, and palisades open to the cover of the tree itself. The palace itself was several dozens of stories high, housing the royal chambers, the gathering rooms, the council's chambers, and the member's quarters, plus the archives, the library, and the quarters for the most trusted advisors and leaders of the Forest Elves who chose to live within the tree itself. Each level of the palace, made up of intricately woven branches and magically carved-out hollows, glowed despite the lack of sunlight that reached the trunk. The top level of the palace, which was nestled in the crook of a major split in the trunk where it began to branch out for the canopy, glowed with the blue light of captured magic.

Orinus, gazing up at the blue glow, rode up to Colna, and pointed at it. "Is that the life force?"

Colna followed Orinus's gaze and smiled. "Yes. If you stand in the center of the dais there, you can look down into the center of the tree itself. It is said that the elves who planted the seed of Elmnas each gave a little of their own life force to help shape the tree. The effect was the hollow, which is sacred to us. Once a year as the tree's new ring is added to its trunk, the hollow glows even brighter, lighting up the entire tree, this open clearing, and penetrates even into the Deep Forest. The magical currents that touch the life force during that time often bless those standing closest to it with abilities."

Grazina smiled and added to the conversation, "One year, it blessed me with the ability to speak with the animals."

Orinus turned to look at the princess. "But you cannot anymore?"

She shook her head. "No. It lasted till the next ring was complete, but it was wonderful to speak with the birds and the creatures who reside with us in the tree and to work alongside the healers to help the sick and hurt animals that we often care for, to be able to calm them, or to better understand their injuries through the communication. Even after I lost

281

it, I have still maintained a connection with most animals that allows me to gain their trust faster. I guess it didn't wear off entirely," she paused in thought before Colna inserted, "I think, though it has not been proven, that the tree's life force enhances the skills we already have within us. In Grazina's case, it made her aware of her own natural affinity with animals because I do not believe she was aware of it prior to that."

Orinus nodded in understanding, but continued to stare up at it as he could feel the way the life of the tree affected the magical currents around it.

He murmured, "I wonder that this is not something that is commonly talked of beyond Elmnas…"

Colna and Grazina glanced at each other.

"Well, while it's not a secret by any means, it is sacred, and so we do naturally guard it as much as we can from the outside world. Most of our elves never leave Deep Forest, so they do not have the opportunity to tell anyone. And traders and travelers? Most do not seem to care about the magical glow. Maybe they assume it is our own magic at work. Or maybe they simply do not care."

The three fell silent as they continued across the clearing and took in the rest of the tree before them. Built among and into the roots were homes and shops, so perfectly woven into the root system and constructed so flawlessly it appeared the roots had grown the homes and shops. Then just beyond the edges of the roots were gardens and fields of every kind of food imaginable. And in the fields, hundreds of elves were working.

Grazina teared up at the sight of all the elves and her home. Had she been gone so long? She noted how much was very much as she remembered it, but the more she saw, the more subtle changes she also saw. She smiled in sudden pride. This was her home. As nervous as she was, she realized with a definite feeling of wholeness that she was home again, and that was where she belonged.

*"When Elmnas was but a seedling, we gathered
about it, the elves united. We sang songs that
forced it to sway and dance, to reach for the sky, to
move faster than nature. When Elmnas was a
willowy sapling, we gathered about it, the elves in
sync. We danced about it and raised up prayers to
Kudhe to bless this beloved tree, a remnant from a
time we cannot return to. When Elmnas reached its
full glory, we gathered about it. We elves are no
longer of one blood and one mind. We mourned
our differences, but we celebrated them too. At the
roots of The Great Tree, we buried our past and we
sowed seeds for a future where we might be united
once more. Ah, Elmnas, protected by our Forest
Elves, how we long to rest in the shadow of your
branches once more. Lord Kudhe, let it be."*
~ *Prayer of the Wanderer, the White Elf*

39

*T*he group was called to a halt beyond the
fields. At the edge of the first building, a
dozen armed elves waited with their
weapons ready but not drawn. The lead elf of the
guard unit strode toward the group, his eyes boring
into the three leading the way. Glancing over their
weapons before he took in their faces, he finally
looked up and immediately threw himself to the
ground.

"Your Highness!" Calling behind him, he
ordered, "Go to the king immediately and inform him
Princess Grazina has returned and Captain Colna as
well!"

He heard the scrambling run of one of the elves behind him, and he raised himself up off the ground, lifting his eyes to meet those of his princess.

"With hearts as one, My Lady…"

Grazina got off her horse and stepping toward the guard, smiled warmly at him. "With hearts as one. You are?"

"Captain Aurez, captain of the guard." He bowed before the princess and then stood straight noting that all his guard behind him were still bowed on the ground. He snapped his fingers and the guard rose to their feet, putting their weapons away.

Reaching out, he took the reins of Grazina's horse and nodded up at Colna, who watched the exchange without comment. Aurez took in the rest of the group, noting his general's absence.

"General…?"

Colna interrupted him quietly, "Died heroically in battle."

Aurez instantly lowered his gaze and touched his chest with his closed fist in honor of Valero. "May the gods grant him eternal peace."

Colna said nothing as a tear slipped down her cheek. Aurez raised his eyes to meet hers with compassion and sincere remorse. She smiled lightly at the man then cleared her throat. "We are all weary, Captain, and we have wounded among us. Will you please lead us in and have someone see that healers are brought to assist our healer with our wounded?"

Aurez snapped to attention and turned to give orders.

Just as he finished, a runner from the palace raced up to them. "The king wishes for them to be brought directly to him and the queen. Without delay."

Aurez nodded and looked at Grazina and Colna, ignoring Orinus. "Those wounded who cannot walk will go to our healers, but the rest of you must come with me."

Excitement and nervousness rippled through the group, but following Grazina and Colna's example, everyone except Stranick got off their horses or climbed off the wagon and followed Aurez, who was leading the way through the lanes between the roots and up the wide stairs that wrapped the trunk up to the lower levels of the palace.

The group lingered in a large open-air space outside the throne room. Colna sat with Estryl, who had to sit and rest her body after the laborious climb up the side of the tree. Aldrina wrung her hands nervously, equally worried about Stranick and Virconia, who were not well enough to join the group, and anxious over meeting her aunt and uncle for the first time. While anxiety ran through her, Orinus paced the space, his own curiosity tempering his nervousness at meeting the rulers of the Forest Elves. Tristal also paced though her pacing was from a desire to rush along to Wargate to give her reports and begin planning strategies and defenses against the rising attacks she was certain were driven by the White Lord.

The door to the throne room swung inward and Captain Aurez stepped out. "Princess, will you please come with me? The king and queen would like to greet you privately first."

Grazina, who had been standing at a rail overlooking the Elven city below, turned to face the captain. She took a deep breath to steady her nerves and nodded as she walked toward him. She noted Colna rise, but she waved her back and tilted her head as she shrugged her shoulders, indicating to her old friend that she would be fine.

She stepped through the door and it shut quietly behind her, leaving her new friends to resume their own internal emotions as they waited to join her.

After nearly an hour, the door opened again. The group, now all seated together on low benches, rose as Grazina came back into the open-air space. Colna smiled widely at the appearance of her friend. Grazina had left them in her traveling clothes. She had been dirty and unkempt, but now, standing before them, she was transformed. Standing in a long lavender gown with her hair washed and put up in the elegant fashion of the elves of the royal house, she looked every bit the princess they knew her to be. She smiled at the group and motioned for them to follow her.

They silently obeyed and walked behind her into the throne room and then allowed her to position them in a line before the thrones. She took point in front of them and waited in silence.

From a side door, they watched as the king and queen joined them, guards hidden in alcoves snapping to attention, heard but not seen. The king and queen stood before their thrones and sat in unison, both still emotional from their reunion with their daughter. After taking a breath to steady her voice, also still emotional, Grazina bowed to her parents and waved a hand at the group assembled behind her.

"My Lord and Lady, I would like to introduce you to the people who I have met on my journey home. Their own journeys were leading them here to seek guidance, to give report, and to seek your help. May I introduce them each to you now?"

King Mronas nodded and waved to someone standing off to the side. "Bartholomew, would you please join us and document this?"

The group noted the older elf as he moved out of the shadows, a tablet in his arms.

Grazina moved to the end of the line. At a signal from Bartholomew that he was ready to write, she began to introduce the group, one by one. Once she got to the end of the line, she turned to face her parents.

"Not with us at the moment are the injured who are being helped by our healers. There is a Drow ranger by the name of Virconia, sent by King Aris. And another Silver Dwarf called Stranick, who is brother to Estryl. Then there are our deceased." She drew quiet and noted the emotions playing over the faces of both Colna and Estryl. She stepped toward the thrones of her parents and in a quieter, gentler voice pronounced, "General Valero Ald-Bric was killed in battle, fighting heroically to get to me and fulfill his mission given by you. He will be missed…" She paused and waited for the unbidden gasps that echoed from the alcoves for Valero had been beloved by all the Elven troops. Then she looked at Estryl before looking back to her parents.

"We also lost Elder Martan of the Silver Dwarves who was killed during an attack on his caravan. He had been entrusted with bringing Estryl to the Forest Elves in search of knowledge and training. On behalf of our new friends, and all the elves of Elmnas, I ask that due honors be given to both our fallen general and this fallen elder."

King Mronas rose to his feet and stepped down to stand in front of Colna. "My dear friend, I have no words to convey the heavy loss we all share with you. You can be certain we will honor our friend and our warrior as is due him."

He took Colna's hand and squeezed it gently, watching emotions roll through her eyes that she struggled to keep from her face. As a tear ran down her cheek betraying her, he pressed his forehead to hers and whispered an Elven prayer.

Then he stepped away and moved to stand in front of Estryl, who leaned heavily on a crutch tucked under her arm. "And you, Estryl, our honored guest, I assure you that we will honor Elder Martan as you see fit. If you wish him to be sent along to the Silver Isles, we will see it done with all expediency. You have but to tell us what you think is best."

Estryl met the Elven king's clear gaze. In his eyes, she saw sincere remorse and gentleness, but deeper within she saw a strong and willful presence, comforting and intimidating both at once. She lowered her eyes. "I'm not certain what my people would prefer. If I could send word…"

The king nodded. "It will be sent at once. Bartholomew will see to it."

He turned to step back up to his throne but then thought better of it. He instead turned to face

Aldrina, noting that she seemed to want to melt into the floor.

Standing in front of her, he gently reached out and raised her chin so that they were looking into each other's eyes. He felt her tense up, and then force herself to relax.

He smiled at her. "You look so much like your mother,'" he whispered barely loud enough for her to hear, certain no one else heard either. The blood rushed to her face as she realized he would not allow her to ignore her heritage. She closed her eyes, unable to look at him. He dropped his hand and moved away. When she opened her eyes, he was back on his throne, holding his wife's hand. Together they rose.

"The queen and I would like to spend a few days getting to know our daughter again. During these three days, we invite you all to rest in quiet and peace among our people. Recover. Heal. Mourn. Rest. We will meet with you all again, I promise."

The king noted Tristal's sudden anxiety. He raised a hand toward her, suspecting she was eager to be on her way. "I have no doubt you all have reports to share with us and to send to your own people. I also have reports to share with each of you concerning events I am certain you are as of yet unaware of. But for now, I see you each need food, baths, sleep, healers…. So please, take these days to get those things."

Abruptly he turned and led his queen out of the room, followed by Bartholomew.

As the group watched them leave, Aurez stepped forward from the side of the room. "Princess, I have been directed to lead you to your quarters, while your friends are shown to their own quarters for the next few days."

Grazina turned to the group. "I am sorry I have to leave you now. But I will try my best to see each of you as soon as I'm able." Without another word, she turned to follow Captain Aurez, while the others were led out of the throne room by another guard.

*"It is said that Siki, our Father, created Inda,
our first sun with its red hues to remind us upon
waking to be grateful that our blood still pumps in
our veins. It is also said that Cria, our Mother,
created Sola, our second sun, with its blue hues to
remind us upon setting that death is but a heartbeat
away. Thank the Creators; we live under their
combined purple hues that teach us to count our
blessings and to live so that the rising is a blessing
and the setting is an encouragement."*
~ Queen Myralli, *A Mother's Heart*

40

*T*he three days passed quickly for the travel
weary group. During their arranged time
in seclusion, in order to prevent rumors
and gossip from spreading regarding the events of
their travels, the group were forced to interact more
closely with each other. They found that they
differed in so many ways but were also drawn
together. As they relaxed in the comfortable
surroundings, they found they had formed a bond
even in their short times together.

Aldrina, along with some of the Willows that
lived among the Forest Elves, worked diligently to
heal Virconia, Stranick, and Estryl more completely.
As a result, all three were out of bed and interacting
with the rest of the group as they gathered for meals
or simply enjoyed strolling the promenades that
joined their rooms and common area.

In an effort to minimize news spreading before the
king and council had had time to sort through it and
decide how they should react, Colna and Layni were

292

ordered to remain among the group as well. Colna spent a great deal of her time watching over Layni.

She sat on a cushioned sofa and watched as Layni paced the balcony, trailing her hand along the rail, her lips moving but no sound escaping her lips.

"She witnessed something that broke her."

Colna snapped her attention to Virconia who sat gently beside her, her voice low so it wouldn't carry across the common space. Colna stared at the Drow trying to discern if there was something behind the simple comment. Seeing no malice and sensing nothing more than an observation being made, Colna relaxed and nodded.

"She had not been battle tested prior to this. This was supposed to be a simple mission. We knew there were creatures on the move, but we had no idea to such an extent or that they would be so organized. Our lack of preparation…" she paused as the thought continued on within her, *killed my love and broke poor Layni.*

Virconia knew that the general had been Colna's mate even though she had not met him. Seeing how broken Layni was, Virconia could not help but wonder what it was that caused the other three—Colna, Orinus, and Tristal—to keep it together so well. Or were they hiding their own trauma?

Colna turned to face Virconia. "Our travels were very similar. Abrupt. Violent. Unexpected. Yet here we all remain." She waved her hand around the room, her voice louder than she intended, and the others all paused to look at her as she spoke. "Here we remain. We. While the greatest of us lies dead. And the purest of us paces broken." A grimace spread across her face, and Virconia could see the tears brimming in the archer's eyes even as everyone

293

else stiffened and looked away at the pain and honest regret they shared with Colna.

Colna, paying no attention to the others and their discomfort, bore into Virconia. "What makes us so special that the gods allowed us to live? What is so special about me? Can you tell me? What about you? What is so important about you that you're still with us? Why are we untainted while that young woman sees monsters and demons on a clear sunny day? Why are we so unaffected?"

Virconia blinked at Colna's questions. How many times had she wondered the very same thing as she witnessed the violence of the world? She stared back at Colna, her red eyes meeting Colna's green.

"I don't know, Colna," she said quietly. She glanced at Layni who had stopped pacing and stood in silence, just staring at Colna as though seeing her for the first time. In a sudden flurry of movement, Layni dashed to Colna's side and threw herself at the older elf, crying madly and asking to be held. The others moved to pull Layni away, but Virconia stopped them with a raised hand, motioning them all to stand back. They all looked down at Colna, who leaned over Layni, brushing her hair out of her face, crying and whispering to the younger elf. Virconia stood up and pulled a blanket that had been placed beside the sofa over Colna's shoulders. Colna looked up at her, the well of tears flowing without check, her face twisted in a mask of profound anger and grief. But she nodded her thanks to the Drow, who then turned to the others and motioned them to go to the other side of the room.

Later that day, Captain Aurez entered the common area to find the group scattered about and understandably subdued. Colna rose to meet him, having gained control of her emotions once more. "Captain?"

He bowed slightly and motioned at the others. "I have been directed to bring you all before the council, one at a time, so that an accounting of your different travels can be logged and decided over."

Colna nodded. "I understand. Who do they want to see first?"

Aurez looked past Colna at the group and then back at her, a sheepish look on his face. "They'd like to see Layni first. There is concern that her current condition could…"

Colna sighed deeply, but she understood. "Very well, but I have decided to accept responsibility for her. May I join her?"

Aurez shifted on his feet and frowned, but after a moment's consideration, nodded. "They might not allow you in the chambers with her, but you can wait outside so if your assistance is needed, you will be readily available."

Colna nodded, then turned to the group. "We are to be interviewed now. This is routine," she said as she noted the alarm in some of the faces that looked to her. "I will go with Layni first. Then Captain Aurez will call you each as the council and our king demands."

Moving to Layni, who sat rocking on the edge of a chair, Colna took her hand and led her out of the room ahead of Captain Aurez. He glanced around the room at the faces representing other races and cultures. As he closed the door on them, he hoped whatever they had to tell was something that Mythnium could endure.

Tristal slapped the table in frustration as Orinus won another round of cards. "You play dirty, mage," she accused.

Orinus smiled crookedly at the White Elf and then shrugged. "If you can't catch me cheating, then it didn't happen. No?"

Tristal glared at him and then tossed another silver coin on the table. "Again."

Orinus laughed, truly enjoying the banter and distraction. He shuffled the cards and was about to divide them out when Estryl approached. "Can we join the game?" she asked and nodded over her shoulder to indicate Stranick behind her.

Tristal looked irritated, but Orinus spread his arms wide and motioned for them to take the two remaining chairs. "Toss in a coin to get your cards. Winner gets the pot at the end of each round."

Estryl sat opposite Stranick and the two gathered their cards as Orinus passed them out.

Tristal leaned in and peered at them both. "You dwarves do know how to play, right? I don't want to have to explain…"

"Yes, Tiny," responded Stranick, surly at the way Tristal sneered at his race, "we know how to play." He winked at his sister whose eyebrows raised even as Tristal tensed at being called "Tiny." "I hope you are ready to lose whatever coins you have left." He looked at Orinus and continued, "And beware, mage, we dwarves don't take kindly to cheaters."

Orinus chuckled and nodded.

As the game began and the bets and plays moved around the table, Estryl pondered out loud. "Now that they know everything we know, what do you think will happen?" She looked at Orinus for an answer.

Orinus stared at his cards, not letting on that he heard her question. But as he laid out the cards he was playing that round, he looked at the dwarf woman and leaned back in his chair.

"I imagine that Tristal's request to contact Wargate has already been granted. With what we have learned about the attack on Farcaste Reach and this rumor of a dragon reborn, you can bet that the Forest Elves and all the leaders of all our peoples will want to know and prepare."

Tristal snorted. "No one is prepared. Not even my people. Not even the Drow, by my guess." She glanced over at Virconia who sat alone in a corner, content to observe everyone else. Her lids were low over her eyes, making it hard to tell if she was still awake or taking a nap.

Tristal turned back to face the others at the table. "If the White Lord truly has a dragon now, we will be hard pressed to keep him exiled to Mygras."

Orinus nodded. "I agree."

"Well, thanks, mage, because I needed your vali-…"

The door to the common area swung open once more. Grazina and Aldrina stepped into the room. Everyone stood and moved before them.

Grazina stood quietly while Aldrina looked as though she were scared out of her mind. Orinus stepped toward her. "Aldrina, are you okay?"

"What? Oh… yes… Sorry."

Tristal looked at them both and exclaimed, "You are family! You two…You're related!"

The others glanced at her as she stared at the women in shock. They turned back and suddenly saw the similarities in the women for themselves.

Estryl broke the silence and stepped to Aldrina's side. "Is it true?"

Aldrina nodded and looked desperate, like she was ready to run away.

Estryl took her hand. "Not sisters, surely."

Grazina, noting her cousin's silence, responded for her. "Aldrina is not my sister. She is, however, my cousin. She is the rightful ruler of the Ebony Isles."

At the announcement, Aldrina visibly withdrew into herself while everyone else reacted with surprise and then excitement. Estryl though could see how terrified Aldrina was. She held her friend's hand and squeezed it gently then leaned in and looked up into her friend's face.

"Did you know?" she asked.

Aldrina nodded miserably. "Olphara guessed it long ago. She informed the king and had tried to convince me to return to Elmnas, but I chose to become a healer…. Now that I am here…"

Grazina put her arm around Aldrina. "I understand the burden you carry. It is what drove me away from my home for so long. No one here will push you to do something you are not ready or willing to do."

Aldrina looked into her cousin's eyes and saw truth reflected there. She smiled and then looked at the group. "I don't know if the king and queen will announce my heritage, but I ask that you all please keep it just among us for now. Until I decide…"

Estryl, still standing at her side, smiled widely up at her. "I knew it the moment I met you! You are special. You are a healer. You are of royal blood. I knew it. I just didn't know exactly what. No matter what you choose, we are here for you."

Grazina added, "We are here with you."

*"How Mythnium trembled. How suddenly small
did our great world feel. On the wings of rumors,
Mygras was not far enough for we learned that the
White Lord had gained an ally, an ally straight out
of our world's crumbled past."*
~ *King Aris of the Drow*

41

*M*ronas sat at the center of the long table that was shaped like a crescent moon. Myralli sat on his left, Grazina on his right, and Bartholomew to her right. The rest of the Elven council members sat along the same side, and they all welcomed the Willows before them with concerned stares.

Olphara stood tall among her clan leaders. She was exhausted and dirty from weeks of traveling both below and above ground, hoping that the White Lord gave up his pursuit of them though they really had no way of knowing.

Beside her on a litter piled with blankets and cushions to help him sit upright was an even more weary Pruzin. Their travels made it impossible for the healers to fully focus their attentions on him in their rush to get to Elmnas.

Mronas stared at the two old elves and at the six leaders behind them. The remaining two dozen that had survived the attack from the White Lord were being ministered to down on the ground level, most of them fearful to enter the tree itself.

"Your Majesties," Pruzin started, his speech brittle and coarse, "the White Lord has a Red Dragon."

"That can't be!" argued one of the elves seated far down the table. "Dragons haven't existed since before the Cataclysm, and we simply aren't certain they existed even then!"

Pruzin shifted on his litter and stared at the elf. "Are you calling me a liar?"

The elf gritted his teeth but said nothing, so Pruzin looked back at the king and queen.

"I saw it with my own eyes. I understand the hesitation to believe that they exist, even one. Had I not seen it for myself with these two eyes, I would doubt it as well. But I can assure you, that dragon is real. It is big. Big enough that it tore down the doors of the tower at Farcaste Reach just by leaning against them. Furthermore, it does in fact breath fire. The legends surrounding Red Dragons, at least, are true."

Silence hung over the council chamber as everyone weighed the historian's words. There was no doubt he was telling the truth. The facts were etched in his recovering body, on his weary face still bruised from the beatings at the direction of the White Lord. There was no denying that the White Lord was growing bolder. He had ventured far enough inland to attack Olphara's camp and to lay siege to Farcaste Reach. The actions themselves bore witness to a bold confidence that must have driven the White Lord to begin his reach north once again.

After several long minutes, Myralli rose to her feet and addressed the room. "In light of the weariness of our guests following the events that led them to us, I suggest we break for now and meet again tomorrow. Let us allow the people of Olphara's clan a chance to rest, eat, wash, and mourn their dead."

"My Queen, I second your suggestion, but as tomorrow is the Celebration of Passing for Valero, let us meet again two days hence."

Myralli smiled down at Bartholomew, thankful for the reminder of the passing of their own, and she looked to Olphara and Pruzin. "You are welcome here, and we are grateful for the journey you took to bring us this news. We know it cost you, and we cannot repay you the lives the journey cost. Please, accept our hospitality as we welcome you, our cousins, our blood, back to the tree of our heritage. Please know all your people are welcome among us. My personal guard will show you to your quarters and you need but ask if you lack for anything."

Olphara bowed deeply, and Pruzin bowed his head as guards scooped to pick up his litter and carry him out of the chambers.

"Hold one moment, please, Olphara," interrupted King Mronas.

Olphara turned back to look at the king while Pruzin was carried out. "I thought you would be pleased to know that Aldrina has safely arrived in the company of the dwarf and her brother."

Olphara smiled weakly at the news and she bowed again. "Thank you, my lord. I am glad to hear it. I would be pleased to see her again if that is possible."

The king nodded. "I will see that she knows where to find you."

Olphara bowed her head and left the room, leaving the royal family and the council to talk amongst themselves.

Aldrina watched the Ceremony of Passing from the balcony where she stood behind the king and queen. Beside her stood Grazina on one side and her great-uncle Bartholomew on the other. High above the rest of the Forest Elves who were gathered to honor their beloved General Valero, they watched in silence. The balcony on which they were standing overlooked the ceremonial grounds where every festival and major event was celebrated. Aldrina noted how the roots of the tree had spread around the large area in an oval. The ridges in the roots provided stairs and rows of seats all the way around so that it appeared as though the entire population had gathered within them.

In the center of the ceremonial grounds, a large pyre had been built that held the bodies of the general and of the Dwarven elder, who was being honored as a hero at the request of the Silver Dwarves. They wished his body to be returned to Hux, the god of the dwarves, and welcomed into the Great Halls of the Craftsman. Aldrina watched as three figures in robes of different colors stepped up on a raised platform. The first was the priestess of death, a high priestess devoted to Sayki, the goddess of death. Dressed in robes of white that were trimmed in brilliant gold and red, she lifted her arms to quiet the waiting crowd. Once the crowd was quiet, she turned toward the pyre and began to sing the "Song of Passing," a song that spoke of the legends and heroes of old, and asked Sayki to open the gates to the spirits of Valero and Martan that they may be received by the gods.

Once the high priestess of Sayki concluded the main portion of her song, a high priest stepped forward while the high priestess kept singing her

303

song, slightly subdued. The high priest, dressed in green robes trimmed with gold and blue, lifted his arms to the pyre and chanted a long chant to Kudhe, the god of the elves. He chanted asking that Kudhe welcome Valero to the Endless Forests of Eternity where Valero might rest in peace and wait to be reunited with his loved ones. Then he too stepped back and allowed a short priest in robes of black and purple trimmed with silver and white to step forward yelling loud chants to Hux.

Once the Dwarven priest finished his portion of the ceremony, the three lifted fiery torches from waiting stands and set the pyre ablaze. As the flames ripped through the pyre, the waiting elves gathered broke into a mournful song that Aldrina had never heard before. She glanced at Grazina and saw that her cousin had tears on her cheeks. Looking at the king and queen, and even her uncle, she noted they all mourned the passing of the elf they called Valero. Seeing the pain of their loss, sensing deep within her that their grief was genuine, her heart warmed to her new family, and she gained respect for them.

As she watched the entire Elven community of Elmnas mourn for a single elf and a dwarf that was a stranger to most of them, she noted a shift in herself. These were a people to stand with, to stand beside, to stand for. Unbidden, she wondered, Are the people of the Ebony Isles like this? Were they? Under the rule of this General Duwo, were they suffering? Or being divided?

She shook her head and then saw Bartholomew observing her closely. "As you come to know your people, you will find it harder and harder to turn away from the duty you inherit in honor of your people."

Aldrina blanched, feeling like he had read her mind, but she said nothing. Instead, she lowered her eyes back to the ending of the ceremony. She knew that the old elf was right. It would be harder. The longer she remained among them, the harder it would be to run. The harder it would be for her to just be a healer. But then she looked over at Grazina, the princess who ran, and she wondered what had brought her cousin back.

Meanwhile, around the massive trunk on the other side of the Elven city, Colna sat in the small yard of the house she had shared with Valero. Layni sat on the ground at her feet, and Colna hummed a tune to comfort Layni as she combed the younger elf's hair. With each stroke of the brush, Colna felt more and more responsible for Layni, who teetered on the edge of madness. Faint echoes from the Ceremony of Passing drifted over the city, and from the opposite side of the tree, Colna closed her eyes and envisioned Valero there with her. Her chest tightened as she recalled one of their last tender conversations early in the morning before they rose. They had talked of children. Now those children would never be.

Layni jerked under Colna's hands, jolting her to the present. "Shhhh, Layni. Shhhh…. You're okay."

Layni said nothing. She simply rocked from side to side, her eyes focused on something Colna could not see.

Colna leaned forward and whispered in the young elf's ear, "You are safe, child. Together, we are safe. You're with me now, and I will not leave you."

As she sat back upright and continued brushing Layni's hair, she looked at the letter on the table beside her, a letter to the Elven council resigning from her position among the guard to live a life of seclusion with Layni. She looked beyond the letter to a large pack waiting next to the door. Once she was done brushing and braiding Layni's hair, they would begin their journey deeper into the Deep Forest to a cabin Valero had built them at the base of the Walker Mountains on the western shores of Folgen Lake. There, she hoped, she and Layni could begin a new life.

Tell us of the dragons of old.
Sing us the songs of the mighty beasts.
Let us dream of them,
see visions of them,
remember them.
~Children's Dragon Song

42

After a few weeks, Estryl had gotten permission from the Elven council to set up a forge outside the perimeter of the great tree where she could keep learning her craft between her lessons with the Elven craftsmen. She and Stranick were hard at work helping Elven smiths craft blades, arrows, swords, and shields as a result of deliberations following their reports and the reports from Olphara and Pruzin. She thought of Pruzin as she worked on a blade. The old Willow was a resilient old elf. After the torture he endured, he had mostly healed and was now working with the Forest Elves to send a delegation to Farcaste Reach to rebuild and restore the tower and its precious histories. He had also made great effort to make sure Estryl was introduced to Elven elders who could help her learn more about her skill.

While she was lost in thoughts of her own, Orinus lounged on the ground nearby with his eyes closed. He so enjoyed watching how Estryl worked with magic. With his senses he could hear her singing and see the magical currents all around her dance and wave, moving together and apart outside of her, then within her body, then coming out of her hands, to her tools, and into the item she was working on. Every piece that she completed was perfectly designed with unexpected sigils and markings; for some, entire scenes depicted some element of nature that the owner felt most attuned to.

In just the short time that she and Stranick had been working, word had spread through Elmnas of her unique gift, and she was set to meet King Mronas again later that day. It was rumored that he wished her to make something for him, but if Estryl was nervous about taking on such a prestigious task, she gave no sign.

Orinus recalled his own audience with the king and council, and many of his initial fears had been relieved. He had wondered how much of his reputation preceded him. He didn't mind so much if the elves here feared him. A little healthy fear was a good thing, in his opinion, but he was not ready to be cast out away from the group, and he had no intention of trying to plead his case, a case he did not fully understand himself.

That first formal meeting had laid his fears to rest, but the second private meeting confirmed that he had nothing to fear from the Forest Elves. The meeting with the king had been incredibly laid back. Captain Aurez had led him to a small library where the king sat alone staring at a map. Orinus had stood in silence for several minutes before the king addressed him, and then he spoke only of his gratitude in helping locate the princess to see her safely home. Orinus had laughed out loud for he realized that the king knew Grazina had already been on her way home, and Orinus and the rest had simply stumbled onto her. With the realization that he had just passed a test of sorts, Orinus had stood in silence, but the king met Orinus's gaze. With a solemn promise, he swore that Orinus was welcome in Elmnas for as long as he liked. Then, just like that, the visit was ended, and Orinus was led back to the ground level where he had been given more than adequate accommodations in rooms he shared with Tristal, Estryl, and Stranick.

He smiled at his recollection of that meeting and then began to wonder how everyone else was doing. It had been several days since they had gotten together, he realized, and determined to make a point of having everyone meet within a day or so. He wasn't sure why, but he felt that each of them was going to be needed and soon. He pondered that for a moment, but then something caught his attention. At first, he thought he was feeling a surge in Estryl's magic, but when he opened his eyes, he saw that she and Stranick were no longer working, but were staring up at the sky beyond the canopy of the great tree.

Orinus followed their gaze and attuned his senses for what he was feeling was moving closer and whatever it was had the biggest push on magical currents he had ever felt. He stared but didn't see anything; then he heard a strange sound.

A deep *fwap fwap fwap* came from just over the top of the forest trees and the tops started to sway toward the great tree as though something were blowing them over.

As the deep sound grew closer, the magical currents grew even more intense, and Orinus drew as much as he could within himself. As he prepared to defend against whatever was approaching, he finally saw it move past the tops of the trees and make a wide loop between the canopy of the great tree and the top of the forest.

Orinus gaped in shock and wonder, and all around him, he heard horns, alarms, and cries of either excitement or fear; he could not tell which.

Flying above them—huge, menacing, and beautiful—was a giant Black Dragon.

$\mathcal{L}$ibitina stood at the edge of the coast where the water lapped the rocky beach and washed over her talons. She looked north over the ocean that was curtained with a fog so thick she could see the winds moving the water vapors in circles and vortexes, intimating a violence in the air that could consume anything that dared attempt to pass through.

Turning her attention to the tiny day-old Blue Dragon that stood sheltered by her thick front leg, she moved her head down to peer at it.

It sat on its haunches, flexing its leathery wings in the breeze off the water, but met her ruby red glare with his own icy blue stare.

This is the way? she asked.

I can feel them as strongly as you can. You know it is.

She touched her nose to its wings.

Your wings can't handle those winds.

The little dragon turned its head to examine its wings.

I will fly in your wake. If it proves too much, I will catch a ride.

She sensed the humor in the young one's thoughts and saw an image of it perched on her back. She scowled and huffed smoke at it, causing it to step backward out of the shelter of her leg so that the wind caught its wings and pushed it roughly away from her. She watched as it kept its head down and worked its wings in the wind. It finally got control and flew/hopped back to the shelter of her much larger body.

When do you want to go?

The little Blue Dragon turned its own gaze out to the thick fog, sensing that the fog was there by design. *I don't know about you, but I'd rather fly in the day than at night. At Inda's first light?*

Libitina nodded in agreement.

Together the Red and Blue Dragons watched as Sola, the second sun, set on the eastern horizon. Its blue hues cut through even the dense ground clouds, making the fog appear icy and cold. Then they both turned back toward the higher beach to settle in for the journey that would take them away from Mygras and away from the White Lord.

GLOSSARY

Species and Races

Dwarves

Deep Dwarves – native to the caves of the Walker Mountains; tribal society; live up to 600 years; short, stocky, fair complexion; masters of stonework

Silver Dwarves – native to the Silver Isles; complex society; live up to 600 years; short, stocky, ruddy complexion; masters of metalwork

Elves

Drow – Dark Elves; native to Netherland; monarchal society; as advanced as Forest Elves; main city is Ervenhall; live up to 400 years; medium height, slight but muscular build, dark skin; known for their red eyes; considered a malevolent race

Forest Elves – native to Deep Forest; more advanced monarchal society; main city is Elmnas; live up to 900 years; medium height, slender build, fair complexion; respected by Mythos society, in general

White Elves – native to Walker Mountains; tribal society; medium lifespan of up to 200 years; very short, very pale complexion, muscular; known as a warrior race

Willow Elves – scattered across Mythos; nomadic society; medium lifespan of up to 200 years; medium height, lithe build, fair to ruddy complexion; focused on working as healers and protectors of collected history of Mythnium

Dragons

Drake – evolved humanoid race of dragons now extinct; unknown lifespan; medium height, scaly skin; had been master craftsmen and artists

Demiods – extinct lizard-like dragons; unknown lifespan; small stature, scaly skin, still have wings; servantile

Imperial – thought to be extinct; four classes: Black, Blue, Purple, Red; unknown lifespan; get up to four wagon lengths long, stand a story high at shoulder on all fours; communicate telepathically

Fairies

Giants

North – native to northern part of Mythos; reclusive; no established society; two stories tall, muscular, blue-grey skin; fierce, territorial

Rock – native to the southern part of the Walker Mountains and into the Alisyan Mountains; nomadic, follow chieftains; two stories tall, muscular, gray rocklike skin; warmongers

Goblins – scattered across Mythnium, mainly mountainous regions; nomadic society; short, wiry, pale; considered a nuisance race; typically avoid large groups

Heridon – endangered; only one known remains; part Drake, part human, part elf; suspected lifespan of 900 years; known specimen is taller than the tallest human, pebbly skin, lizard-like facial features; historical traces mostly lost or forgotten

Humans – scattered across Mythnium; societies very dependent on area; short lifespan of up to 100 years; height varies, but typically taller than most elves, build varies, complexion directly related to areas they live in; ethnicity and culture shaped by time and environment

Merfolk – humanoid with fish tails; live exclusively underwater in oceans and seas; very little-known regarding lifespan, culture, history; suspected to have subspecies and various cultures

Mulig – scattered across Mythnium; nomadic, typically found near sources of fresh water; short lifespan of up to 30 years; froglike humanoid, medium height, stocky, muscular, brown flabby skin; not very intelligent; prone to causing trouble, fighting, stealing, marauding

Orc

Rana – scattered across Mythnium; tribal (known as schools) located only near fresh or salt water or in swampy areas; fish-like humanoids believed to be related to merpeople; medium height, slender, scales for skin, fish faces with large eyes, breathe with gills and lungs (amphibious); emotionally telepathic; rarely survive outside their "school;" peaceful, gentle

Trolls

GODS

Father creator- Siki
Mother creator - Cria
War - Peran (M)
Hunt - Dali (F)
Wisdom - Igma (F)
Death - Sayki (F)
Harvest - Skeru (M)
Fertility - Asuna (F)
Dwarves - Hux (M)
Elves - Kudhe (M)
Dragons - Zeni (F)
Heridon - Naga (F)
Fairies - Ose (M)
Drow - Mura (F)
Merfolk - Cracia (F)
Rana - Cracia (F)
Mulig - Muli (F)
Giant - Tsufa (F)
Orc - Grix (M)
Troll - Hmor (M)
Goblin - Plueg (M)

SIGILS

Ab-nar – nature; life
Bah-nar – water
Ja-nar - air
Poz-nar - fire
Ur-nar - earth

My Thanks

Thank you, dear reader, for taking the time to read these accounts from Mythnium. I hope you enjoyed your journey through Mythnium and that you rejoin these incredible characters as their journey continues in following books.

I would be incredibly honored if you left a review of your journey into Mythnium on Amazon and/or Goodreads. Reviews are an important tool that other readers use to determine the next book they will pick up, and they are essential to me as an author.

Additionally, if you are interested in learning more about Mythnium and staying up to date on future books, events, and promotions, please *like* and *follow* World of Mythnium on the following sites:

Instagram: @worldofmythnium
World of Mythnium: www.mythnium.com
Facebook: @authorc.borden.14

With hearts as one,

C. Borden

Short Stories from Mythnium

Available in e-book and paperback on Amazon.com

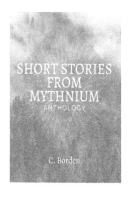 Enter the world of Mythnium through these tales of heroism, discovery, and realization with elves, dwarves, humans and more who play significant roles in the continual battle between good and evil. Each of these short stories introduces you to Mythnium's races, creatures, and magic, while hinting at something dark on the horizon. This anthology takes you on eight journeys into the lives of characters who come from different backgrounds, different cultures, and different races giving fantasy fans snapshots into the world of Mythnium and opening doors to a place of magic, danger, intrigue, romance, and adventure.

C. Borden fell in love with fantasy and science

fiction as a young girl when a family member introduced her to <u>Dune</u> and the <u>Wheel of Time</u> series.

Drawing inspiration from her favorite authors, author colleagues, family, friends, and from the various places she has lived or traveled, her works include life-like characters, places readers wish they could visit, and story lines that pull the reader in and wanting more.

C. Borden lives in the mountains of Montana where she enjoys reading, writing, traveling, and dabbling in nature photography. When she is not writing fantasy, fiction, or Christian-related works, she is most likely enjoying the outdoors with friends and family, helping another author get their ideas on paper, or curled up with a good book from one of her favorite authors.

You can follow C. Borden on Facebook. Just search for "Author C. Borden" to follow her updates on all her writing projects even beyond Mythnium.

*C*OMPANIONS OF *D*RAGONS

*A*WAKENINGS: *B*OOK *T*WO

*P*ROLOGUE

*H*e stood in the large ring that had housed Libitina and the dragon egg. Inwardly fuming that the Red Dragon had stolen the egg and disappeared, he tried to find her by searching the magical currents. He realized he wasted his time because, after a week of trying, it was obvious that she was good at masking her trail and was likely too far away for him to track. Past the point of raging, following several days of wanton destruction around his citadel every time he got no word from his spy network, killing nearly all the messengers who brought him no news, he stared around the large space of the ring and tried to discern what had motivated her to leave so abruptly. He could not help but wonder, and the questions gave rise to his growing doubts and suspicions.

Doubts added to his fury. Fury clouded his mind. He knew it, and yet he seemed unable to get the rage under control; while he was controlling it outwardly, it was uncontained within him, and he felt as though all the plans he had been working toward were coming unraveled.

He made a mental note to seek Naga's help during their next communion, though he worried over that as well, for the last time he sought communion with his god, Naga had not responded. The loss of Libitina, the egg, and the quietness of his god made him uncertain. So, the ugly cycle of doubt-filled rage continued.

Turning to leave the ring, he looked out the wide doors and saw several messengers racing up the rise from the Citadel and docks beyond it to meet him.

The first one, a manipulative sailor that hopped from one ship to another as a regular course of his work, arrived in front of the White Lord first. Dropping to his knees, his eyes downcast, he waited for the White Lord to address him, while seconds later a second and third messenger dropped to the ground beside him, their eyes also staring at the ground.

The gravel crunched under the heavy stride of the White Lord, and in their peripheral vision, they could see his feet, the large toe claw of his left foot tapping in annoyance.

"What have you to report, Irgus?"

To be continued...

Printed in Great Britain
by Amazon

77585957R00185